I0593164

Abstract

Nothing is as it seems

Jeannette Maree

Copyright © Jeanette Maree 2023

All rights reserved.

The right of Jeanette Maree to be identified as the author of this Work has been asserted by her in accordance with sections 77 and 78 of the Copyright, Designs and Patents Act 1988.

This book is a work of fiction and any resemblance to actual persons, living or dead, is purely coincidental. Research References within the book are fictitious.

No part of this publication may be reproduced, stored in a retrieval system, copied in any form or by any means, electronic, mechanical, photocopying, recording or otherwise transmitted without written permission from the publisher. You must not circulate this book in any format.

Cover Design by Brittany Wilson | Brittwilsonart.com

Contact: Jenmaree2003@yahoo.com

Luke 8:17

Whatever is hidden away will be brought out into the open and whatever is covered up will be found and brought into the light

Also by Jeannette Maree

I Belong to Me (Louise Ayden)
Remember To Breathe
Plum blossom

Acknowledgements

Many thanks to:
Jenny M Black and Elizabeth Becka

Seven days left of 2017.

Each year, Eva Rennie had made a ritual of listing her New Year goals since the year 2000. She picked up her pen and held it in her right hand, twisting the pen between her fingers for several seconds, hesitating to commit to a list. *'I shall leave it to chance, this year,'* she thought, laying the pen upon the opened, blank notebook on the table in front of her. Leaning back in her chair, she rested her hands in her lap.

'Wishing for more is foolish,' she reasoned, 'especially when I have everything I need.'

'Do you plan to be alone forever?' her inner voice whispered.

'I don't need more heartaches', she mused.

Chapter 1

In the summer of 2016, tall, eye-catching Josh Rennie ducked out of the office to buy a coffee at his favourite cafe across the street. Standing at the lights, he glanced at his watch. A client was due in twenty minutes. He had to hurry. The lights turned green and he dashed forward before anyone else. Halfway across the road, something caught his attention. He looked to his left. The driver of a white van ran the red light and was heading his way. The impact was sudden and fatal.

Josh's death devastated his wife, Eva. Thirty-five years of married life shattered in an instant. She missed him and contemplating the future without her husband felt terrifying to her. Having to keep her emotions in check in the company of her son, Harry, and daughter-in-law, Montana, and some of her friends was a struggle. She loathed their expression of 'Oh, you poor thing.'

Two months earlier, Harry married his childhood sweetheart, Montana Davis. Since Montana was an only child and both of her parents had passed away, Eva wanted to do something special for Montana to commemorate the day. She made a small octagonal origami box.

Montana adored Eva's gift. She put it on display at the wedding reception and as she had expected, every woman there wanted one. Eva was inundated with requests for her beautiful boxes, triggering a business opportunity.

Josh gave Eva a sceptical look. "How on earth are you going to fill all those orders, hon?"

She shrugged. "I'll find a way."

Before leaving for work that fateful morning, Josh said, "Well, if there's anything I can do to help, just tell me, okay?"

As he kissed her goodbye, she was unaware that it was their last kiss.

Full of enthusiasm for her new project, Eva headed to the shower, to her bedroom to dress, the kitchen to make coffee, then to Josh's home office, where she spent all morning working on a business plan.

At noon, the phone rang. Eva was about to let it go to message bank, then changed her mind.

"Hello?"

She listened to the person at the other end of the line. The phone fell from her hand seconds before she collapsed on the floor from shock.

Eva stirred at the sound of her son's voice when he picked her up and cradled his mother in his arms. She had no idea how long she had been lying on the floor.

"Mum, Mum?" Harry choked back tears. "I can't lose you both on the same day."

Eva was groggy; she blinked several times, dazed. A voice echoed in her head, *'So sorry to have to notify you … Your husband was in a fatal …'*

She wiped her tear-soaked face with the back of her hand. "Your father … is dead!" she repeated several times, clutching Harry's shirt, understanding the wretchedness of that moment. She rested her head against her son's chest, resigning to the worst.

"I know Mum," he said, his voice full of emotion, hugging her. "I came as soon as I heard."

Days and months passed unnoticed. Eva became a shadow of herself. Enduring each day with little thought of what she did, just existing. Life had lost its lustre. Grief overwhelmed her. Evenings gave some relief. Medication helped her sleep. However, the heartache returned each morning.

The phone rang day and night. Her message bank was full of concerned friend's voices expressing their condolences or extending invitations to lunch and other functions. They went unanswered. The phone eventually fell silent.

Only Harry called every day to ask the same question, "How are you, Mum?" and got the same answer, "I'm fine, darling. How are you and Montana?"

Then one morning, a magpie perched on the terrace balustrade watching Eva drink her coffee. The magpie made loud, fluty sounds as its eyes followed her every movement. Eva sighted the bird out of the periphery of her eye. She took care not to frighten it. Reaching for the bread container, she pulled a piece of crust from the loaf inside. She expected the bird to fly away with the sound of the screen door opening. Instead, it jumped off the railing, ran to her and accepted the bread she offered. Up close, its markings were easier to see. The bird was female. Male's hoods are vibrant white. This magpie's hood was white, running to a greyish colour.

The magpie returned in the afternoon with her chick and a male bird. Eva assumed they were family. Having little knowledge about native birds, she knew, however, if they came back, she should feed them meat rather than bread. That meant a trip to the supermarket. She had not left the house in many months.

Chapter 2

The carpark at Manly Village was full. Eva had forgotten how busy it was at midday. She was ready to give up looking for a parking bay and go home. Up ahead, two cars pulled out, one after the other. She swung into one of the vacant spaces; another car drove in beside her. Instead of getting out of her car right away, Eva sat staring through the windscreen at nothing in particular.

'I can't recall the last time I was here,' she thought. 'I remember it being a pleasure to shop here, though. Seeing old friends and saying hello.' Fear seized her. 'I cannot face anyone, yet.'

With a shaky hand, she started the engine and then she killed it. A slim woman with shoulder-length, raven hair pummelled her window.

As the window buzzed down, the woman's lovely features creased into a broad smile.

"How are you, Eva?" she trumpeted with such enthusiasm Eva drew backwards. Before Eva found her voice, the woman said, "It's about bloody time you crawled out from under that *pity* blanket."

"Tell me what you're thinking, Danika!" Eva barked back.

"It's been long enough, don't you think? If I hadn't bumped into you today, I would have been on your doorstep Monday morning, anyway," Danika Bryce declared. She then smiled. Her large green eyes softened when she said, "Get out of the car so your bestie can give you a hug!"

Without thinking, Eva obeyed.

"I am buying lunch," said Danika, giving her friend the once over. "By the look of you, you could use a good feed."

Danika linked arms with Eva. "C'mon," she said. Eva stiffened at first and then relaxed. It was pointless to resist. Danika was unchangeable!

Danika still had a firm grip on Eva as they walked across the street and climbed the stairs to The Deck restaurant, above the Celtic Corner café. A waiter greeted them at the door. He asked where they would prefer to sit.

"Outside." replied Danika.

"This way," he said with a smile, tucking two menus under his arms. They followed him through the dimly lit lounge area out onto the balcony. A table for two with tall chairs gave access to encompassing views of the town and part of Manly Marina at the end of Cambridge Parade. The sky was cloudless; the breeze was pleasant on their bare arms.

"What have you been doing to keep yourself occupied all this time?" Danika asked. "I cannot imagine you curled up on the couch devouring Tim Tams all day."

Eva said nothing. She looked at Danika: brash and straight to the point, although with good intentions. People either loved Danika or loathed her. Eva liked her. She trusted her. Eva leaned forward and spoke loud enough for Danika to hear her over the street noise.

"It's taken me a while, but I have figured out what I want to do now that," she paused, two beats, then took a gulp of air and continued, "now that Josh isn't here," she said in one breath. "I'm working on a business plan to sell online the octagonal boxes I make."

Danika, ignoring Eva's hesitation, knew her friend needed no more pity. She needed strength. "Ok. Now tell me what you have in mind. Perhaps I can help. If you recall, I was in marketing for many years." She paused and smiled. "You can pay me when you make your first million!"

Both laughed aloud.

Eva foraged in her bag for her reading glasses. She slipped them on and perused the menu when she saw the waiter heading their way. They ordered salmon salad, cappuccino and bottled water.

Eva was in the middle of explaining her business plan when their meals arrived. Both went silent and sat back in their seat. The waiter placed the food in front of them. He smiled and asked if they needed anything else before he left.

Tucking into her salad, Danika said, "You were saying?"

Eva continued, explaining the method of how she made the paper sheets: the texture, their strength and their size, etc. "Size really matters in this case," Eva giggled, holding a forkful of salad ready to pop into her mouth.

Danika smiled and then waited until Eva had finished sharing her business concepts before asking questions during a second cappuccino and a slice of mud cake.

Eva took the last sip of her coffee, wiped her mouth with the edge of a paper napkin and sat back. "Well?" she said, looking at her friend. "There you have it."

Danika said nothing for a moment. She was running the information over in her mind. "Hmm! Not quite."

Eva responded with a questioning look.

"You left out your market target, time involved in making a box, your profit margin, marketing ..."

"My targets are brides and anniversaries. The boxes are unique and expensive. Each box will have its own identification number to attest its authenticity, dated and linked to a limited-edition code ..."

Danika nodded as Eva continued. Although only half-listening and impressed with Eva's ideas, her sudden transformation had astounded Danika; Eva had changed within the hour. Her eyes sparkled when she spoke. It had been a long time since she had seen that in her friend.

"What made you come to Manly Village, today?" Danika asked, interrupting.

"Excuse me?" Eva replied, puzzled.

"What was the reason that brought you to the Village?"

"Why?"

"Because," Danika said, "right now I am witnessing a phenomenon."

Eva did not respond.

Danika waited.

Eva sighed, twiddling her reading glasses, which she had placed on the table earlier. "To be honest, Dani, I am tired of being sad. The boxes are my ticket out of my *pity* party."

"I am not apologising for that remark, either," Danika replied.

Eva half smiled.

Danika studied Eva. "It's more than that. Why are you here? You can have anything you need delivered."

"Oh my gosh, Maggie," Eva gasped. "I almost forgot her. I have to go." Eva pushed her chair away from the table and stood. "I've shopping to do," she said, hurrying away.

"Who's Maggie?" Danika called out.

"Come to my place tomorrow, 10 am," she replied, rushing away. "You will meet her then. Oh, and thanks for lunch. Bye Dani!"

Chapter 3

On her way home, Danika sat tall in the driver's seat and then, leaning forward, she switched on the radio. The cabin vibrated with country music. Her fingers danced on the steering wheel in time with the tune, as she sang along with Tim McGraw. In the middle of the song, Danika stopped singing.

'Maggie? Hmm, I wonder who she is. Must be someone very special,' she mused, then shrugged. As she turned into her driveway, the mobile buzzed in her bag. Danika parked and fished around for the phone, found it and glanced at the screen.

"G'day Hon!"

"Hey, ma."

"How are you, sweetheart?"

"All's well here. Just wanted to say 'Hi'. What are you doing?"

"All good here too, hon," without missing a beat, Danika said, "Oh, yes, I have some news. I ran into Eva at Manly Village this afternoon ..."

Abigail Bryce, known to her friends as Abbi, was a thirty-year-old of average height, with a flawless olive complexion, dark curly hair and hazel eyes.

"Wait, wait, Mum," Abbi cut in, "I'll come over. You can tell me then. I have something to tell you, too. See you soon."

The mobile went dead.

When Abbi arrived, she could hear her mother singing as she moved about in the kitchen, cupboards opening and closing and the tinker of crockery.

"Hey ma," Abbi called from the doorway.

"Hey sweetie," Danika beamed, "Coffee? It's ready."

Abbi smiled. "You are so predictable, ma."

Danika smiled, shrugging. "You should take comfort in that."

"Oh, I do, ma. I do."

Danika picked up two brightly coloured mugs from the bench and carried them to the table.

"Okay, now what is it you want to tell me?" she said, sitting down, wrapping her hands around her mug.

Abbi pulled out a chair from the table and sat opposite. "I have met someone on social media."

Danika looked puzzled. "What about Leo, what's-his-name?"

Abbi flicked her dark locks aside, releasing an exasperated sigh. "Brandt, Leo Brandt, ma. You never remember his name."

Danika said nothing. She quelled the impulse to respond; she was thinking plenty, though. Danika had not met Leo Brandt; what she knew about him was Abbi's version. Tall, fair and gorgeous, which told her nothing substantial. Following that description came a series of off-again, on-again, off-again with their relationship.

"Anyway, Leo is adamant we are over; said he wants to concentrate on his career."

"And how do you feel about that?"

"Heartbroken! He made me fall in love with him and then he dumped me. How would you expect me to feel, ma?"

Danika sat back in her chair reeling in her mind, as though her daughter had slapped her.

"Well, you know my philosophy, sweetheart. You never lose whatever fate has destined you to have."

"Yeah, yeah, I know, but ..." Abbi stopped, realising it was pointless to debate the subject with her mother. Their philosophy about relationships was worlds apart. After each break-up, Danika would tell Abbi to *move on. He* isn't *Mr Right,* to keep looking. It was not that simple for Abbi. When she fell in love, she gave one hundred percent of herself to the relationship and would persist with trying to mend it to her detriment.

Abbi pulled a tissue from her jacket pocket and wiped her eyes.

"I wish I could cry pretty," she laughed. "I look like crap when I cry."

They both laughed.

"What's his name?"

"Who?"

Abbi thought for a moment. "Oh, oh, you mean the guy I'm talking to on social media?"

Danika nodded.

"His name is Jackson Jefferson McCoy."

Danika smiled. "With a name like that, he has to be American, right?"

"To the core," Abbi grinned. "Armed Forces. He's in Germany at the moment. Jackson returns to America in a few months."

"Got a photo?"

"Yep."

"Well, show me."

Abbi fiddled with her smart phone. "There he is," she said, offering her mother the mobile. The warmth in Abbi's eyes told Danika this man had her daughter's attention.

Danika liked the look of Jackson Jefferson McCoy. His smile was broad and open. His eyes twinkled.

"I like him," she said. "He looks like a 1940's man!"

Abbi looked puzzled.

"A one-woman man. His kind is rare, I can tell you."

"Ma," Abbi said, "we are just friends. That's all!"

"Uh-huh!" Danika smiled.

Chapter 4

At the sound of a car engine, Maggie, her mate and her chick gathered at the back door.

Eva rushed into the kitchen and dropped the shopping on the bench with an exhausted groan. She craned her neck to see if the birds were still there. She smiled. They were there, waiting. Digging deep into one bag, Eva pulled out a packet of freshly ground beef. Maggie and her mate watched through the sliding glass door. A falling leaf had distracted the chick.

Even though the door squeaked opened, the magpies remained where they were, waiting and watching. Eva crouched down and extended her arm. Maggie ran towards Eva's hand and gently grabbed the meat. The male and the chick stood back. Both birds pounced on the morsels Eva tossed to them.

Eva stood up and watched the family tuck into the beef. Her features crinkled with pleasure. Turning to go inside, she stopped. Twisting her torso slightly, her eyes shot downward, toward the sweetest voice that said, "Thank you, Eva."

Maggie was looking up at her. Eva shook herself and muttered, "I must be hallucinating."

Eva watched Maggie and her family from the kitchen window. The longer she remained there, the more she could feel her loneliness dissolving.

The sound of her mobile pinging snapped her back to the present. Glancing up at the wall clock, Eva knew it was Harry. However, she was unaware that her son dreaded calling her. Nothing he said or did would pull her out of her misery. He kept calling because he loved his mother. He never stopped hoping that in his next call with her, she would engage in more conversation.

Just before he spoke, he inhaled, "Hey Mum. How are you?" he asked, slowly exhaling. He was startled when she said, "Wonderful, darling!"

Not believing what he heard, he asked, "Mum? Did you say *wonderful*?"

Eva noted the relief in her son's voice.

"Yes, darling, I said *wonderful*. My day was amazing and wonderful! If you have time," she paused. "I'd love to share it with you."

Harry waved his wife over.

"Just a minute, Mum. Monnie's here with me. I'll put you on speaker."

"Well …" Eva began with her business idea and then went on to how she bumped into Danika at Manly Village.

"You actually left the house and went to Manly Village? That's amazing. I was thinking you'd never leave." He paused. "Never mind. That's great news, Mum!"

Montana put her arm around her husband and laid her head on his shoulder when she saw his tear-filled eyes.

"You've made my day, Mum!"

"I am so very sorry, my darlings. I have been …"

"No apology needed, Mum. Today is the beginning of the rest of our lives."

Eva wiped her eyes. "That it is!" she declared.

Eva went silent.

"Mum?"

"Oh, I was just thinking."

"About?"

"A family of magpies have made camp in the yard." She was about to say the female spoke to her, but changed her mind. *'Surely, I imagined it,'* she concluded. *'Harry would worry that I was losing my mind, if I say anything.'*

"And?"

"And they are delightful. Wonderful company, too."

"I'm so glad you are enjoying life again, Mum. I, we both have been so worried about you."

"Things are back on track now, loves, so worry no more, eh?" Eva said playfully.

"We love you, Mum!" said Montana. "Oh, now that you're a busy businesswoman, please check your calendar to confirm a lunch date with us for Sunday?"

"Just a moment," Eva replied, in singsong fashion, chuckling. "You're in luck. There's a window open."

Montana responded with a hearty giggle.

At the end of the call, Eva recognised the voice of reason taming her extreme grief. Not only had it affected her life, it had affected Harry and Montana's as well.

At the stroke of ten the following day, Eva opened the front door.

"Good morning, Dani!" She beamed.

"A mind reader, too?" responded Danika.

"You are, without doubt, the most punctual person I know," Eva replied with a grin and a brief hug. "C'mon through to the kitchen. Coffee is ready. I baked a cake last night. Chocolate. Your favourite, I recall?"

"You've won me." Danika smiled and followed Eva.

Over coffee Danika said, "You've made some changes since I was here last."

"Yes, I have rearranged the furniture and bought a few new things to replace what was sent off to the Salvation Army."

Danika's brow creased. She studied Eva for a moment. "When did all this happen?"

Eva turned to face Danika. "Why do you ask?"

"You're grieving, that's why. A woman grieving the loss of her husband doesn't throw away his favourite chair?"

"My grieving is over!"

"What happened to all this love you have for Josh?"

"I loved him. Still do. Josh was a wonderful provider, kind, as well as an attentive husband. An amazing father too, but ..."

"But what?"

"Truth is, he just couldn't keep it in his pants."

Danika dropped her head.

"Oh Dani," Eva paused, "not you, too!"

Danika raised her hands. "No, no, no! I doused his *come on* the minute it happened. Married men are off limits," she said. "That was years ago, Eva," Danika sighed. "I was new to the area when I first met Josh. I was having lunch in Manly when he entered the café. He nodded and said, "hello." On his way out he stopped and introduced himself and then asked if he could join me. I had not noticed the wedding ring at that stage and pointed to the chair opposite. We chatted for a few minutes and by this time I saw the ring. He asked if I would to meet him later for a drink. "Of course," I said, "bring your wife, too."

"Ah ... so that's why he kept a discreet distance from you. I had wondered about that. Josh was always very attentive to attractive women. You're in the *beautiful* category. And ..."

"He was afraid of me." Danika interrupted. "Or of what I might tell you."

"Why didn't you?"

"Why didn't I what?"

"Tell me my husband had made a pass at you."

"It was long before we became friends and Josh never repeated that mistake again, at least not with me."

Eva was silent.

"Why did you not leave, Josh? You knew he was a player. Why did you stay and play happy families?"

"He was still a wonderful man, regardless of his infidelities."

"But you wasted almost a year grieving over a lie."

"No. It wasn't a lie." Eva's voice was full of emotion. "I had lost my companion and a life familiar to me. It was a safe life! I felt secure! Facing the future alone scared me to death!"

"You're not alone, Eva. You've *never* been alone!" Danika said, a tad irritated. She had no time for self-pity. Danika was thinking how her past had been no picnic. Yet, she survived it.

"I know that now," Eva fired back. "And that's why I need to be productive. Not to waste what time I have left. Who knows what's ahead of us, Dani? Stones or diamonds; and another thing, no one can guarantee me, you, or anyone, *tomorrow*!"

Danika nodded. "I can't argue with that."

Both went silent for an entire minute. The only sound in the room was the ticking of the wall clock. Danika looked up at the time and then checked her watch.

"What time is your friend arriving?"

Eva's brow creased. "What friend? I'm not expecting anyone."

"Maggie?"

"Ah yes, Maggie." Eva grinned.

She got up from the table, gathered the mugs and plates together and placed them on the sink. She opened the fridge door and took out a small ball of meat from a container. She then moved toward the screen door.

"Follow me," Eva said.

This time Danika obeyed without question.

Sitting on the porch balustrade was Maggie. Her mate and chick were picking in the yard. They stopped when they saw Eva and ran over to join Maggie.

Danika's lips parted and her eyes widened, then her features crinkled with delight.

"So, this is Maggie?" she whispered.

Maggie looked up at Danika.

Eva nodded. "The others are her family; husband and baby. *It's until death do they part* with them. Magpies can live twenty to thirty years in the same area. Maggie and her family are now my extended family. Yesterday, you asked me what brought me to the village. Well, they did. I needed to get minced beef for them."

"You're right about one thing, Eva."

Eva dropped her head to one side and looked at Danika.

"No one knows how or when situations will change."

"There's more. C'mon," Eva said, heading down to the backyard.

Following close behind Danika whispered, "I think she … ah … Maggie was judging me."

"She probably was."

Danika stopped in her tracks.

Eva looked back over her shoulder. "What is it?"

"You're kidding right?"

Eva looked confused.

"About Maggie judging me?"

"No." Eva replied and carried on walking.

Curiosity urged Danika to follow her.

"There," Eva pointed to the corner of the yard, "is my studio."

The old shed, dilapidated and once falling down, paint cracked and peeling from its boards, doors hanging off rusty old hinges, was now transformed into a warm, inviting little cottage-cum-studio surrounded by lavender and roses.

"I am speechless," said Danika.

"I had planned to tear down the shed and start again," Eva said. "Then changed my mind after speaking to my builder, Lucas Johnson." Eva paused and glanced at Danika. "You remember Lucas, don't you?"

Danika nodded. Unbeknown to anyone, she knew Lucas intimately.

"He said the foundations were solid." Eva shrugged. "Like me, I guess. Solid foundations, but dilapidated within." Eva laughed and continued. "Since its reprieve, the studio has served me well. I love working here."

The women fell into an appreciative silence.

"Well, c'mon in. Look around." Eva said, stepping up onto the veranda. "This is where we will work for however long the business lasts."

Danika looked puzzled. "What do you mean?"

Eva shrugged. "As I often say, who knows anything, these days Dani? Nothing is guaranteed, it's one day at a time, with fingers crossed behind your back."

Danika nodded.

When Danika saw the large navy and white patterned cushions in the two white cane chairs on the veranda, amid colourful blooms in large terracotta pots. She could not resist saying, "That has to be the conference corner?"

"If you want it to be, sure," replied Eva.

The studio was open-plan. Plantation shutters folded back against the northern and southern walls. Natural light streamed through the two large windows. Under the southern window ran a wall-to-wall polished concrete bench. In the middle of the bench was a large double sink.

"This is where I work." Eva said, moving closer to the bench. She touched one of the eight mesh square frames. "Paper liquid is poured into each of these frames and is left to drip dry." Moving along the bench, Eva explained step-by step the procedure of making her unique paper. "Farther along, as you can see by the pile of dried sheets, is where I cut the paper to size with the guillotine."

"Oh, that guillotine looks intimidating," Danika remarked.

Eva nodded. "It's very sharp. Be mindful of that whenever you're near it," she warned and continued, "And here is where I assemble the boxes and paint them."

"Oh, I will be mindful of the guillotine," Danika said, backing away from it while doing her best to absorb all Eva had told her. "Wow! I am impressed!"

"It took a few weeks of trial and error before I came up with the perfect formula for a batch of rose scented paper sheets," said Eva, with a note of pride. "I must follow a specific recipe; otherwise, the paper will fall apart," she added. Picking up a sheet, holding it up to her nose and closing her eyes, Eva sniffed the paper. "Hmm, that fragrance is divine," she said, handing it to Danika. "Here, what do you think? Isn't it lovely?"

"Yes, it is." Danika smiled, breathing in the perfume. "It's amazing! And how do you make the boxes?"

"Origami style, folding each sheet to slide inside one another. One week I assemble several dozen boxes and the next I decorate them with intricate spring flowers in watercolours."

Danika was too enthralled to interrupt Eva with questions.

"I have embroidered irises in the corners of these delicate white linen handkerchiefs." Eva said, holding one up to show Danika. "If you remember, I did the same for Montana on her wedding day."

Danika nodded. "I remember. The box and everything in it were beautiful, representing the tradition of 'Something old, something new, something borrowed and something blue.' Your handmade paper and exquisite artwork made an ordinary octagonal box extraordinary."

Eva smiled her thanks.

Danika stood back to admire all that had gone into creating this wonderful workplace. There was also a compact kitchen and powder room. "Wow!" she said appreciatively. Turning to the northern window, inclining her head, Danika remarked, "That's my space over there I take it. The computer and office equipment are a dead giveaway."

"I hope you have everything you need ..."

"All this is amazing, Eva!"

"I have commissioned Lucas to build a large, silky oak table for the middle of the room. This table," she pointed at that space, "is on loan until mine is ready," Then with a sweeping of her hand, she said, her tone full of emotion, "All this is thanks to Josh."

Danika stifled her curiosity and said nothing.

"It floored me when the insurance company contacted me." Eva took a breath. Her eyes glistened. "Anyway," Eva cleared her throat, "as I had said, Josh was always an excellent provider."

Silence fell between them.

"There's a bottle of red in the cupboard." Eva announced with gusto, startling Danika. "Let's open it and toast Josh!"

On the veranda, in the cool spring afternoon, both women lounged in the white cane chairs, sipping their wine in peaceful silence, unperturbed by the muffled traffic sounds in the distance.

"Ah, this is the life," Danika said. "An excellent way to kick-start the work ahead."

"Now?" Eva groaned. "Must we talk about work right now? My brain has retired for the day."

Danika shook her head. "I am ready to go! So many ideas are running around in my head."

"That's awesome, but?" Eva gave Danika a pleading look.

"Okay." Danika raised her hands, surrendering. "First thing tomorrow then, right?"

"Right," agreed Eva, putting the wineglass to her lips. "Tomorrow," she whispered.

An hour into their rest and relaxation, Danika heard her mobile buzzing. She got up to answer it. The buzzing was persistent while she shuffled around inside the bag. Danika knew the caller must be Abbi.

"Hi ma? Are you ok?" asked Abbi. "You took a while to answer."

"I'm fine sweetie. It took a few minutes to find the damn phone. Is everything okay with you?"

"Are you busy?"

"I'll be home in about 10 minutes."

"Mind if I come over?"

"Sure. See you soon," Danika said, ending the call.

"Is everything okay?" Eva asked.

"That was Abbi. She is on her way over to my place."

"How is Abbi? I haven't seen her since, ah, since the funeral."

"I'm about to find out."

"Still running the moment she calls, I see."

"Prerequisite for being a mother." Danika shrugged. "Don't get up. Stay where you are and enjoy this gorgeous ambience." As a sudden thought, turning back to Eva, Danika asked. "Mind if I contact the others to let them know the phoenix has risen."

Eva raised her glass and smiled. "You sure can. Please organise a get together. It has been too long."

Danika nodded. "Indeed, it has. They understand."

"I must apologise for ignoring them all this time," said Eva, looking into her wine glass. "Dani, did you know for several months after the funeral, Chelsea left delicious meals, on the doorstep for me?"

Danika shook her head.

"I would have withered away had she not been so thoughtful. Cooking was the last thing on my mind. She made all of my favourites and still leaves treats now and then." Eva paused. "I feel horribly embarrassed; not once did I call and thank her."

"Well, now you can." Danika replied.

"Hey, Dani?"

"Yes?"

"It's spring!"

"And?"

"Chelsea's Spring Luncheon!" Eva's intonation changed. "Sadly, I missed last year's."

"The luncheon was postponed."

"What?" Eva's eyes widen.

As she left, Danika called out, "Work tomorrow!"

Danika headed up the pathway, then stopped and turned around and walked back to the studio.

"Oh! Back so soon?" Eva giggled.

"Which treats?"

Eva stared at Danika.

"Chelsea left for you?"

"Oh, oh, yes." Eva smiled with delight. "The double chocolate crunch, you know, the ones ..."

"I know the ones you mean." Danika interrupted. "They are my favourites too!" she said, with a twinkle in her eye. "If I, were you, I would have called Chelsea and thanked her the moment I opened the box."

When Eva dropped her lip, she reminded Danika of a child.

"I guess you had a valid reason for not calling," Danika said. "But you don't anymore."

Eva looked up at Danika as she picked up her mobile. "I am calling her now."

"Good girl." Danika waited until Eva's call connected.

"Hi Chelsea," Eva smiled and paused. "Yeah, yeah, I'm fine …"

As Danika walked away, Eva's laughter faded into the mix of sounds around her.

Chapter 5

"Peru?" said Danika.

"Yes. I'm taking a month off work to trek around Peru," Abbi said.

Danika studied her daughter for a moment. "You are going to Peru *alone* to trek around the country? Is that Right?"

"Yes!" Abbi declared. "For the first time in my life I'm stepping out of my comfort zone. The *first time* comes only once. I have to do this for me."

Danika said nothing for a moment. She was digesting the situation. *'OMG! She doesn't speak a word of Spanish.'*

"Rudi, a former workmate, has invited me to visit him and his wife," Abbi said, interrupting Danika's thoughts. "They're part of a conservation group in the Amazon. We remained in contact after he left Australia. You've met Rudi and liked him, ma." Abbi sighed. "I told you, several times, about the work Rudi and his wife are doing there."

Danika did not miss the irritation in her daughter's voice.

"Abbi, I have met so many of your friends over the years. Unless I see them often, they become a blur."

It did not appear as if Abbi heard her mother's comment because she said, with insurmountable excitement. "Ma, I'll get to hold a sloth. You know how much I love sloths! How amazing is that?"

Danika smiled. "Yes, I do. You promise to send a message every day and heaps of photos so I don't worry, ok?"

"Ma, I'll be fine. I'm not a child! Jackson will track me all the way on social media. If I don't contact him, he'll send out a search party."

"Can he do that?"

"He said he can."

"Well, it's your life to live. Best to do it full throttle because we never know what tomorrow will bring."

Abbi reached for her mother's hand. She squeezed it. "Thanks, ma, for always supporting me. You taught me not to be afraid; to explore all that life offers."

Danika smiled. "It's a prerequisite for being a mother, hon."

"What about you, ma?"

Danika thought Abbi's question was odd, since she rarely showed any interest in what she was doing unless Danika mentioned it.

"What about me?"

"Eva's business?"

"Oh yes, well ..."

It was late by the time Abbi had left. During the brief drive through Manly Village and along the foreshore to Lota, without warning, snapshots of the past flashed into her mind, images of her mother's youthful face – eyes swollen and blood from her cut lip. Guilt still gnawed at her for being helpless to protect her mother. *'Being a four-year-old sucks!'*

Abbi steered her car to the curb and let the engine idle while she inhaled and exhaled several times. Her mother's words echoed in her head. *'Emotional pain and the humiliation of abuse stains your soul. It's implanted in you, becomes part of you. Trust is open to scrutiny. Suspicion loiters at the back of your mind, like a thief about to rob you of any peace. Despite that, you manage it and get on with life.'*

Abbi's heart thumped hard in her chest. *Why am I thinking about that now?* She ran a hand over her eyes. When steady, she drove home.

Long after Abbi had left, Danika sat at the table, listening to her daughter's voice swirl around inside her head. Her excitement was unmeasurable. Danika felt a sense of relief shroud her like a warm cloak. Independence had emboldened her daughter's adventurous nature; thankful the past had not broken Abbi's spirit.

Danika suddenly remembered she had not messaged her friends about Eva. To her surprise, when she picked up her phone from the bedstand she found messages from them, expressing how thrilled they were to hear Eva was well. Danika smiled, guessing Chelsea had contacted them right after Eva's call.

Chelsea Harrison, the proverbial social director, could create spectacular morning teas, luncheons and get-togethers at a moment's notice. Tall and stylish, she charmed her friends into 'willing helpers' with her engaging smile. Part of Chelsea's text read ... *morning tea here, this coming Friday, 10am.*

'Things are back on track,' Danika thought, climbing into bed. She turned out the light and slid down under the feather-filled doona. Seconds later, she sat up and switched the light back on. Hearing Lucas Johnson's name earlier had whipped up old memories like a whirlpool. Their history went back twelve years. He was the husband of one of her friends. She supported him through his divorce because she knew both sides of the story. His wife boasted to Danika of her many conquests, unaware of her friendship with Lucas. Danika stayed neutral viewing the couple as miscast characters in a tragic comedy, only no one was laughing.

It was difficult to say when *feelings* developed between them. It was too subtle to pinpoint, but they agreed it would be a mistake to take it farther. A relationship would not have worked for either of them; too many obstacles were in the way.

Sometime later, Lucas moved to Western Australia. His ex-wife and two sons went down south to her family. Danika later learned Lucas had remarried. He and his second wife divorced nine years later. She knew he had recently returned to Manly. She also knew he had opened a carpentry business prior to Eva telling her about the table she ordered. He had never been far from her thoughts. She wondered if the feelings they had for each other all those years ago were still there. In his absence, his image had invaded her thoughts without warning, like an unwanted visitor, forcing her to recall all that she loved about him and all of what she had lost - his voice gentle, yet masculine; hands calloused yet tender at his touch and the smile that lit up his eyes the moment he saw her. She believed all of that had become a distant memory. She reached over to turn off the light. Lying there in the dark Danika thought about her past relationships and understood why all of them had failed. Her heart belonged to someone else. *'The next time I see him, that question will be answered, once and for all.'*

Maureen Manning, a sweet-face, petite woman in her late fifties, was also reading Chelsea's email. She was a freelance photographer. Chelsea had introduced Maureen to Josh at a *Cancer Foundation Fundraiser* after he mentioned he was looking for a photographer who understood what *composition* was.

Josh contacted Maureen after Chelsea showed him the photos she took at the fundraiser.

"Your work is excellent. You have an eye for detail," he said, genuinely impressed. "I'm looking for a talented photographer, if you're interested?"

Contact then was over the phone or via email. Maureen would go to the address Josh sent to her; do the shoot, check the photos and then send the best to Josh for his approval.

Maureen's professional life was uncomplicated, unlike her private life. Her husband, Barry Manning, a surly, moody man with unpredictable outbursts, sapped Maureen's energy and confidence in his company; she became fearful and subservient. She hated and feared her husband. Too afraid to leave; she believed he would find and kill her.

Josh discovered the truth of Maureen's domestic situation the day he came by her house unannounced to drop off flowers; a thank you for a job well done. There was no answer when he knocked on the front door. He put the flowers in a shaded part of the porch and was about to leave.

Maureen, watching him through the window, ran to the door and flung it open. "No, no, you can't leave them!" she screamed.

Josh froze. His eyes widened in horror at her behaviour and appearance.

"Please, please take them away. Please!" she begged him.

"These … these," he stammered, offering her the flowers, "are to thank you f… for …"

"I can't take them," she said, talking over the top of his words. "Please go away!"

"No!" Josh fired back. "Look at you, you're in danger. Whoever beat you so savagely is, without doubt, a psychopath. Your husband did this!" It was a statement not a question.

Maureen nodded.

"Where is he now?"

"He has just left to deliver a load to a Sydney warehouse," came her weak reply.

"Gather your belongings together."

"I have no place to go!" she shouted, backing away from him. "If my husband can't find me, he has threatened to harm my family."

"Where's your family?"

"My mother and my cousin live in Cairns."

"OK. I'll see that they're safe. Now do as I say. Get your things. I know of a place where you can stay."

A few days later, the police contacted Maureen to inform her of her husband's death. "He had fallen asleep at the wheel on his return trip to Brisbane," they said. The news of Barry's death came as a shock. Maureen was unsure if she should cheer or cry. She did neither. Instead, she called Josh.

"That's unfortunate," was his response.

She said nothing.

"Are you okay?" he asked. "Is there anything you need?" And so began their two-year relationship.

Maureen was reluctant to attend the morning tea. She could not face Eva after betraying her. She could not decline the invitation without attracting unwanted attention either.

Chapter 6

"You sure have caused a stir." Danika remarked on coming into the studio the next morning.

Eva looked up at Danika. She stopped folding a paper sheet. "Moi?" she said, pointing to herself.

"Yes, you," Danika said, shaking her head, laughing. "Can you live with not being the *centre* of attention, now that you're all better?"

"It will be difficult, but I shall try," Eva replied.

Danika headed for her desk, sat down and switched on the computer. "We should start working on your business profile today. I'll need a photo, background info, etc."

"A photo?"

"Yes."

"Must we have my photo for the profile?"

"Yes, we must! It's your business, Eva."

"I loathe the idea of being so exposed."

Danika gave Eva a questioning look. "Any other suggestions?"

"Yes. You could be the face of the company!"

The terror in Danika's eyes shocked Eva. "I can't," she said. Her words were just audible as she folded her hands to her chest.

Eva stopped what she was doing. Grabbed a chair, dragged it closer to Danika and sat down facing her.

"Hon, are you okay?"

"Yes. I'm fine," she lied. "But I cannot be the *face* of your business, Eva. I just can't."

Eva went silent.

"Ok, hon, you're right. It's my responsibility."

Eva stood up, replaced the chair, went back to her workstation and carried on folding paper sheets in silence. Concerned for Danika, Eva worried she had upset her. Thinking back over the years, Eva realised she knew very little about Danika. They had met at a function many years ago and continued to cross paths thereafter. Danika was not like most women. Although oozing with beauty and confidence, she refrained from self-promotion to the point of being an enigma. Eva observed Danika from across the room. She watched her drop her hands onto her lap and slumped back in her chair and swing the chair around to face the computer only to stare through the window. It was so unlike the woman she knew or thought she knew.

Maggie was on the studio window sill watching what was happening inside – Eva dragging a chair over to Danika, sitting down to face her and talking for a few minutes. Eva returning the chair back from where she took it and moving back to her workstation to finish folding the paper sheets. Maggie reacted to the tension in the air, warbling with concern. When Danika noticed the bird looking at her, she opened her desk draw and yanked out her bag.

"Mind if I do this tomorrow?" she asked, then got up and left.

"Not at … all" Eva stammered. "See you tomorrow," she called out.

Danika waved without turning.

The magpie flew after Danika. She landed on the front fence to watch her car disappear down the street. Returning to the studio, Maggie perched on the sill of Eva's opened window, startling her.

"Oh, hello Maggie, how are you this lovely morning?" Eva said. "Well, it was a lovely morning until I upset Dani. I am such a clot. Why did I make such a bloody fuss about *my* photo?" she paused. "I didn't mean to. If I were as beautiful as Dani, I wouldn't have minded being the face of my company and perhaps Josh would have not have been a cheating liar." Eva paused. "If I was not beautiful enough for my husband, why would I be good enough to represent this business?"

Maggie moved closer. Almost in a whisper she said, "You are beautiful, Eva. You were not the problem. The truth of the matter is Josh felt inadequate."

Eva stopped what she was doing and stared at the bird. "Now, I'm not sure if you said that Maggie or if I am imagining that you are talking to me. Whatever, but it makes perfect sense. It would explain why Josh was anal, not just about his appearance, about everything."

Danika drove to the foreshore and parked on the roadside at Pandanus Beach. Taking a moment to gather her thoughts, she then stepped out of the car and strolled across the lawn to a bench seat facing the Bay. She breathed in deeply several times. *'Ah, that's better',* she thought, looking around. Her gaze swept all directions. *'This place is magical, the way it comforts my spirit.'*

She sat back and watched people from various lifestyles take advantage of a glorious day. Young mothers pushing baby-buggies, couples strolling hand in hand, people walking dogs, elderly groups sitting under enormous pine trees chatting to each other.

An Asian couple hurrying by, carrying fishing rods and equipment, ignored Danika. A young woman chasing after her run-away pup came in to view. She gave Danika a questioning look. Danika pointed in the direction where the pup had gone. The young woman shouted her thanks and ran off down the pathway, sighting her wayward pet.

Pushing all thoughts from her mind, Danika took in her surroundings. The warm air was summer's way of announcing it was on its way. Some summers were brutal, causing death and destruction with devastating bushfires, droughts and floods. You either loved summer or hated it. Danika loved summer and the freedom from heavy winter clothes.

Squawking seagulls caught her attention. A smile escaped while watching them windsurf above her, wishing she had something to reward them for their performance. The tide was out, which triggered her to recall a comment made by an old-timer who had lived in the area all his life.

"People," he said, "complain when the tide is out. Blind to all that beauty visible when the tide's out. All they see is an open space. I dunno," he said, shaking his head in disgust. "Some people just don't know how to appreciate nature!"

After that conversation, Danika went to the foreshore to have a look. She discovered that the old-timer was correct. There was much to see. From that day onwards, whenever the tide was out, she made a point of perusing the rock pools. She was never disappointed.

With that thought in mind, she got up and walked to the path's edge. There was so much activity: small sand crabs scurried around water pools and shells; tiny fish and other life moving about in crevasses. Sunlight hitting watery gaps and cracks made everything sparkle. A gentle breeze ruffled her hair. She caught a whiff of salty air and thought, *'How blessed I am to have all this beauty at my fingertips.'*

Danika went back to the bench seat and sat down. She carried on observing the world around her. Taking note that people walking past were smiling. Over in the park, parents played with their children. Dogs romped about barking for their owners to throw them a ball. Laughter and joyful squeals filled the air. Traffic hubbub merged with the rhythm of life; it was a beautiful noise.

Feeling better, Danika sat forward and covered her mouth with her hand. *'Oh, heck, I owe Eva an apology. I have to explain everything to her right away.'*

"Are you talking to that bird?" Danika asked, coming through the door.

"N ... not really," Eva stammered.

Silence fell between them.

"Are you okay? I didn't mean to upset you."

Danika nodded. "I'm fine. You didn't upset me. The past did. If we are going to be working together, there's something I must tell you."

"O-kay."

Danika sat down across from Eva. The room felt still as Eva waited for Danika to speak.

"My name isn't Danika Bryce."

Eva's eyes widened as her jaw dropped open.

Danika gave her a moment to recover before continuing. "My real name is *Jane Hopkins.* My eyes are blue and my hair is blond. I am wearing green contact lenses. Here, see," Danika said, slipping out a contact lens to show her.

"So, your beautiful black hair isn't natural?" All Eva could say.

Danika shook her head.

"What possessed you to go to such extremes?"

"My life, mine and Abbi's life were in danger."

"W ... what?" Eva stuttered, trying to comprehend what she was hearing. "How?"

Danika got up and went to the fridge. She grabbed a bottle of wine from the side door, two glasses from the cupboard and took them to the table. She opened the bottle and filled both glasses.

"Here," she said, pushing a glass in front of Eva. "You will need this."

Eva, too stunned to talk, wrapped her hand around her glass and took a very long swig. "Holy moly, Danika," Eva said, wiping her mouth with the back of her hand. "I guessed something was amiss, but nothing as crazy as this." Eva paused. The wine was affecting her speech. "Jane?" she slurred and giggled. "You do not look like a *Jane.*"

Danika smiled.

"Ok," Eva said, taking another long swig of her wine. "Tell me where, why, what and all of that."

Danika shook her head. "No point now. You wouldn't remember a thing I said when you sobered up. Tomorrow, I'll tell you everything."

Eva's eyes closed as she laid her head on the table. "Okay," she muttered. "I feel sleepy right now."

Danika shook Eva awake enough to help her over to the cherry red leather couch in the corner. The couch was new. Danika could not recall seeing it there earlier. Then realised it must have been delivered while she was at the foreshore. After Eva flopped down and melted in to the soft leather, Danika grabbed the lightweight shawl hanging from a chair and draped it over her. Then washed the glasses and put the wine back in the fridge and left, closing the door quietly behind her.

Eva stirred and mumbled as she tossed and turned in sleep. She then shot upright in fright. Eyes wide, darting about the studio. Nothing looked out of place. *'How did I get here?'* she thought, resting her head in both hands. *'Are the nightmares returning?'*

"What the bloody hell was I thinking, unloading on Eva like that?" Danika yelled, driving home. "And filling her glass so full," she barked, pounding the steering wheel, spewing obscenities. "She's on antidepressants! Why did I not remember that? Now, I have put her life in danger too!"

Danika swung the car around and drove back to Eva's place.

Eva was slouched over, holding her head in her hands, when Danika arrived. "Oh Dani, I just had the worst nightmare. My head is aching."

Danika knelt down beside Eva. "Are you okay?"

Eva nodded. "I think so. My head feels as though I have been hit with a sledgehammer, though. I'm fine other than that."

"What happened?"

"Not sure," Eva said, running her hands through her hair. "Everything is fuzzy. The dream. No. It was a nightmare I had, is fuzzy."

"What can you remember?"

"It was strange."

"How so?"

Eva stared at Danika. "It was about you. You were telling me you have different colour eyes; your hair is not yours."

Danika said nothing, just stared back at Eva.

"Like I said, Dani, it was weird."

Danika still said nothing.

"You were here earlier, weren't you?"

Danika nodded.

"We had a glass of wine, right?"

"Yes." Danika said. "I think I poured you too much wine."

"And I drank it too fast. Mixing so much alcohol with my medication would have caused me to hallucinate."

Relief ran through Danika's body. "Are you sure you're, okay?"

"Yes," Eva replied, getting up from the couch. "Stop fussing. It is so unlike you. You'd be telling me to *get over it*," she said, smiling.

"You didn't mention you had bought a couch."

"Oh, I forgot. It was ordered weeks ago. The warehouse delivered it this morning, after you left. Do you like it? I think it's gorgeous. It matches the chair I have in my loungeroom. I love the colour!"

Danika smiled, thinking how the couch had saved the day. Otherwise, Eva would have woken up on the floor.

"What were we celebrating?" Eva asked, wondering off to the kitchenette to make coffee.

Danika studied Eva for a moment. "No celebration," she said, keeping her voice steady, certain Eva had no recollection of their recent conversation. "I felt like having a wine and asked if you'd like to join me."

"Oh, right," Eva answered.

Danika turned her attention to her computer. "I'll be working on your profile today. Do you have a recent photo of yourself?

Eva carried two hand-painted mugs over to Danika's desk. She handed one to Danika and held the other. Sipping the hot brew while leaning against the desk, she gave that question some thought. "Um, no," Eva paused. "There is that group photo of us taken at Chelsea's' luncheon two years ago. You could photo shop me out of that."

"I could but, I won't."

"Why not?"

Danika picked up the camera lying on the desk that Eva used to take photos of her work.

"Stand over there by your work bench and fold papers."

"But I look a mess."

"Eva, you never look a mess. Do as I ask, please?"

Reluctantly, Eva obeyed.

Danika clicked away as Eva worked, moving slowly around the room catching her from different angles. A few moments later, "There, all done," Danika smiled. "Now did that hurt?"

"No, but I feel uncomfortable, though. The camera is never kind to me."

Danika was too busy going through the shots she took to listen to what Eva was saying. "Hmm, I can't pick one."

"See," Eva interrupted. "I told you I ..."

"No, no," Danika cut in. "All of them are amazing. The light and the angle were perfect. Look, see for yourself. They're gorgeous, Eva!"

Eva's eyes widen and features soften into a smile. "They are. I've never looked so good."

Danika shook her head. "Eva, that's what you look like."

A tear slid down Eva's cheek as she looked at Danika. "Then why did Josh cheat on me?"

Danika blurted out, "Because he probably had a small dick and wanted a bigger one. He was an arsehole, an inadequate arsehole!"

Eva's hand shot up to her mouth to stifle shock and laughter.

"Now," Danika said, "can we get on with doing your profile."

Chapter 7

While Eva and Danika were at the studio, working on Eva's profile, Chelsea was sitting in her office planning a menu for the morning tea. At the sound of light tapping on her door, she removed her reading glasses and popped them on her head. Jeffrey, her husband of twenty years, stood in the doorway holding a tray.

"Fancy a cup of tea, darling?" he asked.

"Thank you, sweetheart, perfect timing, as usual."

Chelsea and Jeffrey first met at a cafe in Sydney. Both were on their way to meetings with time to spare and popped into a nearby café for an early lunch. When Jeffrey arrived at the cafe, he placed an order, took a number and sat down at a vacant table. Chelsea entered minutes after him and ordered chicken and avocado on multigrain, took a number and scanned the room for a table; all were occupied.

Jeffrey was texting a message to his secretary telling her he was having lunch before his meeting when he glanced up and noticed a very attractive woman looking around the café, obviously for a vacant table. He stood up, walked halfway towards her to catch her attention by waving.

"You are welcome to share my table if you like."

Hesitating a moment, Chelsea studied the tall man with twinkly blue eyes, dressed in an expensive charcoal suit. She realised it was her only option but to accept his offer. "Thank you," she said, smiling graciously. That's very kind of you."

Chelsea's smile made Jeffrey's heart skip a beat. He introduced himself, offering his hand. "I would love to say, Bond, James Bond, but I'm not that exciting. I'm Jeffrey, Jeffrey Harrison, the company solicitor at Bradly and Mackay, at your service," he beamed, bowing his head slightly.

Chelsea giggled and took Jeffery's hand. "Chelsea Brady, Fundraiser Extraordinaire," she responded, tongue in cheek.

"Good to know one of us is exciting," Jeffrey quipped.

Jeffrey was so amusing Chelsea only ate half of her sandwich, laughing so much. Losing track of time, she had to hurry to her meeting. Before leaving, Jeffrey handed her his business card.

"If ever you need a solicitor, please call me. It was a delight to have met you, Chelsea," he added with all sincerity.

Smiling, she offered him her card. "Christmas is almost here. I am also a Function Planner," she said, before hurrying away.

Several months passed before they crossed paths again at a Cancer Fundraiser Dinner. Jeffrey, for reasons he could not explain, purchased two tickets for the dinner after he had ended his current relationship.

"Hello Jeffrey," said Chelsea, touching him on the shoulder, "How lovely to see you again."

He spun around and clasped Chelsea's hand. "I had hoped you would be here," he said, grasping why he had unwittingly bought the tickets. "Will you join me at my table?"

The invitation came as a complete surprise. Chelsea assumed Jeffrey had brought a companion with him.

"Well, I," she faltered. "I'm working tonight." As she spoke, disappointment wiped away Jeffrey's smile.

"Wait here. Don't move," she said and dashed away. A few minutes later, she returned and guided Jeffrey to a secluded table that overlooked the room.

"This is splendid, my dear. The view is marvellous!" He remarked. "It's like looking through a two-way mirror. We can see the other guests in all their finery enjoying food, wine and music as they dance away the evening, but they cannot see me gazing into your beautiful hazel eyes."

Chelsea giggled and then became serious. "From here," she said, "I can monitor things and spend time with you. My offsider knows where to find me should she need me."

Returning to the present, Chelsea looked at Jeffrey with loving eyes as he poured the tea and handed her a cup and saucer with biscuits she had baked the day before.

"You, my darling, still give me goosebumps as strong as the day when we first met in that Sydney café."

Jeffrey grinned and planted a kiss on the top of her head before settling in the chair opposite her.

"Ah, I remember it well. It was one of the best days of my life!" He paused a moment than asked. "What are your plans for today, darling?

"I'll be home all day," she said, in between sipping her tea and nibbling on a biscuit.

"I'm meeting Johnny Oyster at ten-thirty," he said.

Chelsea nodded. "That's right, I remember. He's involved with the shellfish restoration in Moreton Bay."

Jeffrey nodded, taking a sip of his tea. "I am rather intrigued by it all. From what Johnny has briefed me on the subject, the volunteers are doing a marvellous job. I think I will enjoy washing empty oyster shells and laying them out to dry." Jeffrey paused again. "You know, darling, it takes four months to sterilise the shell before they place them back into the Bay. Each shell provides a home for ten baby oysters." Jeffrey shook his head in amazement. "Can you imagine that?"

Chelsea impishly said, "I'm glad I am not an oyster. It would be awfully crowded in there."

They both laughed.

He continued. "Semiretirement is wonderful. Kicking back and leisurely reading and doing whenever desire takes hold is one thing. I still want to be active outdoors." He paused. "My body craves freedom after being cooped up in an office for all those years." He paused again. "Mind you, I am grateful to be granted the time to enjoy the autumn of my life so far."

Draining the contents of his cup, he glanced at his watch. With a note of great expectation he added, "I had better get cracking if I am to be on time to meet Johnny Oyster."

"Don't worry about the tray," Chelsea said as Jeffrey was about to gather the cups together. "I'll do that."

"If you insist, my darling, I won't argue. 'Time's awastin'," he said, planting a kiss on her lips.

"Enjoy your day!" He called as he closed the door behind him.

Chelsea was smiling. She had not seen Jeffrey that excited in a while. She had often said, there was nothing about her husband that annoyed her. She adored him as much as he did her. Life with him was as perfect as it could be!

She snapped her notebook close. After having written out the last list of delectables for the morning tea she headed for the kitchen. Standing at the sink, looking through the window at her flowers, herbs and vegetable beds, she whispered a prayer of thanks, grateful that fate had led her to the café that day. Had she arrived early for the meeting, she would not have met her future husband.

The house phone's loud ring startled her.

Even before she spoke, the caller said, "I know you are alone," then clicked off.

She knew who it was. *'He will not scare me this time,'* she thought and carried on with the preparations for Friday. Half an hour later, she froze at the sound of banging on the door. When the banging persisted, Chelsea went to the front entrance.

"Go away!" she shouted.

"Chelsea! It's me, Danika. Open the door!"

Danika sighed with relief when the door opened.

Chelsea stood in the doorway, pale and shaking.

"What the hell is going on? You look as if you're about to faint!"

"Someone just called and told me they know I'm home."

"Oh, sorry, that was me. I was in a black spot where the reception was lousy. I said when you picked up, oh good, now I know you are home; I will drop by and give you a hand with the morning tea prep for tomorrow. You always go to so much trouble."

Chelsea raised her hand, beckoning Danika to come in. They walked down the long, wide, tiled hallway leading to the spacious dining room and kitchen in silence. Floor to ceiling glass sliding doors facing the pool and garden allowed speckled sunlight to brighten the darkest corner of the room.

Chelsea dropped onto the leather couch like a rag doll.

Danika went to the sink. Picked up the jug, shook it and then turned it on.

"Oh, forget the tea, Dani. My favourite red is in the pantry. Open it, please. Pour us both a glass. Fill mine to the brim!"

Danika nodded, smiling.

Chelsea rested her head on the back of the couch. A heap of old memories she would rather forget came flooding back into her mind's eye.

Danika stood beside Chelsea and handed her a filled glass. "Here hon, hope this will help with whatever's bothering you."

Chelsea sat up and took the wine from Danika. She sipped it with her eyes closed, appreciating every note.

"Are you ready to tell me what the hell it was that just now turned you into a stranger?"

"It's a stain on my life that I cannot get rid of."

Danika understood what Chelsea meant. She also had a *stain* that she could not get rid of.

"Want to tell me about it?" Danika asked as she sipped her wine. "You know, all stains have enemies. You just have to find someone who can get rid of it for you."

Chelsea said nothing for a long, drawn-out moment.

Standing, she said, "You know what?"

Danika looked puzzled. "What?"

"I'd appreciate a hand with prepping the sandwich fillings."

"That's why I'm here," Danika replied, respecting Chelsea's reluctance to share her secret.

As they stood side-by-side at the kitchen bench, Chelsea asked, "Had a busy day?" As if the last half hour never happened.

Danika nodded. "Yes, I have."

Chelsea turned to look at Danika as she reached for her wine glass.

"What have you been doing?"

"I spent the day with Eva writing up a bio for her social media page."

Chelsea's mouth gaped open. "You what?"

After Danika briefly outlined Eva's plan to sell her handmade boxes online, Chelsea nodded her approval.

"Eva can fill in the details," explained Danika. "I left her to check on the number of *hits* on her page. The photos I took of her are gorgeous. The one we chose, I'm certain it will attract attention."

"The business will keep her busy and her mind off losing Josh," Chelsea said.

"She knows."

"Knows what?"

"Josh was a player."

Chelsea's features froze in horror.

"I'll let her tell you all about it when she's up to it. Okay?"

Chelsea nodded.

The *hits* were coming in fast; a few were interested in the boxes. Dozens more were *friend* request. Eva laughed. '*This is madness,*' she thought as she deleted the friend requests one after the other. Another one popped up as she was about to close the page.

"Will you be my friend?" was the heading beside a small photograph. Curiosity stirred her to click on it. A man in his late forties, with blonde hair, blue eyes and warm smile appeared above the message.

"Hello!" he said.

Eva jumped not expecting him to be online.

"Hello!" she wrote back.

"My name is Marcus Johnson. I am living in Boston, Massachusetts. Do you know where that is?"

"Of course. I was in Boston, two years ago, visiting friends. As you can see on my profile, I am Eva. I imagine it is nice to meet you."

"Why do you say, you imagine it is nice to meet me?"

"I have seen news stories about how devastated women are after some cad has encouraged those women to give them money, with the promise of a loving future together."

"Yes, I also have seen this on the news. As a contractor in the building industry, I travel to other countries for work. The pay is excellent, so I don't need your money."

"That's good because I don't have any money to give you. My lifestyle is very humble."

"You are starting a business, I, see? My wish for you is good fortune."

"Yes, I am. The business is small. More of a *hobby*. Thank you for your good wishes. It is getting late. Good bye!"

Just before Eva closed the page, a message popped up.

"What is a hobby? I will contact you tomorrow you can tell me then."

She did not respond.

Not until later, did Eva realise the oddity of the new *friend* not knowing what a hobby was. She smiled.

Chapter 8

Friday morning on the dot of ten, nine women dressed in all their finery arrived at the gate of the Harrison's lovely home bearing gifts of wine and flowers for their illustrious host and hostess.

No one wanted to be late. No one ever was.

Jeffrey, oozing charm, greeted the women at the door, in the role of Butler, holding a tray of glasses filled to the brim with champagne. The women adored him and pecked his cheek as they crossed the threshold, taking a glass from the tray.

"Good morning, Jeffrey," they said in unison.

"Good morning, ladies," he replied, bowing. "I am honoured to be surrounded by so much beauty, this lovely spring morning."

Eva was the last guest to arrive. Jeffrey whispered to her. "I have juice for you, just in case you are on medication," he winked.

"Oh, you are a darling, Jeffrey," Eva replied, touching his arm.

"I can't take the credit for that wise decision, I'm afraid."

"Ah, okay." Eva nodded.

As Eva headed down the hall to join the others, compliments and admiration for the decor trickled her way. The room, styled in that *old-world* charm, was a spectacular sight.

Chelsea caught sight of Eva entering the room, holding an enormous bouquet of native flowers and a glass of juice, gazing around appraisingly at the transformation that had taken place. Victorian drapes covered the windows, two chandeliers twinkling in the candlelight, hung above the tables dressed in crisp, white linen, fine bone china and silver cutlery. Four, three-tier stands of dainty sandwiches, white chocolate scones with French raspberry conserve, mini cakes with lemon curd, mini caramel tarts and other delicious treats took pride of place on the tables. A table covered in sheer colourful fabric; a crystal ball and a deck of cards lay in waiting, in the farthest corner of the room.

Chelsea wrapped her arms around Eva.

"It's so good to see you."

"You are amazing Chelsea! The room looks wonderful. Nothing is too much trouble for you!!" Eva said, feeling proud they were friends, while taking in all there was to see. "Oh, now that will be interesting," Eva said, pointing to the crystal ball and cards grinning impishly.

Chelsea shrugged. "Just a bit of fun Jeffrey arranged," she said. "I'm so glad you like the theme. Danika and Jeffrey helped me dress the room."

"Like it? I love it!" Eva beamed. "Oh, and thanks for the juice." Eva looked at Chelsea and paused. Her eyes glistened, "I have so much to thank you for, my dear friend. I ..."

"Are those beautiful flowers for me, or are you just going to carry them around all day?" Chelsea asked, interrupting Eva.

"Ok, I get it," Eva said, handing Chelsea the bouquet. "But we will talk later." Eva's tone was serious, then her voice went up a few octaves. "I have so much to share with you. You'll be seeing me sooner rather than later."

Jeffrey left the gathering and went upstairs to his office when Chelsea tapped her glass with a spoon to get everyone's attention. As he ascended the stairs, Chelsea's voice faded. He knew she was thanking the women for coming, as if they were obliging her, when, the truth-be-known, others would have done almost anything to get an invitation to the morning tea. He knew she was saying how happy she was that Eva could join them. Jeffrey missed the part when Eva stood up and thanked Chelsea for her love and support during her *pity party*. He missed the wide-eyes and dropped jaws when Eva blurted out that she was aware Josh had cheated on her and with whom. A few wriggled in their seats at that comment. Eva grinned. "He was a good man regardless," she continued. "I know he loved me. He was kind and would do anything I asked of him. The trouble was that he liked too many other women. However, the past is the past, so let's leave it there, eh?"

The room burst into applause with relief for some. Jeffrey missed all of that, but Chelsea will fill him in later, because time had not allowed him to check the security tapes earlier. Cameras were installed in the house and round the perimeter of the grounds, after several home invasions. They had an idea who the culprit was, but lacked evidence to substantiate this theory. Each evening, Jeffrey would fast-forward the tape of the day to ensure that no unwelcomed visitors had entered the premises. This time, Jeffrey's sharp eyes noticed something odd. Chelsea and Danika's body language alarmed him. He rewound the tape and listened to their conversation. From what he heard, Jeffrey gathered something had happened, but Chelsea was unwilling to discuss it with Danika. The comment Danika made about stains having enemies gave Jeffrey an idea. He opened the secret compartment in his desk and took out a small notebook, found the number he needed and punched it into his mobile.

"Hey, it's been too long, buddy!"

"Too long, mate! Where are you?"

"Home packing, why?"

"Away long?"

"As a matter-of-fact I'm heading down your way. Got a tip about a package a client is looking for. I'm to confirm the package, call it in and I'm done. What do you need?"

"Can't get into it now."

"Ok, I'll check in when I arrive."

"Okay, mate! Travel safe!"

"Always do!"

The mobile went dead.

Jeffrey returned the notebook to its hiding place and went back downstairs. As he stepped off the stairwell, about to join the others, a slim woman of average height and looks he had never seen before came in through the front door. She smiled at him.

"Hello, Jeffrey," she said and kept walking and then sat down at the corner table.

'Who the hell is that?' he thought. *'How in blazes did she get past the security alarm?'*

Puzzled, he dashed out of the front door to check if someone had disarmed the alarm at the gate. Several folds appeared across his forehead when he discovered the alarm had not been touched.

Boisterous chatter and laughter faded as though someone had turned down the volume in the room when the woman of average height and looks entered and sat down at the corner table. Two women whispered to one another, imagining they were in the company of a dominant presence, while others observed the stranger.

The woman raised her right hand. "I am ready. Come," she said, beckoning to Eva.

Raising her brow and smiling at her companions, Eva pushed her chair away from the table and moved to the seat facing the woman in the corner.

She placed both hands over the crystal ball.

"Ask me no questions," she said, gazing into the ball turning cloudy. "I do not have answers. I tell you just what I see in here." She paused. "Do you understand?"

Eva nodded.

"I see a shattered heart." There was a long pause. "Your heart will heal. There is a man with two faces. The voice you hear echoes from afar. Your son and his wife will live a long and happy life. Your heart's desire is closer than you think. Find the diary, find the truth."

The reader's voice droned on in a flat tone, as if reading a badly written script. All the same, Eva was astounded the woman could see any of that in a cloudy glass ball when she could see nothing at all.

The reader lifted her hands off the ball and rested them on the table. She said nothing else, so Eva got up and went back to her seat.

"Well, what did she say?" the others whispered.

Eva was still digesting the reader's words. "She is good," was all Eva could say.

Next was Danika. The reader went through the same routine with her as she had done with Eva.

"You have many secrets."

Danika gasped.

Ignoring Danika's reaction, the reader continued as if in a trance. "A dark shadow is following you. There is light shining through the cracks. This is a good sign, but still take care. Your daughter is standing on a high mountain. She has a long road to travel before she finds happiness. An unexpected visitor will brighten your day, perhaps your life. That is up to you! You are brave, wise and loyal. Your friends support you; one will betray you."

She fell silent and sat back in her chair. Danika saw this as her cue to leave.

As Danika stood to leave, the reader gazed over the heads huddled in low chatter, looking for Chelsea since she was absent. She caught Maureen's attention, unnerving her. Maureen declined the offer of a reading with the shake of her head. The woman insisted with the motion of her hand. With a heavy sigh, Maureen got up and sat down opposite her at the table. Leaning forward, Maureen whispered, "I don't want a reading." The reader ignored her and continued as she had with the others, covering the ball with her hands but did not look into it. Her eyes remained focused on Maureen's face.

"Your spirit is dark."

Maureen squirmed under the reader's penetrating stare. Unwilling to listen to any more, she got up to leave, but before she could, the woman said, "What you have done is unforgivable!"

Acting as though nothing was amiss, Maureen calmly went back to join the others; she was terrified and wanted to leave, but waited awhile and then slipped away while Chelsea was having her reading.

Jeffrey chatted with the guests in Chelsea's absence. The room was full of lively banter. Laughter rose and fell as the reader was telling Chelsea that she must rest without explaining why. *'No questions.'* Her eyes said when Chelsea looked puzzled. "A handsome man is coming your way. Not tall, with blond hair and blue eyes, a knight who slays the dragon."

Chelsea was gobsmacked. She did not understand what any of it meant. The reader got up from the table and left unnoticed. Jeffrey spotted Chelsea sitting alone at the reader's table. He excused himself and went to her.

"Darling, what is it?"

"I am not sure if I should laugh or be alarmed."

"Why?"

Jeffrey paled when Chelsea told him what the woman said.

"Who is she?"

"I don't know who she is. I thought you must have booked her."

"Me? No! Where is she now?"

Jeffrey scanned the room and looked outside while Chelsea checked the powder room.

Danika caught Chelsea heading to the kitchen.

"Is everything ok?"

"Yes, why do you ask?"

"That reader, no one knows who she is or her name. She sure put a gust up Maureen's butt; she could not get out of here fast enough. That woman told me a few things that she could not have known. From your expression, hon, she curled your toes too."

"To be honest, Dani, we don't know who she is."

They looked flabbergasted at each other.

Chapter 9

Maureen's only thought, when she left the group, was to get as far away from Manly as possible. In her haste, she forgot to set the GPS for *home* before driving off down Stratton Terrace. She was unfamiliar with the area having been to Chelsea's home only on two other occasions. Both times were work related. Confused and unsure which way to go, she turned left turn at Cambridge Parade instead of going right, ending up at the Marina at the end of the Esplanade. Her option was to turn left or to turn right. She chose left and drove a short distance along the road. Up ahead was a vacant space at Bayside Park. She stopped. There, she took several deep breaths. With each breath, she relaxed. Gazing at her surroundings, it enthralled her at how lovely the area was; *calming* came to mind.

She wanted to capture the moment, so she grabbed her camera and stepped out of the car. As she snapped away, a rickety voice from behind said, "No doubt your pictures are good, but I bet my next meal that they won't be as good as Dirty George's were."

Maureen spun around to find a big man, bent with time and life, sitting on the bench, near the road crossing, under the shade of a huge Moreton Bay fig tree.

She smiled at him. "Was he a friend of yours?"

The old timer shook his head. "Nah. I was just a kid when Dirty George was around."

"Why do you call him Dirty George?"

"You had to stand down-wind of him," he grinned and continued in a dry, raspy tone, coughing between sentences. "In Dirty George's mind, bathing was unhealthy. His idea of a bath was to stand near a smoky fire to kill whatever infestation he carried. Looking up at Maureen, the old-timer said with pride, "His photography was great, though. Dirty George had nothing like that fangle-dangle stuff you have there," he grinned, scratching his head. "He made his camera out of a butter-box and used an old piece of black cloth he flipped over his head to shut out the light and measured the distance between his subject and the lens for the correct exposure with a knotted string and operated the shutter with another piece of string attached to a pencil after slipping a strip of film into the back of the butter-box, which was mounted on a make-shift tripod." The old man smiled, pausing for breath and staired at the ground, as if he could see the vision in his minds-eye. He glanced up at Maureen and grinned. "George shouted at us to keep still just before he disappeared under the black cloth to take our picture. The photographs Dirty George took of me and my sister are as good as the day he gave them to my mother, over seventy years ago. He charged her two shillings for four photographs."

Maureen sat down on the end of the bench, next to the old fella. He turned to look at her and smiled. "It's been a long time since a pretty lady gave me the time of day."

She returned his smile. "Thank you," she said. "D... Dirty George," she hesitated. "I don't want to call him that, especially since he was such an interesting and resourceful man. What was his proper name?"

"George Cooling," said the old man. "From what I can recall about D ..." he paused and looked apologetically at Maureen. "About George, is his family back in England turfed him out and no one knows what he did to make them so angry. He arrived in the area in the 1930s in a tugboat and later camped under the boat for several years, near a cotton tree, until a fire destroyed it. He was living at the end of Spring Street, now known as Falcon Street. George was known for lighting fires under his bed to keep warm."

"How sad. Was he mentally ill?"

"I recall he had a breakdown at some stage, but wasn't crazy or anything like that. You couldn't whistle around him, though. He hated whistling. It stirred him to anger. Apart from that, he was harmless. George was a gentleman and according to local history, he was educated and could carry on interesting conversations about anything. George played the violin and built a bike out of bits and pieces he found around the place. He was often seen riding the bike around the town. Later on, he built a motorbike with a sidecar. Some say he was a genius. He built a plane out of old scrap metal and got it off the ground, but crashed it into a tree."

"Was he hurt?"

"Yes, but nothing serious."

"Where did he go after the fire destroyed his boat?"

"A local said he moved into a cut-out hollowed log of an enormous tree in Hoffman's paddock at Lota and from there into a tent. Many local say George also lived in a hut in McIntyre's paddock close to Lota creek, probably because a duck befriended him."

Maureen shook her head and then smiled. "I'm glad he had a pet to keep him company."

The old man nodded. "George was shrewd. He would often turn up at the Feige's place at mealtime, asking if Mrs Feige wanted any photos taken. Mrs Feige was my mate, Les Greenhill's grandmother. She would say not today, thanks George. He would then strike up a conversation with family members and keep talking until the meal was ready. They always welcomed George at their home. Most folks back then were kind. Several women like Mrs Feige fed George meals, cake, sandwiches and many cups of tea, even though he stank to high heaven."

"I wish I had been born when life was much simpler," Maureen said.

"Things were much simpler, but life was just as challenging as it is today. We made the best of what we had. It is no different today …"

"What happened to him? Where did he end up?"

"Rumour was that George was burnt to death in his sleep."

Maureen gasped. Her hand shot up and covered her mouth.

"That was just a rumour, not the truth. George had an accident. The authorities took him to the General Hospital, later transferred him to Wondai Hospital where he died October, 26th 1960."

As the GPS guided her back to the city, Maureen's heart was full of regret thinking about what she had done. The reader was right. It was unforgivable! Having to face Chelsea and Eva highlighted that fact.

It was easy to block out everything while residing in a luxury, high-rise apartment overlooking the Brisbane River and Story Bridge, where the chances of running into Eva or Chelsea were slim.

After Josh's death, Maureen carried on as before. Work assignments arrived via email, the same as always; she went to the site, did the shoot, sorted through the photographs, chose the best and sent them to the client. The thing that had changed was Josh no longer visited or stayed overnight with her. Tears leaked from her eyes and spilled down her cheeks, blurring her vision. *'He wanted to leave me. I could not let that happen. I needed him more than Eva did!'*

The terror in Josh's eyes flashed into her mind just before the oncoming car hit her.

The television droned on in the background while Eva rummaged through boxes of Josh's belongings she collected from his office before she sold the business, looking for the mystery diary. Feeling exasperated and tired, ready to give up, Eva planted herself on the chair in view of the television. A clip of a red mangled Toyota flashed across the screen.

Eva heard the reporter say, "The driver died at the scene ..."

Then the phone rang.

"Hello?"

"Have you seen the news?" Danika asked.

"I'm watching it now. That car looks familiar. Do you know who it belongs to?"

"Maureen."

"Oh, oh, my ... She worked for Josh."

"Eva, are you okay?"

"Yes. Just shocked, that's all." She paused. "You just never know when ..."

"C'mon hon, don't go there. We have to take one day at a time and enjoy every moment."

Eva went silent.

"Eva?"

"I'm listening."

"Doesn't seem so to me," Danika replied.

"Something just caught my eye. I'll call you back."

"I'm coming over," Danika said, before the line went dead.

Eva noticed a box different from the others; smaller in size, with different markings on the side. She could not recall packing it. One quick swipe of the Stanley knife, the box popped opened. It was full of old contracts and two legal looking envelopes. Danika came through the backdoor in time to see Eva open the longest envelope. Eva glanced up at Danika, but said nothing as she unfolded the document.

Eva gasped.

"What is it?"

"It's a deed, a remote and a key-card to an apartment in the city. The apartment is in my name." Eva said as her eyes filled with tears, "More deception!"

Danika scanned the room.

"What are you doing with all these boxes?"

Eva shrugged.

"That woman, the reader, told me to look for a diary. I don't keep a diary, so I thought she might have meant Josh."

"Did you find the diary?"

"No, I found these instead," holding up the deed, key-card and remote.

"Shall we see your apartment?"

"What, now?"

"It's as good a time as any. Rush hour and that accident near the Story Bridge should be cleared by now."

Twenty minutes later, Danika steered her car in to the underground carpark of Eva's Kangaroo Point apartment.

"Double garage, hmm."

Eva glanced at Danika as she pressed the remote.

Danika drove in and parked.

"Ready?" she asked opening her door.

Eva shook her head. "I'm afraid of what I will find."

"You are about to discover the truth. C'mon."

Eva sighed and dawdled behind Danika. Her heart thumped in her chest. She swiped the card to the lift. The doors slid open with a huge sigh. Punching in the numbers on the key-card within seconds, they stepped out into what resembled a luxurious real estate magazine. Neither spoke. They wandered around the interior designed, but sterile, apartment in a daze. The panoramic views of the city and of the river were breathtaking.

Danika touched the kitchen bench.

"This is Statuaior marble; it's Italian, the finest marble you can buy. This alone would cost a fortune."

Eva still had not spoken. She leaned up against the bench, shaking her head.

"Who lives here?" she asked, after a long silence.

Danika came out of the bedroom toting a photograph and a diary.

"She does!"

Eva eyed the photograph with contempt.

"Her?" Eva spat, staring at the redhead smiling back at her. "I don't understand. She is not Josh's type. How did she get here?"

"Perhaps the answer is in this."

Danika passed Eva the diary with a pen still attached to it.

She opened it and got comfortable on the couch, turning page after page; it read like a movie script, full of plots, twists and turns.

Danika sat down beside Eva and handed her a glass of red wine.

"Anything interesting?" she asked.

Eva looked at the wine.

"Oh, I found it in the pantry." Danika responded with a grin. "Since you own the place, I poured us small glasses this time. Heaven knows, you, we both need it."

Eva nodded. "We sure do. I'm living in a nightmare."

"Oh sweetie, I would not call this a nightmare." Danika replied with a sweeping hand.

"No, but this diary is," declared Eva with tears welling up.

Danika remained silent while Eva wiped her eyes.

"This bitch trapped Josh in a web of lies. I cannot believe he fell for it."

"What are you talking about?"

"She wanted Josh, so she played the victim. He came by her place to give her flowers for the 'great' work she was doing and found her beaten and bruised. She wrote, *I am not beautiful or tall and slender like Eva, but I have my ways of persuasion. Josh enjoys being the hero. He can be my hero and protect me from my abusive husband. I want him and I will do anything to keep him! I will NEVER let him leave me. NEVER!*"

Eva flipped over a few pages. "Listen to this. *I told Josh I feared for my life. He said he had a place in the city where I could stay. I convinced him I would never be safe anywhere. Barry will find me and kill me. Josh said he has friends who can make sure Barry never harms me again.* Eva flipped two more pages. *Barry is dead. I took care of him. Josh lied.*

It has been months since we have met. I don't understand why Josh won't sleep with me. He stays overnight. We enjoy one another's company, but nothing else. He cares for me. He has said so many times. It is not enough! I want him to love me!

"The rest is about work and the times they spent together. Josh was not her lover," Eva said, feeling relieved. "He was her friend."

She kept reading and then suddenly gasped and dropped the diary as if it were a hot rock.

Danika, who had wondered out onto the balcony to take in the city views, dashed back inside.

"Maureen killed him! She killed him!" Eva was screaming.

Danika wrapped her arms around Eva and rocked her.

"Shhh, it's ok ..."

Through her tears, Eva told Danika how Maureen had hired a van to run Josh down. Eva paused. "That bitch got away with murder. She cold-heartedly planned Josh's death because he told her he loved me. He could be her friend, nothing more."

"Maureen didn't get away with anything, hon; she's dead, killed a few hours ago, in that fatal accident just before the Story Bridge. Karma is a bitch for the wicked."

Half way home, Danika said, "You have to contact the police."

"I know. I was thinking I will do that in the morning."

Neither spoke until they reached Eva's place.

"Are you okay, hon? I can come in and keep you company for a while. Help you tidy those boxes?"

"I'm fine, Dani, but thanks anyway." Eva's words lacked energy. "You look as tired as I feel."

"Yep, I have to be honest and say I am exhausted. See you tomorrow. And if you need anything ..."

"I will." Eva cut in, waving Danika off. She watched the car disappear down the street before going inside. She turned and stood at her front gate, studying the beautiful home where she and Josh shared their life together, raised their son, entertained family and friends and wondered how much of it was real; was the past thirty-five years a lie?

Eva pushed the gate open and went inside.

'Thirty-five years of lies,' she repeated over and over in her mind, trying to understand why until her head ached. She was beyond anger and tears. She was numb and moved about the house like a zombie, sealing all the boxes. The last box was where she found the deed to the apartment. The other envelope was sitting on top. Before taping the box shut, Eva set it aside. She made coffee, then sat down at the kitchen table looking at the envelope, wondering what mystery it held. *'More trouble? More heartache?'* crossed her mind. She scooped it up. It was as thick as an official sealed document without a name or an address. She peeled back the lip and slid the folded article out of its hiding place and into the bright halogen; it was an unfinished letter from Josh.

Darling, if you are reading this, then the inevitable has happened. Maureen has killed me. Sound ludicrous, but 'hell have no fury ...'

She misunderstood a kindness. I foolishly did not see it until it was too late. I hope you can forgive me. I was an idiot. I am so very sorry to have dragged you into my mess. There was never anything between Maureen and me. Never! I continued to keep company with her because she threatened to destroy our marriage; I could not let that happen. Good fortune smiled upon me the day you entered my life, even though I was undeserving of someone as beautiful, as talented as sweet nature as you. Oh, my darling, there is so much more I have to tell you — I don't have time at the moment. I have an appointment with Maureen. Above all, remember I love you! If she listens to reason, perhaps there's no need to finish this letter/confession.

The other pages were blank, but Eva was past caring. Her brain was numb. Her regret was that Josh was not there for her to confront him. Since she could not do that, she reasoned he had paid the price for his stupidity; so, had she!

She poured herself a glass of red wine and went to her room. She showered, slipped on a nightgown and climbed into bed. Although exhausted, she was far from sleeping. Climbing out of bed to retrieve her laptop, she gave it a power boost and clicked onto her social media page.

Among the comments and *likes* regarding the origami boxes were several private messages from Marcus. She opened his first message. He asked if she was enjoying her day. Eva rolled her eyes and cursed, thinking, *'if you only knew!'* She then clicked on the last message. That one sounded panicky asking if she was ok. Was she angry with him? Had he insulted her? He was very sorry if he had ... She smiled. *'He's worried that his fish might have jumped the hook.'*

Now convinced Marcus was a con artist, she proposed his profile photo was a fake, too. This annoyed her that some innocent man was being used to solicit unsuspecting women for a fraudulent purpose. She was determined to know who Marcus, if that is his real name, was. Eva threw back the bedcovers and headed for the kitchen. She had purchased a mobile phone and sim card for Danika to use for the business. But for now, she would use the mobile to contact Marcus and block him from her social media page; their contact would only be via that phone. He had given her his email address so she could find him on a social media he had advocated. She found it and from that page she replied to his messages, explaining that it was easier for him to get in touch with her on that phone. No sooner had she pressed send, "Is everything ok?" popped up, giving her a jolt.

"I was not expecting you to be online. Of course, everything is, ok. I was dealing with a family matter."

"When you didn't reply? I had in my mind you don't like me."

Eva smiled and shook her head.

"I do not know you that well," she replied. "We're just chatting like pen pals."

"What is pen pal?"

"How old are you?"

"42."

"You don't know what a pen pal is?"

"Correct."

"Pen pals are strangers who become friends by exchanging letters, sharing their interests with each other. Like we are doing, only we are chatting via the internet. But if you are looking for romance, Marcus, you have contacted the wrong woman. I am 60 and you are 42."

"It's late. I must go to sleep. We can talk another time."

Eva switched off the laptop and slid down on the bed, pulled up the doona and fell asleep.

Chapter 10

"What a day!" said Jeffery, handing Chelsea a hot brew he had made and sat down on the couch beside her. She took it robotically. Jeffery looked at Chelsea: she was tense, which was out of character. He leaned back, sipped his tea and watched the news while waiting for her to tell him what it was bothering her.

Chelsea was going over in her mind what the reader told her. *'Who on earth could that handsome, short man be? For the life of me, I've met no one resembling that description.'*

She was too preoccupied with this man to notice Jeffrey had joined her and had given her the cup and saucer she held. When she had, she put it down on the coffee table and glanced up at the television; a crumbled, red Toyota flashed across the screen. They listened with disbelief as the reporter announced the driver of the vehicle did not survive. *"There were no passengers,"* he said.

Chelsea turned to Jeffery. "What will I do?"

Jeffrey looked puzzled. "Do?"

"Maureen didn't have any family, so she said."

"Perhaps you should leave that to the authorities."

Chelsea let out a deep sigh and slumped back on the couch.

"Do you want to tell me what's bothering you?"

"I noticed you were startled when I told you what the reader said about the handsome man with blue eyes, short in statue is coming to slay the dragon."

Jeffrey said nothing.

"You know who this man is, don't you?"

"Yes."

"Well, are you going to explain, or do I have to drag it out of you?"

He took a deep breath and took hold of Chelsea's hand.

"Jeffrey, you are scaring me."

"My *law* had a front door and a back door, meaning that I sometimes had to fight fire with fire. The back door was a necessary evil to beat the bad guys at their own game."

Chelsea was listening, wondering where this was going. She tensed up when he said, "Darling, I have a confession to make," then relaxed as he continued. "This morning I listened in on the conversation between you and Danika, while you were busy with the morning tea. Danika's comment about stains having enemies gave me the idea of contacting a colleague, a man I trust implicitly to investigate our trouble-making ghost to find out who his enemies are, so *they* can deal with him. That way, our hands are clean and the stain disappears."

Still silent, Chelsea took her time to digest what Jeffrey was saying. The longer she thought about it, the more she liked it.

"I'm in!" she shouted, adding, "As they say, hell has no fury like a woman scorned. Well, the same can be said of John Patterson, who refused to accept our break-up. That scumbag deserves all he gets. From the day I threw him out of my home, he has spent years seeking revenge and has done his utmost to intimidate, harass, lie and ruin my creditability. That man is a sociopath!"

Chelsea hung her head and then looked up to face Jeffrey. "I am an intelligent woman," she said. "I don't understand what attracted me to him. He was the biggest mistake of my life."

Jeffrey clasped her hand in his. "Darling," he said, brushing his lips across the back of her hand. "We all have kissed a frog before we found our prince or princess. Some find their princess or prince and some get stuck with a frog."

"My frog is still haunting me, hell bent on trying to destroy my creditability and my business." Chelsea slapped the couch. "How dare he contact my new clients with false accusations about how I *fiddled* past clients' accounts! My attention to detail had alerted me to the irregularity in several accounts. I reported my findings to the CEO, which confirmed his suspicions about the fraudulent accountant and he set a trap. Even though I did nothing wrong, that frog marked me as the culprit when repeating the incident to whoever would listen. That bastard cast a shadow over my integrity." Chelsea sighed with frustration. "No doubt he has inflicted more of his lies upon others, too."

"I am counting on it," said Jeffrey.

Chapter 11

Danika felt mentally and physically exhausted by the time she pulled up in her driveway. She rested her head on the steering wheel as the evening's events flashed through her mind. She remained there until she mustered up enough energy to drag herself out of the car and shuffle inside. She dropped the keys on the kitchen table and her bag where she stood and plonked down in the nearest chair. She sprawled across the table with a sigh. Her hand touched her mobile. She sprang up, realising she had left home without it. She cursed. "Abbi will be out of her mind with worry."

There were eight missed calls from her. Abbi's voice mails sounded frantic by the last call. Danika pressed Abbi's number even though it was well past midnight. She answered on the first ring.

"I'm so sorry, honey."

"Ma, I thought ... I couldn't sleep ... I was so worried."

"I know what you thought. That is why I am calling at this hour. No need to worry, I am okay. Eva needed help with something. It is a long, astonishing story. Too late to get into right now. How about you come over tonight and

I'll tell you all about it over dinner? Go to sleep now. See you later. Okay?"

"Okay. Night ma."

"Night hon!"

Abbi placed her mobile on the bedside table and fell back on the pillow. *'If only I could unsee the horrible things I saw as a child,'* she thought, *'I wouldn't worry so much about Mum. She tells me she can look after herself now that she's skilled in self-defence and firearms. I hope she's right. She thinks I was too young to remember anything. I wasn't. I can recall everything and it scares me. This, I could never confide in her or anyone else; it's too dangerous.'*

Her eyes grew heavy as sleep ascended upon her; the deeper she went, shouting, screams and the sound of breaking glass rose to the surface and bounced around in her head until she bolted up in bed breathless and soaked in sweat. She turned on the bedside lamp. Her mobile was ringing. She let it ring a little longer while she caught her breath.

"Hello?"

"Hey, how ya doin'?"

Abbi loved Jackson's drawl. It always made her smile.

"G'day, how are *you* doin'?"

"Aww, you sound all sleepy. Did I wake you?"

"Nope."

"All ready for the big adventure?"

Jackson was shocked when Abbi told him she was going to cancel her trip.

"You cannot not go to Peru. It's a once in a lifetime trip. This opportunity might never come again …"

By the time the call ended, Abbi was in a positive frame of mind and excited about her trip. She just had to trust her mother's judgement that she could protect herself should she need to. Resigning to that, she fell asleep.

Morning arrived faster than Abbi would have liked. She resisted opening her eyes and getting out of bed. Sounds of the world around her coming to life were apparent. She was glad she had not raised the blinds before climbing into bed. The room would have been a blaze of light.

The mobile rang. She frowned, forgetting Jackson said he would call her in the morning.

"Hello?"

"G'morning, lovely lady!"

The smile in Jackson's voice warmed her heart.

"G'morning to you too!"

"Okay, now what are your plans for today?"

"Well, I'm heading off to work soon. Have a few things to do before I go though, like shower and dress, have breakfast," she laughed.

"I won't delay you. Just wanted to make sure you were still feeling …"

"Thank you," Abbi cut in. "Last night was so thoughtful of you …"

"No problem." Jackson said. "I didn't want you to miss out on a lifetime experience, that's all. I guarantee it'll change you in so many ways."

They talked a little while longer before Abbi said she had to get ready for work.

"Ok," said Jackson, unperturbed. "I'll call tonight."

Chapter 12

Eva rose the next morning with a heavy heart and foggy mind. She went through the motions of her morning ritual, showering, dressing and breakfast on auto pilot. The events of the previous day still felt surreal. Discovering that an unhinged woman murdered her husband because he did not love her and that she, herself, owned the luxury million-dollar city apartment Josh's killer, now dead, lived in, would happen only in the movies. In reality, it had happened to her. While mulling all of that over in her mind, a knock at the door startled her. Eva dropped her head into her hands and ran her fingers through her honey curls. She wanted to scream, *'GO AWAY!'* The persistent knocking was hurting her head.

She flung the front door open, about to bark, *'What do you want!'* No words came. Two men in business suits gawked at her. Ignoring her angry expression, the tallest of the two, late fiftyish, wore a suit well-cut, smiled at her. The other man, heavier, older and less dapper, stood behind him, poker faced.

"Our apologies for intruding at this early hour."

Eva said nothing. She was mesmerised by the man in the well-cut suit, by his rich chocolate eyes, smooth, olive skin, salt and pepper hair... *'He was perfect!'* she thought for a split second. *'But of course, he isn't. No one's perfect! He is very impressive, though!'* she mused.

The well-cut suit cleared his throat and held up a small, black folder with his gold shield enclosed.

"I am Senior Detective Sam Ruben and this is Senior Detective Clyde Jones." Jones stepped forward and held up his gold shield in his chubby hand.

"Are you Eva Rennie?" Ruben inquired.

"Yes. Why?"

"May we come in?" he asked, hedging forward.

Eva stood aside to open the door wider. They followed her into the lounge room, where Eva directed them to the couch. She sat on the edge of her high-back, cherry-red leather chair opposite.

"You have a lovely home, Mrs Rennie." Ruben remarked, looking around the immaculate room of neutral shades and textures with splashes of colours in the decor and artwork. One wall was full of books from floor to ceiling. An avid reader himself, the detective was impressed.

Jones shot him a dark look.

"Thank you, Detective." Eva said, softening her voice. "Now, what is the purpose of this, ah, visit?"

"I'll get straight to the point."

"Please do."

"An associate of your late husband, Maureen Manning, was in a fatal accident yesterday afternoon."

Eva remained silent, so the detective continued.

"She has been under investigation for a while."

"Why?"

"A witness to your husband's death called the station a few months ago. He was in a cab, on his way to the airport. He saw the driver's face and jotted down the details in a notebook. He had intended to call the police from the airport, but he got caught up with business calls and forgot about it. It was only when he was looking for something else, he found his pocket notebook."

Both detectives noticed Eva flinch.

"You know this already, don't you?" stated Jones, who had been observing Eva closely. His tone was non-combative.

Eva nodded. "I found out last night while looking for a diary among Josh's things."

"A diary?" Ruben queried.

Eva sighed and leaned back in the chair.

"Would you gentlemen like a coffee?"

"You betcha! Thanks," replied Jones.

She looked at Ruben.

"Yes, thank you."

Maggie was alerted to unfamiliar voices coming from inside the house. She flew to the windowsill and perched herself where she could observe Eva and the strangers. The movement caught Jones' attention. He glanced at the window and saw the bird and immediately dismissed it.

By the time the coffee finished dripping into the glass pot, Eva had the kitchen table set as she would have for friends coming to morning tea; aqua tablecloth and matching crockery, biscuits and patty cakes. The detectives eyed one another. Jones raised his brows. Ruben shrugged and smiled.

"You are going to a lot of trouble, Mrs Rennie. We …"

"Eva," she said, interrupting Ruben. "What I have to tell you, Detective will take a while."

As Eva told them what she had discovered, both men leaned forward to listen. Eva did not know that she was joining all the dots for them.

"That's some incredible story," sprouted Jones.

Ruben narrowed his eyes at his partner.

"Eva," Ruben said and then paused, thinking how much he liked the sound of her name. He also liked her. Very much.

"Yes, Detective?"

"Ahh," Ruben cleared his throat and continued. "You're dressed to go out. Charmingly so, I might add."

Eva smiled and Jones scowled.

"Where were you going?"

"To catch the early train to Roma Police Station to report what I had found."

Eva took Maureen's diary, Josh's letter and the deed to the apartment out of her bag and place them on the table. Ruben reached over and dragged them towards him. Jones picked up Josh's letter, slid it out of its envelope, unfolded it and began reading it while Ruben perused the diary. The room was silent, except for the ticking of the wall clock.

"As you can see, Detectives," Eva said, pointing to the evidence. "My incredible story is very credible."

After the detectives left, Eva called Danika to give her an update regarding the diary, the apartment, Maureen and the two detectives arriving on her doorstep.

"Well, now everything is settled, right?"

"I certainly hope so. I don't expect to see the detectives again." Eva paused.

"Eva, is something wrong?" Danika asked, noting sadness in her voice.

"No. I was just thinking."

"About?"

"Detective Ruben. I like him. Really like him. We had a moment."

"A moment?"

"Yes. A moment. The thing you read in books. *Our eyes locked and wham!!* That kind of moment," she laughed. "Or as in Jane Austen's Pride and Prejudice when Elizabeth's *spirits fluttered* at the idea of Colonel Fitzwilliam visiting her that evening."

"Oh, I see what you mean. Never had that experience myself," she lied, recalling a past regret. "But I get it. Anyway, since this week was so fractured, achieving little, I'll come into the office tomorrow and finish what I've already started."

"Dani, let's enjoy the weekend and see what we can accomplish next week. I need to digest everything. I'm mind boggled!"

"Yes, boss!" Danika replied, saluting the phone.

Travelling back to Roma Street, Jones mocked Ruben in an irritating tone. "You have a lovely home, Mrs Rennie. What the hell was that all about?" Jones barked at Ruben, driving faster than the speed limit allowed.

Ruben said nothing and peered out of the window, watching the world outside the vehicle become a blur. The tone of Jones' voice grated on Ruben's nerves as he ranted about protocol and interviewing people and not getting personal. Other times, he ignored Jones' *feedback* about everything and anything, as his summaries were amusing. Not this time. This time, it was personal. Ruben turned to Jones and said, "You're a bully, Clyde. Shut the fuck up!"

Jones' mouth gaped open. He glanced at Ruben to see if he was serious. The look Ruben gave Jones infuriated him. Jones was about to retort. Before he could, Ruben asked, "Do you ever listen to yourself?"

It shocked Jones to silence when his partner of 18 years said, "How about you tidy up your own shitty life first before you go spilling your pearls of wisdom all over me?"

Jones had no counter; he was about to be divorced for the third time.

They made the rest of the journey in silence.

Chapter 13

That evening, Eva planned a relaxing time watching a couple of videos. She settled in to her chair, picked up the remote, pressed play and the screen came alive. A faint noise coming from inside a drawer of the wall cabinet caught her attention. She knew what it was and shrugged, ignoring it; Marcus was messaging her. The mobile pinged a third time. She threw the remote to one side, got up off the lounge and stomped over to the cabinet to retrieve the mobile. Her eyes widen with surprise. She laughed. Fifty messages! Marcus had sent her fifty messages. Eva held the mobile as she deliberated on whether she would message back.

"Hello!" was her reply.

Marcus immediately responded.

"Hello! Are you ok? I was so worried about you when you did not respond to my texts."

"I'm fine," she said, without explanation.

"What have you been doing all this time?"

"Busy with family and friends."

"Tell me about them," he asked, fishing for information.

"Nothing much to tell, really. We are ordinary people who care about one another. All in good health and try to be good citizens. We're all rather boring." Eva smiled to herself, thinking, *'liar'*. She changed the subject while Marcus was replying to her text. "What music do you like? Books do you read?" Adding that she had to go. A friend had arrived. "Talk later," she said and switched off the phone, found the remote and pressed play.

While Eva was chilling out in front of the television, Jeffery and Chelsea were preparing to meet the *dragon slayer*. It was late in the evening when the front gate buzzed. Jeffery could see who it was through the camera at the gate. Less than a minute later, he was warmly greeting a broad-shouldered, handsome man about mid-fifties, average height, casually dressed in jeans, tee-shirt and an expensive leather jacket. Chelsea noticed he was wearing sneakers, but not a high-end brand. Nothing about this man, said, *dragon slayer*. Even casually dressed, he oozed style and class.

"Darling, let me introduce you to, aah ..." Jeffery turned to his friend and asked. "What name are you using this trip?"

"Ma'am." with hand outstretched, Jeffery's friend said, "Carson Swan, at your service. My buddy," Carson Swan inclined his head towards Jeffery. "And I go way back. I owe him, so I owe you, too. I'll do all I can to make your problem go away."

Chelsea was delightfully charmed by Carson Swan's manner and felt a load fall from her shoulders.

"Thank you, Carson. Please, come and sit down."

"Let's get to the point, Ma'am."

"Chelsea, please."

"Yes, Ma'am. Chelsea."

Chelsea took a huge breath as she was about to begin. Carson Swan knew what that meant and stopped her before she began telling the long version.

"Can you just give me the facts, dates of where and when particular events took place and a photograph of the *subject* and his last known address and who his associates are?"

Chelsea handed Carson Swan two A4 sheets. "Is this what you mean?"

Carson Swan flipped through the notes. He nodded.

"Nice work. Thanks, Chelsea." He stood. "If I need more information, I'll call." Turning to Jeffery, he said, "See ya, buddy." And then left.

"A man of few words," said Chelsea.

"Ah, but he's a man of action!" responded Jeffery with a touch of pride.

"If Carson Swan isn't his real name, then what is?"

"Darling, I don't know. Every time we meet, he is in disguise, never as himself. He completes his assignment then fades away to who knows where until he is needed again.

Chelsea was speechless, but her expression spoke volumes.

"There is nothing for you to worry about."

Chelsea looked directly at Jeffery. "He hurts people."

"He hurts bad people who hurt good people. That scumbag ex of yours has been on the rampage for over twenty years. He has come so close to injuring you severely, several times. That piece of crap has wormed his way out of every offence and court order, coming out of it smelling like a rose, because of the people he knows. He has to be stopped one way or another by the only person who can."

Chelsea nodded. "I know you're right. But what if he gets hurt while trying to protect me?"

Jeffery laughed out loud. "That man's a killing machine."

"What?"

"My friend can take care of himself. I feel sorry for anyone who gets in his way, though."

"What do you know about your infamous Carson Swan?"

"What I know is, he's the best man to have on my side. He is an anomaly. An oafish thug goaded Carson into a fight in a parking lot one evening. The thug blocked our path, demanding our wallets. He towered over Carson. I thought we were done for. Carson told the thug he was going to remove his wallet from his jacket. He nodded to me to do the same. I handed Carson my wallet. He stepped forward, offering the thug the wallets. I must have blinked because, without warning, the criminal was on his back on the ground. I hadn't realised he had a knife until I saw blood oozing from Carson's arm. I insisted he let me take him to the hospital. He refused and demanded I drive him back to his hotel instead. I did. There, I watched him clean and stitch the deep wound without pain relief. He didn't flinch. Some years later, he told me his parents were murdered during a home invasion. He didn't know why. But he found the men who killed his parents."

A questioning expression formed in Chelsea's eyes.

"No, he didn't kill them," responded Jeffery. "I'm sure they would have wished he had, because they'll spend the rest of their lives in nappies and drinking out of straws.

After his parents' demise. His neighbours, a childless Japanese couple, raised him. He was five-years-old. The foster father was a Shihan, a grandmaster who disciplined and rigorously trained the boy in martial arts. Carson's strong as an ox and can bring a man twice his size to his knees in a split second. He's a vegan. Has not tasted sugar that he can recall. Drinks only water." Jeffery sighed. "Never in my life have I met anyone as self-controlled as he. We are the same age, but he looks twenty to thirty years my junior. While working together, I discovered he has access to information only top, world-wide security has. I can only imagine the wealth he gained over the years and the length of his tentacles of contacts."

A few hours after leaving the Harrisons home, the mysterious Mr Carson Swan, master of disguises, was mingling with the inhabitants of Brisbane's Valley backstreets. All traces of style and class gone, replaced with tattoos, scars, body piercing and a menacing attitude. Foot traffic stepped out of his way as he wandered the streets. Occasionally stopping to chat with the homeless; the eyes and ears of the streets and his best source for the information he wanted. It led him to a dingy underground bar.

The four occupants eyed him with suspicion. They looked at each other with raised brows and laughed out loud when the stranger asked for mineral water. Carson Swan stood still with his back to them. Turning, he gave them a thirty-second stare. Their expressions went blank and they turned away. Swan walked to the back of the room and sat down at a table. He waited. An hour passed. Two tall, heavy-set, ominous looking men came in and stood at the entrance. From there, they scanned the room. The leader headed over to the stranger. Without asking or introducing himself, he dragged a chair away from the table and sat down. His offsider stood behind him with arms folded. Carson Swan expected the intimidation and ignored it. Both men loomed over him. Neither knew what nor who they were dealing with. Carson Swan was not thinking about trouble. He was not there for that. He was there to plant a seed.

"So, ya lookin' for a mate of mine?"

"A mate?" Carson Swan smiled. "A mate, eh? Hmm. I guess so."

"Why?"

"Two Mil. That's why."

The guy almost fell off the chair.

"Two Mil? No shit?!"

Carson Swan took a photo from his jacket and placed it on the table.

"Is this your *mate*?"

The man sitting, picked up the photo. The man behind leaned in for a better look. They then looked at each other.

"Okay, how did he get it?"

"That's confidential. The money isn't important. The lesson he needs to learn is. If you get me?"

"Yeah. I get ya."

Carson Swan pushed back his chair and stood up to leave.

"Where ya goin'?"

"I'm done here. Like I said, it's not about the money."

Carson Swan kept walking, leaving both men stunned. Greed was written on their face; they were already counting the dollars.

The alley of the hotel was clear for him to slip in the back way and climb the stairs to his room. He had an hour and a half before leaving for the airport to catch a late flight out of the country. Enough time to remove all traces of the disguise and become David Carrier who had walked from the hotel and blended into the city scene. An expensive leather bag hung from his shoulder. He emptied the contents into several garbage bins while walking around the Valley stopping only at one store. There, he bought a cheap burner phone. After punching in the code, David Carrier sent one message. *Seed planted. Harvest will come sometime soon.* Then removed the sim, crushed it in his hand and tossed it in a bin nearby and the phone in a bin outside the airport.

It was late in the evening when Jeffery's mobile pinged and he read the message. Chelsea was already in bed.

"Well darling, we can breathe easier now. It may take a little time, but I am sure the wait will be worth it."

"Oh, that sounds wonderful! Never knowing what to expect when coming home, when answering the phone or opening emails, these past years have been dreadfully exhausting and frightening. I'll be glad to know the outcome and be done with it; done with that frog! I am so tired." Chelsea laid her head on her pillow and slowly slid under the covers. She was asleep within seconds.

Several weeks later, Jeffery was watching the news while Chelsea prepared the evening meal. Both stopped and listened to a report about an unidentified man, severely beaten and in a coma, was discovered in bushes between the Gold Coast and Brisbane. The description of the man fitted Chelsea's frog. Neither reacted. They carried on with what they were doing.

"Dinner is almost ready, sweetheart."

Jeffery switched off the television.

"Wonderful! I'm famished! How about a delicious bottle of red to go with our meal?"

"That sounds delightful, darling." Chelsea smiled.

Several months later, over coffee, Chelsea mentioned to Danika how tired she has been.

"That's unlike you. You're usually running on energy overload."

"Not lately, I'm afraid. I feel like I've just run a marathon and staggered in last."

"Really?"

Danika's expression was sombre as she studied Chelsea for a moment. "Have you seen your doctor?"

"I've an appointment for the end of the week."

"Good. It's probably iron deficiency," said Danika, disguising her concern. "You certainly don't look ill. A little tired, perhaps and that stands to reason for all that you do."

"Let's talk about something else," Chelsea said. "Tell me about Abbi's trip, which is by far more interesting than my health."

They moved to the lounge and sat opposite each other. Danika took out her mobile and clicked on to her social media page, to where Abbi had posted her Peru photos and then handed the phone to Chelsea. Stunning scenery of the acclaimed Inca trail through the Sacred Valley in the Peruvian Andes highlands lit up the screen. As Chelsea scrolled farther along, the smiling faces of Peruvians dressed in colourful clothing appeared. The joy and vitality of life reflected in their faces; llamas and colonial villages came next. The scene changed to the Amazon River. Photos of Abbi and her friends climbing into a canoe. Abbi at the Conservation Park holding a sloth.

"What has Abbi planned for her next excursion?" Chelsea asked, with her eyes glued to the phone's screen. "It will have to be something spectacular to top this, travelling solo across a foreign country, without speaking a word of Spanish."

"Would you believe she has scored a five-year contract with an Australian export company in New York?"

Chelsea's eyes widened. "No!" she laughed. "That's amazing! When did all this come about?"

"Abbi applied for it a few weeks ago. The position has just been confirmed. She leaves for the States in a couple of weeks."

"Does this have anything to do with Jackson? I like him? Jackson Jefferson McCoy," Chelsea paused and smiled. "How can anyone forget a name like that? His coming all the way to Australia to meet Abbi was a big statement, you know. It's hard to believe it was just a few months ago since he was here. My how time flies!"

"Yes, I know. I like Jackson, too. I hope Abbi can see him for the man that he is. Abbi said her decision to look for work overseas has nothing to do with Jackson. She needs a change of scenery and wants to get as far away as possible from Brisbane; there are too many unpleasant memories here."

Chelsea nodded. "I can understand that."

Danika looked around and realised Jeffery was nowhere to be seen and asked where he was.

Chelsea smiled. "Oh, he is playing nursemaid to oysters."

Danika looked puzzled.

Chelsea returned the mobile to Danika and took a sip of her tea, now cold. As she made her way over to the kitchen to make another brew, she said, "Jeffery has joined OzFish.

Danika looked puzzled. "What and who is Ozfish?"

"Now I'm quoting this OzFish info," said Chelsea, "because Jeffery repeats it so often, when telling friends about the new project, he's involved in. I know it off by heart," she laughed and sucked in a breath and began. "OzFish is a not-for-profit organisation dedicated to helping the millions of Aussie recreational fishermen to take control of the health of their rivers, lakes and estuaries and shore for the future of the sport they love." Chelsea paused looking up at the ceiling trying to recall the rest. "Oh yes, I remember," she said and continued without missing a beat. "OzFish Unlimited partners with them and the broader community to invest time and money into the protection and restoration of our waterways, counteracting decades of degradation. Their mission is to protect and restore fish habitat and support recreational fishermen by working together, to make local fishing grounds healthy, vibrant and more productive. They share ideas on how to improve, restore and protect fish habitat. Seek grants and support for hands-on habitat restoration, provide events, resources, education and research that support fishing groups to achieve local outcomes." She laughed. "I hope that explains what my husband's new interest is?"

"Well done!" said Danika clapping. "I'm sold."

"My knowledge of the project advocates just how passionate Jeffery is. He talks about nothing else these days."

"Are you okay with that?"

"Oh, yes. Jeffery's having a wonderful time making new friends and being part of the solution that preserves marine life."

"What does this group do?"

"Well, they have working bees to wash the oyster shells collected from restaurants and commercial oyster shuckers. After they're dried in the sun for a minimum of four months, the shells are packed in wire baskets. There's also fundraising fishing events, sailing around the bay checking estuaries. Members learn so much about marine life, while caring for local habitat. Most important, they have fun!"

"Since Jeffery does not own a boat, am I correct to assume that he is *crew* on a boat that belongs to a member?"

"Yes. That's right. Anyone can join if you're interested," Chelsea said.

"Are you a member?"

"That was my intention before I felt so exhausted. Once I get my strength back, I'll be on board. Pardon the pun," Chelsea laughed.

Chapter 14

Eight days before Abbi was due to leave Australia, Leo Brandt contacted her saying he missed her and realised he had been rash in ending their relationship. In consequence, Abbi wrestled with the idea of not going to America.

The fury Danika felt towards Leo Brandt's timing remained harnessed when Abbi asked her mother what she should do.

"It's your life, hon, you must choose."

The expression in Abbi's eyes reflected pain.

"But if it were my choice to make." Danika paused and then continued. "I would think an opportunity like this does not come along every day."

Abbi said nothing. She sat still, as if suspended in time.

"What about all the plans you've made and what about Jackson?"

Abbi flinched and look at Danika. "Jackson knows all about Leo. I told him when we first met. He still wants me to come to America. He suggested we share an apartment as friends to give myself time to figure things out. If Leo loves me," he said, "he'll give me that time."

If Jackson had been in the room at the moment, Danika would have hugged him.

"Jackson has a point, hon. Remember, Leo brushed you aside without a second thought, to concentrate on his career, or so he said."

Abbi flashed an ireful look. "What do you mean by that?"

Danika shrugged, resigned to say nothing, but changed her mind. "He broke your heart. He mistreated you, so why should you throw away this amazing opportunity on his whim?"

"Jackson said something the same. Are you and he talking?"

Danika shook her head. "No, but we obviously agree and have your best interest at heart." Danika sighed. "Why not suggest to Leo to give you a year?"

After some probing, Abbi confessed to her mother she and Leo had been in contact for some time. She had even sent him presents on his birthday.

"So, you told him about the job?"

Danika had not met Leo Brandt at this stage, though she was building a dislike towards him and felt he was manipulating Abbi. She had wondered if he was trying to sabotage her trip out of jealousy because Abbi had secured a five-year overseas contract. Or was he insecure about Abbi's friendship with Jackson? Or both? Danika had no alliance with Leo and urged Abbi not to change her plans, that she would later regret it if she did.

Later, together, they packed up Abbi's belongings. There was much sorting to do; what to take and what to discard. Danika was used to Abbi moving house and knew of the few pieces of furniture and kitchen appliances that would go back to her home until Abbi needed them again.

Minutes before boarding the aircraft, Abbi called her mother, in tears, saying she was not sure if she was doing the right thing.

"Sweetheart, believe me, you are!" Danika said. "Have I ever lied to you, or steered you in the wrong direction?"

"No," said Abbi.

"Do you trust me?"

"Yes."

"Then enjoy the trip. Send me a message when you arrive in New York. You will be fine. Trust me, hon. Your life is about to change. The universe has opened many doors for you so, embrace it."

"Love you ma, bye!"

"Love you too, babe!"

The following morning, the sound of a heavy vehicle entering the yard distracted Danika from working. She left her computer and went outside and stood on the veranda just as it pulled up. Unprepared to see the sight before her eyes, she covered her gaping mouth with her hand.

The driver remained seated in the truck; his deep blue eyes lost in furrows, smiling at her through the open window.

"It's been a while, eh darlin'?" said the driver.

That masculine voice was so familiar. The voice she longed to hear again. The voice that melted her heart and made her feel safe. Breathing deeply to steady herself, she nonchalantly flicked her hair to one side and stepped off the veranda, totally composed and walked towards the truck.

"You can't move that table sitting in there," she said officiously. "And you're a couple of days early."

The driver opened the door. As he got out, he reached for her. "Got a hug for your old mate," he said, pulling her closer. He towered over her as she disappeared into his embrace; for those few seconds, two hearts beat in unison. She did not know how much he had been wanting to hold her again. Or that over the years, the many times she popped into his thoughts without invitation; always there at the back of his mind, whether he wanted her there. He came to realise they had unfinished business. Something he wanted to explore, if she was willing.

When she wriggled free, she tilted her head backwards to look into his eyes. "Of course, there's always a hug for you," was her reply, wrapping her arms around him, laughing out loud.

Eva came around the corner of the house in time to witness the scene. Danika pulled away.

"Oh, no, you don't, Dani," said Lucas. "I haven't finished hugging."

Throwing caution to the wind, she moved in closer and wrapped her arms around him again. She gave him a tight squeeze. "There, now let's get to work."

"Getting acquainted, I see," Eva said.

"Nup, getting reacquainted is more like it," Lucas replied with a knowing smile.

His response surprised Danika, but she said nothing. She moved to the back of the truck and undid the ropes securing the tarpaulin around the table, dragging it to the ground.

"Wow!" Eva exclaimed. "This is beautiful, Lucas! Now I understand why it took so long to craft. It is superb!"

Danika looked puzzled.

"What's wrong?" asked Lucas.

"It's huge! Don't tell me you intend to lug that monster inside on your back?"

He laughed. "Not likely. The troops should be here any minute," he said, checking his watch. As he was speaking, two men in a ute drove in to the yard and pulled up alongside the truck.

"Okay fellers," Lucas yelled. "Let's get this baby inside!"

After introductions, the three men made light work of transferring the table from the truck into the studio. Once

Eva was satisfied with where her pride and joy was positioned, the two men left. While she admired the work of art, Danika and Lucas exchanged phone numbers before he left.

Now that they were alone, Danika was bracing herself for an inquisition.

"The table is stunning; it was worth the wait. What do you think, Dani? Isn't it lovely?"

"Lucas is a fine artisan!" was her reply.

Eva looked over at Danika and smiled. "Hmm, I didn't know you two were so … ah … such good friends."

"You should know by now my private life is private!"

"Oh, you have made that very clear over the years. So, I won't pry," Eva said.

"We're just friends."

Eva grinned. "Ooh, hmm, by the way he looked at you, you are telling fibs or blind as a bat."

"Look, sweetie, I'll let you know when I know. Okay? Lucas said he'll call me tonight."

"Ooh?" Eva grinned, walking away singing, "Love is in the air …"

Later that evening, background music drifted around the kitchen while Danika made something to eat. She glanced up at the wall clock several times, expecting Lucas to call any minute, unaware her mobile was on silent and had lit up several times. When the meal was ready, she poured herself a glass of red wine and carried both to the dining room table. She lifted the glass to her lips and then paused. Someone was pounding on her front door.

"Why are you banging on my door?" she asked, "You told me you'd call?"

"I did," Lucas said. "About a dozen times. Knowing what I do and you didn't answer, well, my imagination ran wild. I got here as soon as I could."

"Ahh, my hero," she smiled, softening her voice and opened her arms. "That definitely deserves a hug." He stepped closer and she fell into his embrace. It felt surreal to her being so close to him. Like a dream. But it was not a dream. He was real; holding her. She did not want him to let go. They kissed. Their hearts filled with the passion of lost years and of gratitude for being united again.

"I don't do one-night-stands," he said, carrying her to the bedroom.

"Good, neither do I."

Sometime later, Danika wandered out of her bedroom wearing Lucas's tee-shirt. He followed two steps behind, wearing her cotton kimono. The sleeves came halfway up his arms and the hem to his knees.

"I don't think these purple flowers flatter my skin tone," he complained, mimicking a woman.

Danika laughed, "Here," she said, slipping his tee-shirt over her head and tossing it to him, leaving her naked. "Happy?"

He gave her a mischievous grin as his eyes caressed her body. *'A lovely body at that,'* he thought. "Very," he said. "But you'd better put this on before you catch a cold," he responded with a wink, throwing her the kimono.

Still hamming it up. "It wasn't the size of the robe," he said. "It was the colour."

Danika threw a tea towel at him. "Here, make yourself useful," she laughed. "You made the food go cold, dragging me off to the bedroom to have your way with me."

Chapter 15

While Danika and Lucas made a late-night snack, across the globe in a cabin somewhere in the Montana Mountains, the man with many faces received his next assignment. Two photographs, one female, the other male; both in their late fifties lay on the table. His task was to eliminate one and protect the other. He was returning to Brisbane.

Fourteen kilometres south of Sydney, NSW, Martin Hopkins was discussing his release from prison with his lawyer.

"Now, don't you go doing anything stupid to stuff things up! In four days, you'll be a free man," warned the spiffy lawyer, all decked out in his two thousand dollar, tailored, black suit and handmade Italian leather shoes.

"Yeah, I know." Martin Hopkins said, patting his Bible. "God's looking after me."

The lawyer was not buying any of his *I've found God* bullshit. "Yeah, well, remember you're still breathing because you played by the rules and kept your mouth shut. Those rules still apply. They will always apply. Savvy?"

The lawyer walked over to the entrance of the cell and nodded to the guard to show he was ready to leave. The heavy door opened and closed with a clang. From the other side, the spiffy lawyer said, "I'll pick you up in four days." As he moved along the corridor, his footsteps echoed as he went, fading away to an eery silence.

Hopkins waited patiently for his release. The time left was a split second to the twenty years he had already served. *'One day at a time,'* he thought. *'I've got so many plans. Top of my to-do-list is a visit to Queensland. It took years to find her. Nothing like having friends in high places. Everything is for sale!'* He grinned maliciously.

Mr Spiffy arranged designer casual clothes and loafers to be sent to Hopkins a day before his release. Cat calls and whistles bounced off the walls the morning the guard escorted Hopkins through the prison.

"You'll be back!" shouted an inmate.

"Over my dead body!" Hopkins yelled back.

"Careful what you wish for, Hoppy!" were the last words heard before the door slammed shut.

As Hopkins swaggered through the prison gate, the sun highlighted the silver streaks in his sandy hair. His black-framed glasses added an air of sophistication to his handsome features, which crinkled as he turned back for one last look to give the place the finger, a sign of contempt, before strutting over to his ride.

Mr Spiffy said, "I can honestly say this is the first time I've seen you smile. You scrub up well, too." Adding, "You could actually pass for a gentleman."

"Not much to smile about in there," Hopkins replied, inclining his head towards the prison. "Can we go now?"

They both got in the car and drove away.

"Nice wheels."

"So, you like the vehicle?"

Hopkins nodded. "Didn't take you for a bushy, though."

"Oh, God no! It's not my truck. It's yours!"

"Mine?"

"Look in the back. On the seat is a leather travel bag. Drag it over here and look inside."

A mouth full of obscenities rolled off Hopkins's tongue while viewing the contents.

"There's a fortune in here."

"There is," Mr Spiffy said. "There's also a passport with a new identity, a bank account and credit cards. As promised, you've been compensated for your time; for keeping quiet. Now, if you're smart, you'll ride off into the sunset and make a new start. If you don't, you're a dead man. Understand?"

Hopkins was inspecting his new credentials as Spiffy was laying down the law to him.

Rhys James Winton, investor, DOB: 30/8/1962, height: 180 cm, eyes: blue, hair: brown. "I can carry the height and age, but not the eye or hair colour."

"You'll find colour contact lenses and hair dye inside the bag."

"You thought of everything, haven't you?"

"That's right, *we* have."

"Who is *we*?"

"Never you mind about that. Just keep on the straight and narrow and you'll be sweet."

Hopkins studied the man sitting beside him. *'Too young to be involved in what went down twenty years ago. If he arranged all of this, he would have done a good deal of research.'*

He smiled to himself, well aware of who *'we'* were. He had files as thick as a fist of his own on them; insurance to keep him in the land of the living. *'If the authorities got their hands on the information I have, it might not bring down those bastards, but it would muddy their water,'* he mused, feeling smug. *'Mud thrown always sticks; a dire situation for those posing as good guys.'*

"What makes you think I could pull off being an investor?" Hopkins asked.

"Now that's a silly question," Spiffy grinned. "Have you forgotten your time at university, in your youth? You majored in accountancy."

"Nah, I haven't forgotten. Just wondering how you got that info."

"The same way you got the info on the whereabouts of your ex, which would be very unhealthy should you pursue that avenue. A colossal mistake."

Hopkins shrugged, dismissing the warning. "Where're we going from here?"

"To my office. You can take the vehicle and head off to wherever you like after that."

They made the rest of the journey in silence.

Chapter 16

Six months later, an elderly gentleman in his mid-seventies and Rhys James Winton took up residence in the same apartment building at Adelaide Street in the city of Brisbane. They became acquainted in the gym the morning the elderly man was struggling with bench weights. The younger man rushed to his aid and lifted the weights off him, dropping his glasses when bending down to help the elder up, who caught them before they fell to the floor.

"I guess I'm not as strong as I used to be," admitted the old man, shaking, handing the glasses back after rubbing them on his shirt. With the slip of hand, he attached a minute tracking device to the frame.

"No shame in that," said the younger man, offering his hand. "I'm Rhys Winton. Are you okay?"

The old man laughed, clasping the hand. "Alister Simon. I'm fine. Thanks to you. Just a bruised ego. Glad you came along to save me from strangling myself with that damn thing. No more tights and cape for me after this," he chuckled. Rhys grinned when he got the joke.

"I owe you a beer. A shower and a change of clothes first, though. I'll meet you out front say in twenty minutes?" Alister said, shuffling out of the gym before Rhys could reply.

'Hmm, seems the old man is used to getting his way. He didn't wait for an answer.' thought Rhys. 'He looks harmless enough and it's just a drink.' He shrugged, then dashed upstairs to shower and change too.

"Ah, good. You're punctual," Alister remarked as the younger man walked towards him. "That's a good sign," Alister remarked, nodding at Rhys.

"What is?"

"Punctuality," replied Alister. "Everyone arrives late for appointments these days, with some excuse; always excuses!"

"I guess that was knocked out of me years ago."

Alister's eyes reflected concern. "Knocked out of you, how?"

Clearing his throat, Rhys said, "Ah, my minders," Rhys corrected himself. "My parents." He paused a beat. "Felt like prison guards." With an awkward grin, he continued. "Getting clipped around the ears without warning for stepping out of line kept me pretty much on my toes. I learned never to be late for anything."

Alister listened to Rhys's intonation for resentment, but found none, which surprised him.

"Let's walk over to the Treasury building. It's close to here. Walking is good for the mind, body and spirit. Although, looking at the amount of traffic on the roads, with all this pollution lingering in the air, that philosophy is debatable."

Alister headed off briskly towards Queen Street and then turned left onto George Street. Rhys huffed and puffed alongside, doing his best to keep a stride with him. The ten-minute jaunt took less than five.

"Ha," Alister glanced at Rhys, crimson faced and breathless. "Bet you thought you'd have to carry this old relic too," he quipped.

"Not at all. Didn't think I'd be running a marathon, though."

Arriving at the Treasury Building, Alister took wider strides for a short man and jogged up the steps and waited for his new buddy at the entrance. When he caught up, Alister said, "More treadmill for you, young fella!"

Rhys was seething, feeling the old man was goading him to look foolish. Alister smiled knowingly. By the fury visible in Rhys's eyes, Alister knew he had a short fuse. He had dealt with individuals like him many times. *'Ticking bombs, every one of them', he reasoned. 'Rhys was no different. His anger was the weakness that'll be his downfall.'*

Alister reached up to pat Rhys on the shoulder. "C'mon, buddy," he chuckled, "Drinks and lunch are on me."

The younger man shrugged the hand away. "Yeah, well, you owe me for saving your life." His tone was bitter.

"Rightly so." Alister agreed. He was no longer smiling. "Ryan's on the Park is open." Alister said, matching Rhys's bitter tone, which made him glance at the old man as he strode past him.

"Are you joining me, or are you going to stand there with ruffled feathers?"

The younger man followed, puzzled by the old fella's behaviour. "Don't know why you're pissed; it was you who was taking the micky out of me. Not the other way around, pal."

Alister ignored Rhys's comment as though nothing had happened. Arriving at the restaurant entrance, without waiting to be seated, Alister headed for a table overlooking the park and sat down. Rhys was a few steps behind. After they were seated, an attendant appeared to welcome Alister.

"Good afternoon, Mr Simon," said the attendant, smiling warmly. "Your usual sir?"

"Hello, Sarah. Yes, thank you." Pointing to Rhys, Alister added. "Mr Winton is my guest for lunch. He saved my life. This morning, I almost killed myself in the gym, lifting weights. Mr Winton saved me from myself," he grinned.

Sarah gasped. "Oh my," she whispered, winking at him. "You must take care, Mr Simon. You're my best tipper."

Alister roared with laughter. Rhys could not see the joke, but said nothing. Sarah handed him a menu, telling him she will give him a moment to select something, then hurried away to let the chef know Alister was here.

"You're no stranger here, eh?"

"That's right. This table is permanently reserved. Sarah always serves me. She has done so since my first visit here. She is familiar with my dietary requirements as a vegan. She also knows that I only drink mineral water," he said, pouring water into the glasses on the table. "No other beverage."

Rhys's eyes widened, shaking his head. "Vegan? Rabbit food? Water? Huh! Stuff that! Give me a big fat juicy steak any day. That's my sorta tucker!" he said, as his voice slipped from a well-bred gentleman into a rough-neck. Clearing his throat, he hoped he had not blown his cover, aware Alister was staring at him. Rhys smiled awkwardly. "Well, you get the picture."

Alister nodded. "Yes, I get the picture!"

Rhys studied his companion for a moment. "Do I detect an accent? American or Canadian?"

"Yes, you do. Canadian. But Canada is no longer my home; anywhere I hang my hat or coat is."

"You're Aussie through and through." Alister said, eyeing him through his bushie brows. "You're a little rough around the edges, too. I'm guessing you've done *time*?"

Sarah, appearing beside Rhys, excusing the interruption to take his order, halted the conversation. He apologised he had not looked at the menu, but Alister suggested a thick juicy steak with a side order of vegetables.

Rhys nodded.

"Drinks? Beer, a red or white wine, or champagne?"

"The good stuff will do. No point in letting all this finery go to waste when you're paying."

"By the 'good stuff', can I assume you mean champagne?"

Rhys nodded, looking at Sarah. Before she moved away to allow them to continue their conversation, she topped Alister's glass with mineral water. He thanked her before she left.

During the meal, the men quizzed one another. Since Alister knew he had spent time in prison, Rhys thought it was better to admit he had and wanted to go *straight*. To explain his lifestyle, he invented a story about a relative leaving him money. "I was last of the family line. Lucky last!"

"So, it's just you? No family?"

"Yep! How about you, mate? Family in Canada? Anywhere?"

"No. I'm an orphan, the same as you."

Rhys thought it unusual Alister had not inquired about his time in prison. It bothered him so much that he said, "How come you're not grilling me about my time in the joint?"

"You would tell me if you wanted me to know. Other than that, it's none of my business. Besides, no one is perfect."

Both men had strong opinions of the other, enough to be cautious. Alister glanced around the room. The activity

130

bustled in low key around them. Until two couples engrossed in conversation caught his attention as they entered the room. So absorbed in the topic they were discussing, they caused a collision with one of the staff. The staffer dismissed it with dignity, directing them to the table opposite Alister and Rhys, who eyed the group with raised brows, noting the volume of their chatter. Since neither was in any hurry to leave, Rhys and Alister sat back and eavesdropped.

"Twenty years," the woman said with a smile at the man beside her.

"Yeah, you get less for murder," he quipped. His comment was not malevolent by the twinkle in his eye and the way he looked at the woman.

She slapped him playfully on the arm.

"It almost didn't happen," he said. His voice was full of emotion.

"Why ever not?" inquired the woman sitting opposite him.

"Well ..."

"No, Teddy, let me tell the story." The wife cut in, laying a hand on his arm.

"Ok Sally, my love," he teased. "You lie better than me."

The others smiled, shaking their heads.

"We had been going out for about a year the night Teddy arranged an evening at the club. He seemed nervous. I asked if anything was wrong and he assured me there wasn't, so I embraced the evening with gusto. We had a marvellous time!" she sighed. "Anyway, on the way home, Teddy turned down an alley and parked in front of a brick wall. A brick wall, of all things. She shook her head. I thought the wall was a metaphor. Teddy's way of saying he was breaking up with me." Sally paused for a moment and then continued. "So, I plucked up courage and asked why we were there, bracing myself for the worst. He said nothing for a few minutes and then turned to face me and asked me to marry him. I didn't know what to say. That was the last thing I expected. Shocked, I said no. He said righto, then started the car, did a three-point-turn and we headed home. He didn't mention the proposal again. As the months passed, I realised the inevitable. So, one morning, over breakfast, I said, you won't propose to me again, will you? No, was his reply. Looks like I'll have to ask you to marry me, right? Correct, he said."

Teddy sat back with arms folded, listening, as his wife told the story, nodding and blinking several times. Smug satisfaction lit up his mature features when Sally finished. He reached for her hand and gave it a gentle squeeze. "And they said we wouldn't last."

The other man at the table lifted his glass. "A toast to another twenty wonderful years."

"Hang on. I didn't say they were wonderful years. Who said wonderful years?" Teddy laughed.

Alister smiled at Teddy's comment, looking over at his companion. His expression was grim.

"Something wrong?"

"Nah, just thinking."

"About?"

Rhys did not answer.

"Oh, I think I see. Your wife dumped you."

Rhys shook his head, but said nothing.

The mood was digressing to dark corners. Alister changed course by asking Rhys if he was familiar with the area.

"Why is that?"

"For permanent residence here."

"Sorry, can't help you. I'm a Sydney lad. This is my first trip up this way." Pausing a couple of beats, he continued. "There's plenty of real estate agents around the city," Rhys said, pausing again, as though he had more to say, then changed his mind. He pushed his chair back and stood up. The couple at the table opposite reminded him why he had come to Brisbane.

"Thanks for lunch, mate. I have to make tracks. We're square. See you around."

Alister watched Rhys leave. *'You will, my friend, you certainly will!'* he thought as he removed his mobile phone from his jacket and flicked it open. The tracker was on. Rhys was heading home. Alister followed him a few minutes later. The tracker showed Rhys had not entered the apartment building, but had stopped outside. *'He's monitoring me,'* Alister reasoned as he went inside and took the lift to his apartment. He watched as the tracker moved. Rhys was now in the building. He had entered the other lift and was on his way up. Alister waited at his door until the second lift arrived at his floor. He timed his entrance into the apartment as the doors opened, allowing enough time for Rhys to know which apartment was his. Rhys caught sight of Alister seconds before he closed the door.

In his apartment, Rhys paced the floor for over an hour. Warning bells rang loud and clear in his mind. *'That old bugger is up to something, for sure. But what's that got to do with me?'* Tired of the cat-and-mouse game, he went up to Alister's apartment to confront him. He banged on Alister's door several times before it opened.

"Who are you?" Rhys declared when a man of average height, close-cropped blond hair and piercing blue eyes he had never seen before, stood in the doorway. "Where is Alister?"

"Who's Alister?" the man in the apartment asked.

"The old fella who lives here."

"I live here," the man said calmly.

Rhys studied him for a moment. He could not be a relative of Alister's. This person had chiselled good looks. Alister resembled Fagan from Oliver Twist.

"Is this some kind of joke Alister concocted with you to get me going?"

"I don't know what you are talking about. You're welcome to come in and look for yourself. I assure you there's no Alister living here. I've owned this apartment for two years."

Rhys was dumbfounded. "Nah, that's ok. I believe you." He dropped his head, utterly confused as he walked away. He stopped and half turned. "By the way, I'm Rhys Winton."

"Jack Bradley. Hope you find your guy."

Rhys nodded. "Yeah, me too," he said and left puzzled.

Rhys headed back to the Treasury Building where he and Alister had lunch earlier, recalling the old man saying only Sarah served him because she knew his dietary requirements. She might know Alister well enough to give him some information. He was shocked to discover that no one called Sarah worked in the restaurant. He left dazed. *'What the fuck's going on? The old geezer couldn't just vanish into thin air!'*

Chapter 17

Another summer arrived to scorch the ground bone dry, igniting random bushfires round the country. Driven by extreme temperatures and strong winds, destructive fires spread rapidly, wiping out everything in their path. Day after day, the media reported the destruction of homes and towns nationwide.

Turning away from the news on her computer Danika faced Eva, her voice full of emotion. "I can't listen to the radio, or watch tv or news of any kind anymore. It's too disheartening. Everything is about the fires. The destruction of people's lives. It's difficult to watch those sad faces covered in ash and dirt, telling their story of survival. It breaks my heart. They're so brave! All we can do is donate a few dollars!" Feeling the frustration of helplessness, she asked, "How do we know those survivors are getting the money donated?"

Eva did not respond right away as she pondered that question. "We have to trust the CEOs of the organisations who received that money to do the right thing by those in need."

"Trust is a huge ask when many, many millions of dollars are involved," replied Danika, her voice peppered with doubt.

"Summer is my favourite season. The heat has never bothered me. I find it invigorating while others feel it exhausting. After all this death and destruction, I should feel guilty for looking forward to summer, but I'm not."

"Dani, you can be as hard as nails and yet soft as marshmallow." Eva chuckled. "The seasons will keep coming and leaving; you have no control over that. Embrace them however you like. Life is too short to feel guilty about that. You didn't cause those unmerciful fires or the destruction of anyone's property or life.

"Oh, my goodness. I didn't mean to whine!"

Laughing, Eva said, "Silly girl! I wasn't implying that. Life is abstract. We are abstract; a melting pot of all the experiences we've encountered during our lives; components of who and what we are. Nothing ever remains the same. Situations and people can change from bad to worse, from worse to good in an instant. My life, for one, can be testimony to that. One day married to a cheater and the next day a millionaire. Heck, sweetie, I mean, nothing is ever what it seems."

Chelsea popped into Danika's mind at that moment. She looks a picture of health and yet she has blood cancer. Out of respect for her friend's privacy, Danika refrained from referencing Chelsea's illness as an example of *nothing is what it seems.* She was unsure if Chelsea had told Eva or anyone else about her illness. Turning back to the computer, Danika sighed. "I guess you're right," she said and changed the subject. "Demand for the boxes has just foiled your idea of this being a *hobby*. Without doubt, it's a thriving business already consuming your life. Are you prepared for more of that, boss?"

"So, I've noticed. I'm pacing just fine at the moment. Not sure how long I'll be able to keep up at that pace, though."

"That's because you don't have a life outside of this studio. How about you give that detective a call?"

"Have you lost your mind?" Eva laughed. "That boat has sailed."

"Ah, somehow, I don't think so."

"Why do you say that?"

"I noticed a man sitting under the Moreton Bay fig tree near the road crossing, just up from the marina. He fitted the description you gave me when you first mentioned him. It looked like he was waiting for someone; you perhaps?"

"Are you serious?"

"Very!"

"When was that?"

Danika glanced at her watch. "About this time yesterday and earlier in the week. If you hurry, you can see for yourself if this man is the detective."

Eva hesitated.

Reading her mind, Danika told her she looked great. "You always look great! Go, go, shoo!" she said, pushing her out the door.

Eva was telling herself that she was being silly. The man was not the detective. "But, nothing ventured, nothing gained," she muttered as she steered her car to the waterfront. At that hour, parking was not a problem as it usually was on the weekend. A space opposite the swimming pool area was available, a short distance from where Danika said she had seen the man who resembled the detective sitting under the tree. Eva scanned that section from her vehicle. No one there resembled him. She was about to leave, then changed her mind. "Might as well get a coffee while I'm here," she muttered, getting out of the car.

"How about you join me?" said a familiar voice from behind. "I was hoping to run into you down here."

The detective was casually dressed in jeans and a pale blue polo-shirt. He oozed style and charm. Eva smiled broadly and nervously played with her hair.

"Why do I feel you knew I was here?"

"What makes you say that?"

"Because you looked as if you've been caught with your hand in the bikkie jar!" He teased.

"Guilty!"

"I'm glad, because I have been over this way so often that I can claim native title," he laughed.

"Why not just call? I had hoped you would."

"You did?"

"Yes, I did."

"I'll call next time. Coffee?" he asked, offering his arm.

They strolled arm in arm up Cambridge Parade to the cafe.

"Where are you taking me?" asked the detective.

"To one of my favourite restaurants. It's close by. *The Deck* has a wonderful view of the village and marina from the upstairs balcony."

Once they were seated, Eva said with a sweeping hand. "As promised, a wonderful view of our little village."

He had not taken his eyes off Eva. He was interested in only her.

"The view is perfect from where I'm sitting!"

She smiled. "By the way, how is your partner, Clive Jones, is it?"

"Okay, I guess."

"You guess?"

"I requested a transfer after leaving your place."

"Had you been working together long?" She paused. "Oh, I'm so sorry. It's none of my business. You don't have to answer that."

"I don't have a problem with telling you. Eighteen years. We were fine for most of those years because I chose to not react to the things he said. One day he went too far and that was that."

Eva said nothing. It was clear he wanted to say more.

"A working partnership is like a marriage, only without fringe benefits," he grinned.

Eva nodded and smiled.

"You ignore all the nagging irritations for years. Then one day, you can't do it anymore. You finally see who they really are, gnawing at you until you cannot stand another minute.

"I'm sorry to hear that. It's a shame you can't work things out. Eighteen years is a long time. Detective Jones seemed like a nice enough man. We all have flaws. Anyway, that's your life and your decision to make."

"I welcome your opinion, Eva. Thank you."

"In my job, I get to see humans from every angle. Most would not know the truth if it bit them on the backside. Did you know, according to psychologists, people lie about ten times a day?"

"I'd believe that, especially having been subjected to lies for thirty-five years of my marriage."

"I'm sorry you experienced that from your husband. Life is abstract. Nothing is ever what it seems. For me, life and so many people I know resemble Pablo Picasso's paintings, for example, Women of Algiers. On the surface, the painting looks confusing. But for me, when I look deeper, I see a hypothetical of everything I know and have experienced. That's my opinion. I'm no expert." He shrugged. "It's an opinion, that's all. You might see something else. It doesn't really matter since opinions don't change the world, but they can stimulate minds to open and view the subject from another angle."

"I cannot believe you said that."

"Why?"

"I said exactly the same thing, about life being abstract and that nothing is as it seems to one of my dear friends recently."

"Huh. How about that?" The detective shook his head. "How about that! That's a first."

"A first?"

"Yeah, a first. A woman on the same page as me. How about that," he mumbled, pleased with himself, as pleased as though he had struck gold!

A comfortable silence fell between them. Eva watched as the detective took a moment to absorb his surroundings.

"Manly really is a very quaint village."

"You sound surprised about that."

"Well, yes, I am very surprised. The reason being, I'm noticing this beautiful place for the first time. I wouldn't have contemplated venturing over this way if I had not met you. I'm sure it be would an absolute pleasure to live in such surroundings."

"You sound smitten."

"I am. Not with just the village or the area, Eva. Surely you must have guessed that by now."

She nodded. "I have."

"My work is demanding, but that won't be for long. Retirement is just around the corner. In the meantime, we can get to know each other."

She put her hand on his arm. "One day at a time, Detective. I'm on your team. How about I cook dinner for us tonight? We can start from there."

"How about we cook dinner together, since we're a team? Oh, and by the way, Eva, never in my life have I been so impulsive apart from this time with you. I know you know we had a moment the first time we met. The look in your eyes was clear; as though a bolt of lightning had struck me; imprinting you in my mind. Jones noticed a change in me and began lecturing me about professionalism and stepping over the line. His nagging about what was right and what was wrong angered me, especially when his marriage had crashed and burned for the third time."

Eva was silent. Her heart was full of hope that he desired the same things as she does. She wanted to hear everything he had to say.

"I'm not looking for a perfectly *beautiful* woman, Eva. That's an impossible ask. I want a woman who will stand by me through thick and thin, no matter what, as I will her. A woman whose eyes light up when she sees me, as yours does. A woman who will love me for myself. A woman with a beautiful spirit, who isn't afraid to be her own person ..."

"Have you been reading *my* wish list?"

"Oh, what I would give to see your wish list, Eva"

She smiled. "Apart from what you've already said. I want to add, I never want to have separate bedrooms. If it came to that, we may as well have separate homes, too. It might be suitable for other couples to live that way, but it won't do for me. I have witnessed couples looking smug when announcing their fifty something year anniversary. Yet, not once did I see any sign of affection between any of them. There's only one couple I know of who seem to be genuinely in love and openly display affection for each other. How they feel is reflected in their eyes and in the tone of their words whenever they speak to or about each other. It's refreshing to be in their company. I don't envy them, though."

"You don't?"

"Not at all," she said. "I am happy for them! What works for them probably wouldn't work for me."

"Yes, I see what you mean."

"What it tells me is that it's possible to have a successful relationship. I just have to find the person who is perfect for me. My person!"

"We're definitely on the same page. I, too, want all of that. I'm privy to individuals from all walks of life. The pretence of a perfect marriage is often obvious, more obvious than the *pretenders* realise. Which is fine, if that's the marriage or relationship they settle for. For me, it's all or nothing!"

As they were about to leave the restaurant, Eva said she had to make a stop at the supermarket. "I keep little food in the house these days. Mostly, I eat out with friends or make a snack while working in the studio."

"We can eat here if you like."

"I wouldn't hear of that. Besides, if I'm going to keep you, I need to see how well you can cook." Their laughter was infectious. People in the restaurant looked at them and smiled.

Strolling the supermarket aisles with the detective was far more pleasant than Eva could have imagined. She could not recall ever grocery shopping with Josh. He was always too busy working on a deal or some project. But he was happy to oblige her whenever she asked him to pick up items, on his way home from the office.

Acquaintances waved to Eva when they saw her. They were polite enough not to bother her while in the company of a very attractive man they had not seen before. They smiled their approval instead.

"This feels good," the detective said.

"What does?"

"Cruising the aisles with you. This is another first. I've not shopped with anyone before."

"What, you've never been married or been in a long-term relationship?"

"No long-term relationships. But I was married once. So far back in the past that it doesn't count and only for a moment in time."

"Oh," was all Eva said.

"We were young, too young. I was career focused working the grave-shift, while she was having a good time partying with her friends. She found another bloke and left me."

"That's sad."

"No, it's not. We weren't compatible. It was a relief when she left. Otherwise, I would've had to do, *until death do us part,* to honour my vows had she stayed and that would have been hell on earth for both of us."

"What about Josh? Was he domesticated?"

Eva laughed. "Grocery shopping wasn't on his curriculum vitae."

Chapter 18

Driving home, the detective relived every moment he and Eva shared over in his mind. He could not recall ever enjoying an evening with anyone as much as he had with her; liking the sound of her laughter and graceful movements. Her music and book collection were almost identical to his, except for the few books about craft. That commonality allowed the conversation to flow easily between them. His decision to move to the area seemed practical.

Traffic was light, so he stopped on the shoulder of the road and sent off emails to every real estate agent in Manly. On his way to the office the next morning, an agent called.

Meanwhile, Eva was wondering if last night had been a dream. Wandering into the kitchen to make breakfast, she opened the dishwasher to retrieve her favourite mug. It was full of clean dishes, pots and pans. A smile creased her lovely features. *'So, cooking dinner with the detective wasn't a dream?'*

Hearing activity in the kitchen, Maggie perched herself on the windowsill. She began a short burst of repetitive carolling, attracting Eva's attention.

"Hello, Maggie! How are you this wonderful morning? Have you come for your snack?" Leaning forward, Eva craned her neck to look out of the window for the daughter and husband.

"All alone, today?"

Smiling to herself, she thought, *'If anyone heard me talking to that bird, they'd deem me crazy.'* Throwing her hands in the air, laughing out loud. *'Since when do I give a toss what people think? If a mega supermarket chain can run dumb commercials of a lounge chair spruiking insurance to a couple sitting on their couch reading, then I can talk to a bird and if the bird answers me, I can believe it!'* she laughed again.

While nibbling on toast, Eva was contemplating last night with the detective. *'Hmm, I could get used to spending time with that gorgeous man. After failing with Josh, I should be cautious.'* She paused for a moment. *'Oh, to hell with that! Life is too short for placing obstacles in the way. What an unpalatable thought that is turning away from potential happiness! Besides, that chapter of my life has finished. I'm about to write a whole new story with Detective Samuel Ruben.* "And boy, can he cook!" she said aloud. Maggie flapped her wings at the sudden sound of Eva's voice.

"Okay Maggie, I'll take that as your sign of approval?"

While unloading the dishwasher, Eva's thoughts slipped back to her conversation with the detective.

"Tell me about yourself," he said. His voice was still in her head. She doubted she would ever want it to leave her thoughts. It was a deep voice; smooth and refined. He listened while she told him how her business evolved from a gift to her daughter-in-law and how her long-time friend, Danika, was handling the IT side of the business.

He nodded when she finished talking. "It sounds like you enjoy what you're doing." He paused and glanced over at the bookcase. Eva's eyes followed him. "Is that your friend, Danika, with you in the photo?"

"Yes." Eva got up from the table and went to retrieve it. Handing him the photo, she said, "As you can see in the background, we are in the studio. Next time you come; I'll give you a tour."

The detective did not respond right away. He was studying the photograph. There was something about Eva's friend that bothered him. She looked familiar.

"As you can see by the number of books in my library, I'm a prolific reader. Most of what I read is about war and murder mysteries, probably not the taste of many women – television doesn't interest me at all."

"Yes," he finally said, breaking his concentration from the photograph. "I noticed the extent of your library. We obviously enjoy books by the same authors. But I have to admit, time does not allow me to indulge as often as I would like."

"You haven't mentioned anything about your work. Is it top secret or something like that?" she grinned mischievously.

"Actually, it is something like that and I avoid talking about work. I will say this, not to alarm you, just to be honest with you. My job has its hazards and can be a threat to all I hold dear. That's something you need to consider associating with me, Eva."

She reached for his hand and she said "I don't know you well, but I've had enough life experiences to recognise a good person. You, Detective Samuel Ruben, are a good man. I want to get to know you really well."

"Ahh, so you remember my name?" he grinned as he checked his watch. "It's getting late. I've a full schedule tomorrow. Can I call you later in the day?"

While pouring another coffee before she went to the studio, Eva recalled something about the way Sam looked at the photograph of her and Danika. It felt odd. Being an avid fan of old movies and having had studied subtle subtext of storytelling that spoke louder than words, she was used to how racial tensions were shown without slurs uttered, conflict obvious without raised voices and love apparent without kissing or racy bedroom scenes.

It was the flicker in his eyes and the length of time he looked at the photo that caught her attention. That oddity triggered Eva to recall the dream she had about Danika telling her she had a different name. "What was it? What was that name? Jane something or other." Eva sighed. "I'll ask her when she comes in."

While Eva was busy working in her studio, Detective Ruben was inspecting several properties in the area. The last was an apartment that had been on the market for a while and the owner was eager to liquidate it. The dwelling had a view of the bay and overlooked Wynnum Creek. Partial to apartment living, the detective preferred ownership to leasing. The idea of purchasing a piece of history encouraged him to make his home in the building where the infamous Fishers Hotel once stood. The cash sale enhanced the real estate agent's enthusiasm to rush the paperwork through, which was completed by the end of the day.

Once he had his accommodation sorted, Samuel went back to the office. He punched in Danika's name and description into his computer and came up empty. The day was fast fading to late afternoon and he still had not called Eva. He pressed speed dial and got her voicemail. He left a message apologising for the late call saying he would come by about six, if she did not mind.

Eva was, at that moment, still discussing Danika's situation. They had been talking all afternoon. She was consoling her friend, who was saying she had not dared risk involving or trusting anyone with her secret; failing to mention she had already confided in Lucas.

"Abbi's and my safety were at stake. I couldn't utter a word. Witness protection is a big deal, Eva. Much preparation went into protecting us. More than likely, those who know our real identities and our location are now retired or have passed away. I know for certain, Marty promised to *deal* with me when released from prison, which would have been, from my calculations, eight months ago."

"Your only option, as far as I can see, Dani, is to tell Sam."

"No! I can't do that. He might be one of them."

The terror in Danika's eyes shocked Eva. "Who is 'them'?"

"That's the problem. I don't know. Martin never said. Just that these people were untouchable *bigwigs* with long tentacles that had several coppers on the payroll. Promise me, Eva, you won't say anything to your detective. Promise?"

Eva nodded. "I promise."

The look of relief in Danika's eyes strengthened the promise.

"Will you be able to carry on as usual with this threat hanging over your head?"

"Hmm, I think so. I've done it for over twenty years. I'm sure I can keep the façade going."

"How about you, hon? Keeping secrets from your boyfriend can destroy a relationship."

"I don't know Sam well enough to trust him with your life. If he doesn't understand that, then he isn't *my* person." Eva paused. "As for acting as though nothing is out of the ordinary. Like you, my friend, I'm an Oscar-winning actress. Thirty-five years of living with Josh gave me lots of practice. Just one question."

"What's that?"

"How did you meet your ex-husband?"

Danika looked down at the floor and then looked up at her friend. "Well," she said, hesitating, "we're not married. Not officially. Marty said we didn't need a piece of paper to be *hitched.* He believed because we had been together since we were teenagers, we were already married. I was okay with that. We met at a party. I was sixteen years old. He was eighteen and very handsome. A good guy, then. Kind. I adored him. We ran away together and lived a wild life moving around the country. We even travelled overseas to America. I knew nothing of what he did for a living. Marty told me I didn't need to worry about anything. He would take care of me and he did. I was young and so naïve." Danika paused, thinking back over that time of her life. She shrugged and said, "We laughed a lot and we were happy. Until I questioned things. I wanted to know where the money for our living expenses came from, since he never worked. My curiosity angered him. His reaction frightened me to the point of never challenging him again. When Jade was four years old, Marty beat me up. I can't recall why, but I ended up in the hospital and was forced to say I had fallen down the stairs."

Eva's eyes filled with tears. "I'm so sorry you had to endure that."

Danika waved Eva's words away. "Jade is Abbi's real name."

Eva nodded.

Danika continued. "I knew I was in danger when I overheard Marty talking on the phone about *smudging* someone. He turned around and saw me moving away from the door. I pretended I heard nothing and carried on as usual. A few days later, two detectives were on our doorstep. They told us two of Marty's friends had been murdered. Next thing, we were being escorted to the police station. On the way, I told them Jade was at kindergarten that I had to be back by two-thirty to pick her up. Fear churned in my gut when they said nothing. At the station, Marty and I were separated. As he was being taken away, Marty glanced back at me. The look he gave me said, *keep your mouth shut*! That look sent a shiver down my spine. From one detective, I learned about Marty's criminal history. I was horrified and repeatedly told them I knew nothing about his business dealings. They questioned me for hours and threatened to take Jade away from me. I was terrified I'd never see her again. All I could tell them was that I had asked Marty, just once, how he got his money. He told me to shut up and to not ask questions, or else!"

"Oh, Dani. I can only imagine what you were thinking and feeling," said Eva.

"For a while, I thought I was going to prison. Later, I learned they knew I was not involved. It came as a huge shock and enormous relief they believed me. Only after agreeing to give them information, no matter how insignificant I thought it was, they promised to protect Jade and me from Marty. So, I told them about the phone call I overheard. The rest, you know," Danika said, gathering her things together. "I'll see you tomorrow?"

"Wait Dani, are you okay? I hope talking about this hasn't stirred up a lot of old memories for you."

"I'm fine, mate. I'm not afraid of Marty anymore. I can protect myself. All that self-defence training won't go to waste, I promise you," she grinned. "The fear of the unknown is the danger. That fear is no longer there. I am stronger now."

"Great! Is Lucas coming over tonight?"

"Hmm, yes."

"He knows, doesn't he?"

"Uh-huh, I …"

"No problem, hon. There's no need to explain. Take care! See you tomorrow."

Keeping Danika's secret was something Eva did not hesitate to do, weighing the pros and cons of the situation and that of their friendship, which she valued. The situation was that her friend's safety was at stake. No relationship was more important than someone's life. All the same, Eva worried how she could protect Danika from falling into harm's way. A bodyguard came to mind. She dismissed that as quickly as she had thought of it. 'Perhaps a private investigator?' After giving some thought to that idea, she dismissed that, too. She sighed. 'What then? What can I do to protect Dani?'

Glancing at her wristwatch, the late hour told her she must hurry. Sam was due any minute. She left the half-assembled box on the table and moved towards the exit, switched off the light and closed the door behind her. Before stepping off the veranda, she breathed in deeply, drawing in the scent of lavender and roses. She smiled, thinking, *'It was a beautiful fragrance, as well as therapeutic for her.'*

The evening was warm, humid, peaceful and silent, except for the hum of distant traffic. Life was good. She will try to make Danika's life good, too. Deep in her thoughts, she did not feel the need to hurry. Samuel was important to her, so was their relationship. But caution now ruled. If he was the one, her *person,* then there was no need to rush into anything with him.

Chapter 19

After Danika left the studio, she made a detour to the foreshore to clear her mind. A long walk always refreshed her spirit. She texted Lucas to let him know where she was. He responded, saying he would join her.

'Fish and chips at twilight sound good, eh?'

'That sounds good to me too!' she replied. *'Give me thirty minutes. I'll meet you at Wynnum Creek.'*

'OK, see you at sunset!'

The breeze ruffling her hair and clothing was warm against her skin. She was thinking how good that felt as she slipped her phone in the pocket of her linen slacks and headed toward Wynnum Creek. A favourite place of hers, where in bygone years fishing boats lined up to unload their cargo. The robust activity that was once the heartbeat of the area was now silent. An ambiance of calm had staked its claim.

The times Danika looked across the Creek at the huge block of expensive apartments where the infamous Fisher's Hotel used to be, she felt a sense of loss, as if a part of history had melted into the abyss. Danika had lived in the area long enough to know that this was her forever home. She held dear all of its history and stories long-time residents of the area shared with her over the years. Stories about Fisher's Hotel being the second home of hardworking mariners, jovially boasting of tall tales about their seafaring adventures and the behind-the-hand whispers of debauchery and topless barmaids enticing patrons to consume more alcohol as they kept refilling their empty glasses. It was the meeting place of many men. If a wife could not find a wayward husband, Fisher's Hotel was the first place she would look. Danika respected the sentimentality that strongly featured in the reminiscing.

She turned away from the apartment building and looked out at the bay, the colour of a sapphire stretching as far as the eye could see; symbolic of beauty, prosperity and inner peace. She understood why people come here and park; the view and inner peace had claimed their spirit at first sight, as it had hers. At her lowest ebb, this place would always come to mind. She felt the essence of the bay pull her there, where she experienced *satori,* enlightenment to whatever bothered her.

The mobile pinged in her pocket, letting her know a message had arrived. Hoping it was from Lucas, she pulled out the phone to check. A broad smile crinkled her face as the joy of seeing him percolated. Their relationship still felt surreal. A dream. Danika turned toward the parked cars and waved when she sighted him. He waved back and hurried to her, carrying two small square cartons and two take-away coffees purchased from a local café. The afternoon sun was behind him, cocooning his large, strong frame in an angelic glow for just a few seconds. She smiled, thinking Lucas was a good man with a kind heart, but far from angelic. Like she had done, he did things he was not proud of while surviving hazardous circumstances – his remorse was his absolution, as was hers.

Danika did not know how eager Lucas was to see her. That she had been on his mind all day and every day since their first night together; a love unspoken. His grandfather once told him that the right woman by a man's side can bring out the best in him. But the wrong woman could destroy him.

"How will I know the difference?" the younger Lucas asked.

"You'll know when she becomes more important than yourself and you become more important than herself."

Lucas smiled inwardly, thinking how ironic it was that he remembered his grandfather's comment at that moment. *'Perhaps,'* he shrugged, *'it was a sign of the old man's approval.'*

"You look pleased with yourself," Danika remarked when he reached her and planted a kiss on the top of her head.

"I guess I am. Who wouldn't? Spending time with the most amazing woman I know is something to gloat about."

"Wow, you're such a charmer!" she said and then placed the container and coffee he had just handed to her on the bench seat and then moved in closer with open arms. "You're amazing too!" She said and kissed him.

They ate in comfortable silence in the twilight and watched the world around them. Foot traffic was high in numbers, being the best time of the evening to stroll along the esplanade or to share a picnic with loved ones.

When they finished eating, Lucas gathered the rubbish together and carried it over to the bin. Congregating seagulls scrounging chips scattered in flight, squawking in protest.

"Next time, I'll bring an extra box for you guys," he said and Danika laughed.

Sitting down next to her, Lucas put his arm around Danika and gently drew her closer.

"You know you don't have to be brave around me, don't you?"

She gave him a questioning look.

"Something is bothering you, babe. I can feel it. Your energy is low. And I know it has nothing to do with me because I couldn't help but notice the light in your eyes when you saw me walking towards you. Your eyes shone like headlights!"

She nudged him with her shoulder. "Pretty sure of yourself." She said nothing for a moment and he waited patiently.

"An odd thing happened today," she said.

"Okay and?"

"As you know, Eva is dating the detective."

"Uh-huh."

"He may have recognised me."

"How?"

"Last night, he saw a photo of Eva and me. He told her I look familiar."

"Yeah, so do about a million other people."

"I'm not so sure."

Lucas looked puzzled.

"Last year, I was about to tell Eva everything." Danika sighed. "Oh, to cut a long story short, while I was confessing, she gulped down a full glass of wine and with the mix of her anti-depressants and alcohol, she zonked out."

"So, that's when you told Eva?"

"No."

"How come?"

"She woke up a few hours later with a hangover … and thought she had dreamed what I told her. I didn't correct her. But the detective's interests in my photo triggered Eva to remember *that* day. I hated the idea of lying to her again. I value her friendship too much to deceive her for a second time. I had to tell her everything this morning. Loyal friends are as rare as hen's teeth these days. We talked for hours and she guessed you know, too."

"How did she respond to you being incognito?"

"At first, Eva suggested I tell the detective so he could protect me and then agreed not to say anything to him after I explained the people involved had coppers on their payroll. She said she trusted him, but didn't know him well enough to trust him with my life."

"Good call. How does my girl feel?" he asked, drawing her closer to him with the arm already around her.

"Me? Oh, I'm fine. Relieved Abbi's overseas right now. And grateful to have you in my corner. Just knowing you're there is enough."

"That's a given," he said, resting his head on hers as they looked out at the bay.

Chapter 20

Detective Ruben arrived at Eva's place in high spirits, eager to share his news about buying his new digs with her. He knocked on the front door and called out through the screen door.

"It's open," Eva shouted. "I'm in the kitchen."

"Hey, how are you? Do you not know the dangers of leaving a door unlocked?" he said, entering the kitchen, pecking her lightly on the cheek as she leaned backwards to receive it.

"Help yourself to beer or wine in the fridge. I'll join you," she smiled. "I'm aware of the dangers of an unlocked door. I left it open for you. I've only just come in myself. How was your day?" she asked without missing a beat.

"Ok, point taken. My day was great!" he grinned mischievously.

Eva caught his tone and looked over at him. "Ok, what have you been up to?"

"I bought a two-bedroom apartment on Fox street ..."

"Where Fisher's Hotel used to be?" she asked, interrupting him.

"Yes!"

"Wow! Can you imagine all that history under foot?" She paused. "There might even be a ghost or two hanging about. After all, it was an infamous place," she teased.

He laughed too, responding, "I've never met a ghost. If there's any wandering around, I'll get that chance," he quipped, handing her a wine glass. "Chardonnay 2017, hmm, you've got good taste."

The detective turned around and leaned against the sink, watching Eva stir chicken strips around the pan with one hand and tossing herbs and garlic in with the other. The aroma was wonderful! "Mmm, that smells good!"

"It has just occurred to me, Samuel," Eva said, emptying the contents of the pan into a serving bowl. "I know very little about you, but you know all there is to know about me. Grab the salad from the fridge, please?"

"Okay. Now what do you want to know?" he asked, taking the salad from the refrigerator and setting it on the table.

"Everything!"

The rest of the evening was taken up with the detective sharing his life story. Starting from his youngest childhood memory. "I'd always wanted to make the world around me a better place for as long as I can remember. My parents weren't happy people. I think they hated each other. Our home wasn't a nice place to be. So, I left at age fourteen. I was luckier than most, though."

"In what way?"

"I had a part-time job and I loved learning. I thought leaving home had put an end to my education, until an old man, a regular at the café where I worked, asked where I saw myself in five years. I told him I wasn't sure because I had left home and could not afford school tuition. He laughed and told me I didn't need school to get an education. There was a library full of information on any and every subject there was, if I was really interested in an education. I saw the wisdom in his words and so I spent my spare time at the library reading everything on law and human rights, coincidently I breezed through university. After graduating, I realised I did not want to be a lawyer. I joined the police force instead."

"How did you pay for your university tuition?"

"Part-time hospitality and," pausing for a moment, he reluctantly continued, unsure of what Eva would think, "I was a male dancer."

She was about the take a sip of her wine and stopped midway. "You were a what?"

"The money was too good to pass up. Most weeks, I made close to three thousand dollars." Shaking his head, amazed, he added, "Women lose their minds at ladies' nights. They go crazy, throwing money at all of us." He stopped talking and glanced at Eva. By the expression in her eyes, he could tell what she was thinking. "No, I did not sleep with any of them. For me, it was just a job. Besides that, I had plans for the future. I wanted nothing foiling them. Because I didn't mingle with the women after hours, the guys thought I was gay. That did not deter the ladies from throwing their money at me, for which I am grateful."

"Wow! I wasn't expecting that."

"I was young. It was a means to an end goal."

Eva said nothing for a few minutes. She took a sip from the wineglass and looked directly at the detective, who thought his confession had ended their relationship. "Do you do encores?" she asked. He sighed with relief as they both laughed.

"So, I'm forgiven?"

"For what?"

"My past?"

"You are joking, right?"

"Just wanted to be clear about that."

"Let's just say, if you strip for anyone else, that'll be a deal breaker. Your life before *us* has nothing to do with the present, as long as you have broken no laws. But, there's no point in letting all that experience go to waste, though," she smiled provocatively.

The detective mirrored her smile, thinking he was about to have an adventurous evening, which was quashed with Eva's next question. "Now tell me how a detective can afford that apartment?"

"Wow! That came out of left field. I'm not on the take, if that's what you're implying," he said.

"I wasn't implying anything, Detective Ruben. But that's reassuring to know," she quipped.

"I follow the stock market. I've made a killing, buying and selling shares and investing in bitcoin some years ago. My portfolio is very healthy. I can show you, if you like."

"Okay, one day," Eva said, flippantly, "We can compare notes."

Eva wanted to ask questions about his work, but thought better of it, sensing she should back off. Gathering up the dishes for the dishwasher, Eva declared she had work to do, that she had orders to finish before going to bed. The detective took that as his cue to leave, wondering what had just happened.

Closing the door after he left, Eva felt annoyed with herself. Playing games was not her style. *'But Dani's life is at risk if I've misjudged him and he is one of them. I don't know what I should do.'*

It took a few minutes for Eva to register her mobile phone was ringing. She answered without looking at the screen.

"Hello?"

"Eva, it's me." The detective said, his voice was full of concern. "Is there something wrong?"

"No! No. I was preoccupied with work in the studio," she lied.

"So, we're good?"

"Yes, we are," she said.

Later, as Eva was getting ready for bed, the forgotten mobile pinged. She opened the draw it was in and took it out. Looking at the screen, she thought, 'Damn! *I had forgotten about him.*' Eva sent Marcus a message telling him she didn't have the time to continue their friendship and not to contact her again. Seconds before she had her finger on the off button, he was calling her. She let it ring out, but he called again. She gave in and answered. "Marcus, I don't have time for this. I have other things to worry about."

He began sobbing. "I need your help, Eva. There's no one else I can turn to." Without taking a breath, he continued telling her a long story about how his business was successful. "The contractors haven't paid their accounts and now I'm in trouble. If they paid me, I would've cleared all of my debts. The people I borrowed the money from, to start my business, want me to pay back what I owe them. I only have a few days left to get the money. I fear for my life, Eva. My friends gave me most of what I owe, but I'm short thirty thousand dollars to make up the difference. Will you loan me that money? I'll pay you back as soon as I can."

Eva laughed.

"Why are you laughing?" He screamed. "These people will kill me if I don't pay them what I owe."

"You can't be serious, Marcus. I don't have that kind of money. My life is simple. I live modestly."

"You have a house. You can get a loan to help me. You said you were my friend. Pen pals. That's being a friend."

"My real friends would never ask me to risk my home to pay their debts. No, I won't do that! Don't call me again!" she said and turned off the phone and climbed into bed. Switching off the light, she muttered. "What a load of crap! He actually expected me to fall for that bullshit and give him thirty thousand dollars?"

Chapter 21

Detective Ruben did not go home. Instead, he went back to his office to catch up on paperwork. While sitting at his desk, the overhead halogen pulsed. Ruben leaned back in his chair to look up at the light, deep in thought. The flickering did not bother him. It soothed him as he concentrated on Danika's image in the photograph, still clear in his mind. It troubled him he could not place her. He knew he had seen her before, but where had that been, was the question. He let out an enormous sigh and then turned his attention to the files on his desk. While sorting through them, a note page fell on to the floor. He bent down and scooped it up, about to drop the sheet on top of the file, instead he glanced at it.

It was a message from a parole officer, about an ex-con released from prison over eight months ago who had vanished; a key witness to several unsolved murders. Ruben cursed several times. He then punched in the ex-con's name into the computer. Martin Hopkins' photo and criminal history appeared on the screen. There was an ex-wife, Jane Hopkins and a ten-year-old daughter, Jade. The wife was a witness for the prosecution. Her testimony put

Hopkins away for twenty years for the murder of his two business partners. The detective scrolled down, looking for a photo of Jane Hopkins. Reading through the file, he discovered the wife and daughter were in witness protection. He did the calculations in his mind and came up with ages for them. The wife would be close to sixty and the daughter would be thirty years old. He was not sure if Danika had any children, let alone a daughter. But his gut told him he was on the right track.

Lounging back in his chair, Ruben felt a great satisfaction with some pieces of the puzzle coming together. He then sat up ram-rod straight as a thought struck him; Eva could be in danger if Danika is the ex-wife and Hopkins comes looking for payback. Ruben stood and began pacing the floor. *'I don't know if Danika is Jane Hopkins for sure. All I'm going on is a gut feeling I hope will lead me to the truth.'*

Ruben's next dilemma was how to broach that possibility with Eva. *'Or maybe she already knows and is keeping quiet for Danika's sake?'* He would say nothing for now, just monitor Eva and Danika instead. What bothered the detective most was Hopkins travelling under the radar. He could have changed his appearance, which gave Ruben an idea. He copied ten photos of Martin Hopkins and changed the images into individual composites with glasses, without glasses, different hair colour and styles.

Facial hair, non-facial hair and so on. Each composite was unlike any of the others.

Gathering the photos up about to slip them inside his briefcase, Ruben stopped for a moment, second guessing his actions. When convinced he was right, Ruben closed the briefcase and left the building.

The following morning, Eva stood at the kitchen sink, holding the jug under the tap. Her thoughts were like a pig's breakfast thinking about Danika, Marcus and the detective. The jug overflowing snapped her attention to the present. Tipping the excess water out, she watched the liquid circle the drain and disappear. *'Relationships can be like that,'* she mused. *'Go down the gurgler with a blink of an eye.'* Eva wrestled with her negativity. She had earned no gold star for her past relationships.

At the table, as she nibbled on her toast smothered with home-made berry jam and sipping her coffee, she laughed out loud as a thought came to her. There had been only one failed relationship; her marriage. "That was not of my doing!" she declared to the empty room. "I like the detective," she said with conviction. "And I trust him! But I will remain cautious all the same because my choice of husband could be called into question."

Later, in the studio, Eva said as much to Danika. Danika thought about what Eva said and concluded she would trust her judgment. "I know you're aware of the seriousness and consequences of what could happen to me if the detective was one of *them*. Well, I believe you would not jeopardise my safety."

Eva nodded.

"I have both you and Lucas looking out for me. I pray no harm comes to either of you when Martin finds me. He will, you know. It's just a case of when. He will be in for a surprise. He won't be expecting me to be ready for him."

"In the meantime, we'll remain alert as we carry on as usual," Eva said. "No point wasting energy on something that may not happen."

Danika agreed, then asked had she been in touch with Chelsea, subtly inquiring if she knew about her illness.

"Yes, I called her yesterday," Eva said. "We didn't talk for long. The medication she is taking saps her energy. Chelsea told me why she kept her illness from me for so long, though."

Danika looked at the floor.

"The same reason you did, I expect," said Eva.

"I'm sorry. We …"

"I understand. You two have to stop treating me like I'll break. I can deal with whatever comes along now that I'm over the shock of Josh's misdeeds and my fake marriage."

"Talking like that tells me you have not recovered. You're still angry at Josh, Eva."

"I know. I want to be angry with him until I decide I'm not. Okay?"

Danika nodded. "Fair enough."

"One day, I'll wake up and won't be pissed with him. That day is not here yet. But that doesn't mean I can't be there for my friends when they need support. I'm here for you Dani because we are like sisters. The same goes for Chelsea."

"Okay, I hear you. But Chelsea's illness is more dire than my situation."

"Your problem is a work in progress," said Eva and they both laughed.

"Now, how is our friend? She's been dealing with this blood cancer for over a year. Chelsea said all she does is sleep. But I'm not so sure about that. I drove by her house the other day and noticed her garden has lacked no attention. It is just as perfect as it ever was," said Eva.

"I know she has good days in between the not so good days. That's when she gets stuck into her gardening and gets things done. Pushing through her pain and exhaustion is her saving grace," Danika said. "Another thing, for someone with a serious illness Chelsea looks wonderful! The weight she has lost suits her. But there are days when she is beyond tired from the effects of the medication. Her cast iron will won't allow her life to be governed by this illness, which is admirable."

"Is there a cure for ... I've forgotten the name of the disease?"

"Polycythaemia Vera," Danika said. "It's a type of blood cancer. No, there's no cure as yet, just medication management. Chelsea's a smart lady. She's not about to put her wellbeing in the hands of strangers, even if they are so-called experts in their field; *experts* have been known to be wrong. She has researched the subject thoroughly and is confident she can work with her specialist to regulate her medication to suit her. No doctor knows a patient's body better than the patient."

"Do the doctors know how Chelsea contracted PV?" Eva asked.

"No. But Chelsea worked in a laboratory years ago while living in London. That could be the link. No one can be certain of that. She said it was too long ago for an inquiry and it won't change anything."

They both went quiet and carried on working, deep in their own thoughts. Eva painted spring flowers on a box while Danika tapped away at the computer keyboard. Scent from the roses and lavender in terracotta pots on the veranda floated in to the studio. Eva drew in a deep breath. "Ahh, I love that fragrant mix. It's like a pick-me-up tonic!" she said.

Danika swung her chair around and studied her friend. "You've got something on your mind."

"What makes you say that?"

"You've got that look."

"What look?"

"That distant gaze you get when you're worried."

Eva said nothing.

"Okay," Danika shrugged, turning back to her computer. "If you don't want to talk about it, that's fine,"

"Well, there is something."

Danika swung back around. Facing Eva, she asked, "What would that be?"

Eva kept working on the box in silence while Danika watched her.

"I did something really stupid," Eva said.

"Okay?"

Silence.

Eva put the box down and cleared her throat. "Want a coffee?"

"Uh-huh." Danika nodded. "I'll make it."

"No, I need to do something while I talk."

Danika sighed. "Okay."

Eva went to the kitchenette. As she talked, she opened and closed cupboards and filled the jug with water. "Remember when you set up my social page for the business?"

"Mm-mm."

"I also mentioned the many friend requests I received."

"And you deleted them."

"Yes, I did. All but one."

Danika sank back in her chair. "And?"

"I was bored and lonely then. At first, it seemed like fun. It didn't take long before I saw *red flags and* realised he was a con. This infuriated me. I wondered who the poor bugger in the profile photo was. I played along, hoping to find out more about this person. Keeping the conversation short. Divulging nothing personal when he asked about my family, or myself."

"Are you still talking to this imposter?"

"No. Well, not in the sense of friendly chatter. I told him, Marcus, that's what he calls himself, that I didn't have time to talk with him any longer as I was too busy."

"Okay. And?"

"Marcus was persistent in his calling. After a while, I answered to reiterate my non interest in being his *friend*. He begged me to listen to him, not to turn the phone off because he was in fear of his life."

"What reason did he give to explain his fear?"

"His story is he borrowed a large sum of money to start up his construction business. The business has gone bust because the contractors did not pay their bills and now he must pay back the money he owes to the people he borrowed from. He said, friends have already loaned him most of the money, but he is short thirty thousand dollars. I laughed when he asked me if I would loan him the money. He retorted with anger. So, I hung up on him."

Danika's eyes popped. "He asked you for thirty thousand dollars!"

"Uh-huh. I feel foolish for thinking chatting with a stranger was harmless. After realising Marcus was a conman using a fake identity. I played along, pretending to be his newfound friend, hoping to find out who the person in the profile photo he was using was. I guess that was a dumb idea!"

"Okay, I'll check him out and block him from getting in contact with you again."

"Oh, I have already done that."

"You may think you have. You never know with these people. They're very cunning bastards. I'll make sure he can't access your social media page nor business or personal contacts. Now, destroy that sim card. Anything else I should know?"

Eva shook her head.

"With your permission, I'll monitor all of your emails for the next few weeks and sporadically over the next few months. Just to ensure everything else is clear." Danika paused. "Are you going to mention this to the detective?"

"I was just thinking about that. Do you think I should?"

"If it were me, I'd tell Lucas. But that's your call. Secrets can ruin a relationship, if you recall."

Eva said nothing. She was weighing up the pros and cons of the situation. The detective's dancing days came to mind, which was pre-her as much as her chats with the conman were pre-him even though only by a few days. She felt absolved. "You're right Dani. I'll mention it to him."

Danika smiled. "Mention it? Hmm, that's a good idea."

"What?"

"Nothing. Oh, I almost forgot," Danika said, glad for a chance to change the subject. "I'm going to the local Senior's Expo tomorrow morning. You're welcome to join me. Mingling with the crowd is good for business, not that we need more business at the moment. But many enterprises have sliding scales. The idea is to keep things on an even keel."

"Well, since I slipped into the senior zone last month, I guess I qualify."

"And you said nothing?"

"I didn't want any fuss. I forbade the kids to say a word to anyone. They agreed only if they celebrated with me at my favourite French restaurant in South Brisbane."

"Okay, I forgive you, since I let my birthday slide, too." Danika laughed.

"Oh?"

Danika raised both hands, palm out. "We won't go there, okay?"

Eva nodded and took a sip of her coffee, now cold.

Chapter 22

The following day was overcast and blowy by the time Eva and Danika met up at Bride Street, at the back entrance of St Peter's Anglican Church, where the Expo was.

High temperatures of the previous few days had dropped several degrees. Cooler weather was a welcome relief to the humidity and heat. Despite threatening, dark clouds lingering over the town, the Expo attracted interest. Storms were common in spring. People kept a watchful eye on the weather to avoid being caught in a torrential downpour that sent them scurrying to a nearby shelter. The clouds seemed less threatening as the morning wore on, but the persistent wind became stronger. Secured perimeter tents stood firm, as gathering crowds meandered the grounds, stopping to either collect pamphlets available to seniors regarding services they or loved ones might need, or to chat with friends.

As Eva and Danika ambled among the tents, a voice from behind said, "Hello Dani!" They both turned to see who it was. Danika smiled as she greeted Mary Castle, a friend from one of the local women's groups, of which Danika was a member.

"Are you manning our stall?" Mary asked. Looking at Eva, Mary introduced herself.

"Not this time," replied Danika. "Mary, this is my friend and boss, Eva Rennie."

Mary smiled, nodding. "How good is that? Your boss is also your friend. That's helpful for when asking for a raise," she teased.

"Oh, you've been keeping too much company with Dani, I see," Eva replied with a smile.

Mary laughed. "You bet I have, Eva. Dani dragged me out of my miserable shell. Before I met her, I was afraid of my shadow. She encouraged me to be brave, to say what I think and to stand up for what I believe in. Also, how to have fun. Dani convinced me I have a right to express my opinion as much as anyone. And if people don't agree with me, then that's their right too."

"Yes. Dani's a good egg. She pulled me out of the doldrums, too."

"Excuse me ladies, I'm right here," said Danika. "C'mon. How about we find the cafeteria and get that tea and bikkies the Expo flyer promised?"

Wine would have been better than coffee under these circumstances," said Danika, as they carried their cups to an outside table.

"What circumstances are they?" Eva asked.

"A gals get together!"

"Oh, yes!" said her friends in unison.

At the table, the trio observed their surroundings in silence. Mary was trying to place Eva, thinking she was familiar. Then she remembered.

"Eva," Mary said, "I recall your husband was Josh Rennie. Right?"

"Mary." Danika was about to say something. Eva laid a hand on her arm to stop her. Mary looked puzzled.

"It's okay, Dani."

"Did I say something wrong?"

"No. You didn't, Mary. Yes, Josh was my husband."

"I was about to say that I am sorry for your loss. I apologise if that was inappropriate."

"It's okay, Mary. Thank you. You did nothing wrong."

"If I may say so, you two were a power couple. I met your husband once. He was very charming."

Eva smiled, giving nothing away. "Yes, he was very charming. Where did you meet Josh?"

"Oh gosh, it was years ago, I recall, it was at a local politician meet and greet at the foreshore. You were present, talking to an elegantly dressed older woman. I didn't get to meet you, but I've seen you and your husband out and about together. You seemed like a lovely couple. People like to see that, it ensures confidence."

Danika's eyes remained on Eva while Mary spoke. Eva caught her and gave her the, *I'm okay look,* so she sat back and listened to the conversation.

"Yes, it does, even if interpreted incorrectly."

"Nothing is ever as it seems, I often say. People see what they want to see, Eva. And believe what they want to believe in order to feel comfortable. The world is changing and no one wants to talk about it."

"Changes take place every day, Mary. Change is good!"

"Not this change, Eva."

Eva looked puzzled.

Danika broke in, "Mary's into conspiracy theories. Has been for over a decade. Right?"

"I'm not really. I'm into conspiracy truth. Many truths are deemed as conspiracy theories to confuse and to cause doubt in people's minds. The truth is horrible, the conscious mind cannot grasp or accept it."

"What is the truth, Mary?"

"How would you react to a New World Order?"

"Not well. I very much like the status quo! Oh, we could improve on human rights and ..."

Mary cut in. "What if I said, you could lose your freedom and all of your rights as a citizen?"

Danika sat forward. "What are you saying?"

"I'm saying if people cannot see what's happening around them and in other countries at the moment, then that's exactly what will happen."

"One thing for certain is, our mainstream media cannot be trusted. Television stations and media outlets are owned by mega-media giants who control what we see and hear from morning to late evening. Propaganda. All of it! There are only a few selected shows I enjoy and then off goes the idiot box. The rest is brain numbing trash for the lower socioeconomic audience."

"I agree with you about the garbage shows. That's why my TV is never on. I prefer to listen to music. I'm a sucker for crooners and classical music. Michael, Frank, Nat, Pavarotti and Andre, just to name a few of my favourites." Danika shrugged. "So, for me, I guess that had me tuned *out* of the world around me and I was one of the many who wasn't paying attention. Probably why so many like myself haven't noticed the subtle changes around us. Now that you've drawn my attention to this, I will take notice of local and world events."

"Same here," Eva agreed.

"I know of a few independent news sites where you can keep up-to-date. They report the truth and factual events." Mary said, digging around in her shoulder bag for a pen and notebook. She scribbled something on the notepad and then handed pages to Eva and Danika. "Here are their contact details and websites. Have a look and see what you think."

Eva noticed Danika had a far-away look on her face as she took the notepaper.

"Dani, are you okay?"

"What? Oh, yes. I'm fine. Just thinking about something my ex had said years ago. Something I dismissed as crazy talk. But now I'm not so sure it was crazy after what you've said, Mary."

"What did he say?

"He said he knew people who would one day control the planet. Sounds farfetched, I know, that's why I laughed at him. My ex didn't laugh, though. H said he knew their secret and would be safe from them as long as he had the files."

Eva and Mary stared at Danika with unbelieving eyes.

Looking at her friends, Danika said, "The way you two are looking at me in disbelief, is how I reacted when Marty said what he'd said."

"Where is your ex now?" asked Mary with a note of excitement. "Can you get in touch with him to find out what he meant?"

"Not likely, mate. He's a dangerous man. I want nothing to do with him."

Mary stared at Danika. "Oh, I'm sorry. I didn't know."

"It's okay, of course you couldn't have known. Don't worry about it." Danika shrugged. "I'll do my best to remember if he'd said anything else. Also, I'll do research of my own and see what I come up with." Danika rose from her seat. "I'm getting another coffee. Any orders?"

Both declined.

As Danika entered the cafeteria, a man bumped into her. The stranger smiled and apologised. His magnetic blue eyes mesmerised her; she was awestruck by his good looks. "You're too young to be at a Seniors Expo," she said unintentionally. "Oh," her hand shot to her mouth. "I'm so sorry. I've no business saying that. I don't know you."

He smiled. "I could say the same of you. About being too young to be here. How about I get you a coffee and you can tell me what brought you here? Afterwards, you can decide whether you want to know me."

Danika blushed. When she recovered, an expression of surprise travelled across her face. "How did you know I was about to get coffee? Without waiting for his reply, she asked him if he was new to the area. He told her he had guessed about the coffee and had arrived in Brisbane eight months ago and then introduced himself as Jack Bradley from Quebec. "I bought an apartment in the city," he said. "Since I don't know Brisbane, I thought I'd start by exploring the city. From there, I've been visiting the surrounding suburbs as a matter of interest and mostly because I have an abundance of time, now that I've retired."

"Retired?!" Danika paused. "Oh, there I go again, asking personal questions. My apologies once again."

Jack laughed. "No apology needed."

"I'll have that coffee and then introduce you to my friends," she said, moving inside. "They'll be wondering where I am."

Jack nodded and followed her. She ordered her coffee. The woman behind the counter looked at Jack. "Same for you?"

"No. just water if you please. Merci!" The woman smiled, charmed by Jack's accent.

As they headed over to the others, another woman had joined her friends. It was difficult to tell who it was as she was facing away from Danika.

Mary nudged Eva when she saw Danika heading back with a very attractive man. "Do you know who he is?" she whispered.

"No. I'd remember if I had seen him before."

"Oh, there you are, so you haven't left town," Mary chuckled.

"No, just picking up strangers, as you can see," she laughed, looking back at Jack.

The other woman at the table turned around. "Danika," she said, "it's lovely to see you. I haven't seen you in a while. Are you keeping well?"

"Irene! How nice to see you? Yes, it has been a while. I'm well. Thank you."

Danika turned to Jack Bradley and said, "This lovely lady is not just one of Wynnum, Manly icons of the Arts. She was also involved with Meals on Wheels in the late sixties. Thirty-five-cents meals for the elderly, back then, bought a hearty three courses." Danika looked at Jack. "Of course, you wouldn't know what that is, being a stranger in town. But that service was life-changing for many. We're very fortunate to live in an area full of wonderful history. So, Jack, I would like to introduce you to the multi-talented Irene Baxter. Irene, this is Jack Bradley, a visitor in town."

Jack offered his hand. "It's a pleasure to meet an icon, Irene. I'm just a simple man leading an uninteresting life."

Irene smiled. "I'm sure there is more to you than you are telling, Jack."

Danika broke in. "Irene has an amazing story to tell. Her life's woven into the fabric of this town's history, which should be preserved for future generations. With encouragement, I'm sure Irene will write a book."

"I agree," said Eva

"So do I," said Mary.

"Well, that's the fourth yes with my vote," said Jack.

They all laughed.

"I can hardly say no after such rousing support now, can I?" replied Irene, getting up from the table. "If you'll excuse me, I have a few more friends to see before I head off home." She grinned. "To write that book."

After Irene said goodbye and headed for another group huddled together, Danika called out, "I'll come by next week to read the first chapter."

Irene nodded, waving as she faded into the gathering crowd.

Chapter 23

The women turned their focus to Jack Bradley after Irene left. Eva sat back, picked up her water bottle and took a sip.

"What brings you to this neck of the woods, Jack?" she asked.

He studied Eva for a moment and decided he liked her forthright approach. "Well, I'm retired, originally from Quebec, now living in Brisbane. I bought an apartment in the city several months ago and now, I'm looking around surrounding towns, familiarising myself with the area; my new home."

"What brought you here today, to the Expo?"

"People I met during my travels around the city suggested I visit the bay area. They told me how beautiful it was. The description they gave me was too enticing to ignore. Since I have time on my hands, I thought today is the day I would drive here to see the Bay. I parked my car in the train station carpark. The easiest place to remember where my car was while I took my morning vigil around the town. On my way to the foreshore, I saw the sign out front and came in to see what a senior expo was. Also, it's a good way to meet the people of the area. My closest buddies live in Canada. I've met many people visiting craft markets on weekends, while discovering new places to revisit. Life's too short to waste time lounging around a pool, working on a tan. As you can see, I don't need a tan."

The women smiled while admiring his movie star good looks; cropped, dark hair, intense blue eyes and flawless olive skin and perfect smile.

"What's your line of business, Eva? Assuming you have a business?"

"Yes, I do, Jack. More of an on-line hobby than a business," she said.

Jack glanced at his watch. "I'd like to know more about your hobby, Eva," he said, getting up from the table. "Can we save that for another time? It's been a pleasure meeting you lovely ladies," he said, smiling warmly at each of them. "Sadly, I must leave. I have a meeting I can't miss and I want to drive along the esplanade on my way out." He paused. "Brisbane is a great city, but you have struck gold living here. From what I've already seen, the bay views are spectacular! I envy you."

Mary, who had been silent, said, "You could always pack up and move to here, Jack."

He looked at the attractive, petite redhead. He liked the way her eyes sparkled when she smiled. "That's worth considering, Mary," he replied, handing the three of them his card. "Just in case you need another guest at your next party."

They watched in silence as Jack Bradley left the church grounds.

"Wow! What an impressive man!" Mary said. "I hope I see him again."

"Somehow, I think you will. He didn't eye us the way he eyed you, Mary."

Dismissing Danika's remark, Mary asked, "Do you recall what business Jack said he had retired from?"

Eva and Danika shrugged. "Don't think he said," Eva replied.

As Jack walked backed to the station to collect his car, he analysed his impression of Eva, Danika and Mary. All three were uniquely beautiful women and looked younger than their years. He assumed life had slapped all three in the face at some point, recovering with a greater understanding of what their purpose in life was; even if it was as simple as being grateful for the things they have. *They are alert and intelligent; and more than likely very curious about me.* He would return, now he had found what he was looking for. An element of surprise unsettled him, feeling an attraction to Danika. He sensed he knew her!

At the train station parking area, Jack let the motor idle for a moment, taking in his surroundings. A train pulled in. He switched off the engine and watched as some passengers disembarked and the others waiting climbed aboard. People fascinated him with the way they interacted with one another. They also frustrated him, reason enough to prefer his own company when off duty. He had no need or room in his life for relationships. It was a complication he avoided. The work he did required total freedom to travel at a moment's notice.

Heavy rain and wind swept through the town minutes after the church grounds were cleared of all evidence of the expo, drenching everything in sight. Eva went home. She had a few things to do before the detective arrived that evening. Danika and Mary opted to meet up at their favourite café, Flowers on the Bay, just up the street from the church, on Bay Terrace. Danika wanted to learn more about Mary's *conspiracy truth*, as she called it. Whatever it was, she wanted to know what Mary knew.

The owner of the charming café was an attractive young Iranian woman named Mata. Her warm, friendly manner welcomed customers as if they were long-time friends. A calming ambiance embraced everyone at the point of entry. Vases of fresh flowers of various varieties stood on a large white wooden table in the middle of the room; a focal point of the café. The fragrance from the flora was pleasant to the senses. Mata's recall of Danika and Mary's favourite sweet-treat impressed them. She also sat them at the table nearest to the flowers. Mary believed they had a calming effect on her, as she often felt overwhelmed by the world events; few bothered to notice.

Danika and Mary were frequent visitors to the café.

They usually arrived at the lull of trade, so Mata could take a break and join them. From their first meeting, a bond of friendship had formed. Mary's inquisitive nature took over on their second visit. She invited Mata to join them.

"Dani and I have been admiring the way you have styled your café," Mary said. "It's lovely. The way you have mixed white on white furniture and mirrors and adding the splash of colour with fresh flowers is a wonderful idea. This presents a serene ambiance." Mary paused. "Oh, of course, the cakes and desserts are delicious!"

Danika added, "Your café is unique. I notice your customers reflect this by the way they are dressed."

The three women scanned the room. "As you can see. Everyone is smartly attired. That's a compliment to you."

Before Mata could reply, Mary said. "Everyone has a story. I'm willing to bet you have a story to tell, too."

Mata looked at her. "It is interesting how I was originally perceived as a refugee."

"How do you mean?"

"Recently, a customer asked me where was I from. When I said Iran (Persia), she replied, she had seen no one from Iran before. I thought her comment was odd, since many of my countrymen live in Wynnum and Manly. Some of them come in for coffee," Mata shrugged.

"I understand," said Mary. "Some of us take people at face value, while others assume a lot especially, about migrants, out of ignorance. We can thank the media for that with their constant negative reporting. I don't watch the news anymore. How often do they report positive stories about anything or about emigrants arriving in Australia as a successful applicant, having learned English to pass the immigration test to find work and or start a business? *Feel good* commentary is not their priority."

By the time they arrived at the cafe, all the tables were occupied. Then Danika spotted a vacant table at the back of the room. She tapped Mary on the arm and pointed to it. They headed for it and sat down as Mata hurried by, carrying coffee and a generous slice of apple pie and cream. Both women eyed the pie.

"There goes my diet," said Danika.

"Mine too."

"Ah heck, life is too short to worry about that these days, anyway." Leaning forward, Danika said, "I'm really interested to know about your conspiracy *truths*."

"That surprises me. We've known one another for many years and yet, I know nothing about your past. Where you lived before here."

"Is that a problem?" Danika cut in. "It's no secret I'm a private person."

"No, It's not a problem. I'm surprised. You said you wanted me to tell you what I know. Well, most people dismiss what I know as fantasy and absolute nonsense. I was equally surprised Eva seemed interested in what I had to say, too. It was good to meet her. I've seen you two in here several times."

"You should have joined us. I would've introduced you to her."

"I didn't have the confidence. There's a time for everything. It just wasn't the right time back then. Anyway, I'm often dismissed as a nutter when I ..."

Danika cut in a second time. "Let me be the judge of that."

"Okay," Mary said. "Have you heard of David Icke or Alex Jones?"

"Yes. Both are known as infamous conspiracy theorists."

Mary smiled. "The media deemed them as that. I read *Robot Rebellion*, when it was published in 1994. The book grabbed my attention because I could see what David Icke was saying as possible. William A Ward said, *if you can imagine it, you can achieve it. If you can dream it, you can become it.* That's what I saw in Icke's book; it was possible a Babylonian Brotherhood was trying to control the world. You need to read the book to get the gist of what I am telling you."

"I'll get the book and read it. My gut tells me David Icke has a better understanding of the future than any of us can imagine. I've seen a couple of his videos and thought them interesting and believable and possible!"

"Oh," Mary's eyes widened. "Wow! If ever I mention David Icke or Alex Jones, I was met with a blank stare or shouted down to stop the conspiracy BS! Even laughed at when trying to explain what it's all about."

"I've heard Alex Jones talking about similar topics as David Icke. To be honest, I was busy with my life *situations* to take too much notice of what they said. But the idea of this being BS had not occurred to me. There are too many things happening in our society I'm not comfortable with. For example, the breakdown in family values and especially minority groups dictating to the community what we should think. I don't care what people do or call themselves, as long as they don't impose their opinions on me. That angers me!" said Danika. "I believe billionaire cults and big pharma are reasons for great concern. No one is paying attention to them and the pills they push. My elderly friends take at least six to eight pills three times a day. I shudder in horror. Doctors conditioned their patients to believe they cannot function without their pills. Just with the few elders I know, the pharmaceutical industry would pull in thousands of dollars yearly. The thing is, none of these people are ever in good health. Had they chosen natural remedies and healthier diets, would they be? Most doctors know little or nothing about nutrition. Ignorance isn't bliss. Ignorance is dangerous! Patients are subtly brainwashed into trusting their physicians, blindly following their advice."

Danika shrugged. "That's their choice, I guess. Having a *choice* is what it's all about, isn't it? I know of one friend who questions everything her doctors tell her; about the medication she is given; what the side effects are and so on. She then goes home and does her own research."

Mary shook her head. "Well, aren't you full of surprises? Never in my wildest dreams would I have ever thought you would make such bold statements like that."

"I may refrain from commenting about your, what some would call, radical views. Not once have I dismissed anything you've said. Instead, I researched them and found valid information. Although, I'm not vocal about what's happening around the world. My eyes are open wide. Believe me when I say, I notice a lot. Also, Marty, my ex bragged about being safe as long as he kept his files hidden. As I mentioned before, he told me he knew of a plan some people had about world domination, which went right over my head."

Mary nodded.

"That was over twenty years ago. He never talked about his business or the people he knew. I thought the drugs and booze had scrambled his brain."

"But you don't think that anymore?" Mary stated.

"No, I don't. I'm not sure what to think." Danika looked at Mary. "I heard him say to the police, when they caught him, he had done the world a favour by getting rid of those two bastards." Nodding, Danika said, "I think I now understand what he was talking about." Danika gasped. "My testimony put him in prison for twenty years."

Mary was frozen in her seat. She took a breath before she said, trying to lighten the conversation. "Ah, so, that explains why you're a 'private' person. You've a hidden past?"

Danika nodded.

"Well, you can tell me all about that another time, if you so choose." Mary paused. "I'll get you a heap of information to read about our Constitution being illegally changed."

Danika's eyes widened. "What?"

"Australia is currently operating as a corporate state with an ABN, not as a Commonwealth Government." Mary watched Danika as she gasped in horror. "Wait," said Mary, There's more. "Anything to do with the Crown was removed by the State of Western Australia on the first of January, two thousand and four. It was a declaration of war on the people of the Commonwealth. Also, they are doing everything they can to get rid of cash and replace it with digital currency. Every transaction we make will be monitored. Our every move will be monitored as well. I know this is a lot to take in, so I'll email you all the information I have to substantiate what I am saying."

"That's astounding!"

"Exactly! My initial thought when I was shown this information. Media are silent about this, which implicates them as traitors too. Australians are in for the fight of their lives and of their freedom. They've had things too good for far too long. And have left the politics to others to worry about and to those running the country. Complacency is a dangerous vice!"

"Can we not talk about this right now? I'll have to read what you send me and then take a moment for all of this to sink in. My brain hurts. My heart hurts knowing we are being governed by criminals."

"Yes, we are. Australia is being controlled by the United Nations and every politician, minster and lawyers are aware of it too. They are all traitors for keeping silent!"

Mata appeared at their table full of smiles, unaware the country she believed to be the land of the free, isn't!

"Your usual, or the apple pie I noticed you both salivating over?" She teased.

Mary looked at Danika, still reeling from information overload. "I think it will be the apple pie and coffee today."

Danika nodded.

After apologising to them for having to wait, Mata dashed off to fill their orders.

"How's Abbi going in New York?" Mary asked, to lighten the conversation. "She's still there, I take it?"

"Hmm, yes, Abbi's still in New York. She has a five-year contract. The past two years have sped by without notice. It's mind boggling how time just zips by. She seems happy. And loves her job!"

"How are you going without her? You two are very close. Just like Lucy and I were." Mary paused long enough for Danika to notice she seemed sad.

"Were?" Danika asked. "What do you mean, were? Has something happened to Lucy and the baby?"

Mary took a deep breath. "Lucy cut me out of her and Millie's life."

"What?" Danika shouted loud enough to turn heads. "Why?"

"My fault." Mary said, looking at the glass on the table as she moved it around.

Danika said nothing. She waited.

"There are so many reasons.

"You were so close. We all saw how devoted you two were."

"Every action has consequences. I'm paying the price for that. I adore Millie. She's a sweet child. We bonded immediately. We were close for nine months of her life. I had the privilege of holding her just hours after her birth. When she was unsettled, I sang her to sleep. I will treasure that time. It's all I have of my darling granddaughter and the many photos of us together."

"Oh Mary, that's so sad. My heart hurts for you. I want to cry."

"Oh, I'm fine now and am coping with the loss better than expected. My son, Will, is my rock. He has been very supportive. The silver lining in this scenario is I can pursue other interests. Perhaps, one day, I might even have a weekend away at a lovely bed-and-breakfast in the country; something I've always wanted to do. For now, my time is absorbed researching current global affairs. Keeping busy distracts me from dwelling on the disintegration of the relationship. Maybe time will heal the situation? I don't know what the future holds for us. Perhaps the universe separated us so we could grow as individuals. After all, Lucy consumed a lot of my time and I did not mind that." Mary paused. "Anyway," she sighed heavily. "I'm now free to do whatever I want to do whenever I like. All's not lost!"

"I'm speechless." Was all Danika could say.

Silence fell between them as they ate their dessert.

"Mmm, this is delicious!" said Mary.

Danika nodded her appreciation.

"How is Lucas? All good there?" Mary asked in between bites.

"Uh-huh," Danika had a mouth full of pie. "Yes. We agreed to take it one day at a time with no expectation. No pressure that way."

Mary grinned. "You've been together what, almost two years now?"

"Uh-huh! Lucas is away at the moment. He usually calls every night when he goes on trips. It's odd that he has only called once this week. Not sure what to think. But I'm not getting my knickers in a knot over it. I'll find out when he comes home," she said, giving nothing away.

Chapter 24

Eva arrived home as the storm hit. The weather was the farthest thing from her thoughts. She was thinking about Jack Bradley. *'Who the hell was he?'* Although she liked Jack, her instinct sounded alarm bells. *'Perhaps I'm overly concerned about Dani's safety. Perhaps I'm overreacting?'* she told herself, trying to shake off her suspicion.

Towards evening, Eva looked up at the kitchen clock, checking to see how much time she had before Harry, Montana and Sam arrived for dinner. Previously, when Eva told them what she did during her day, she would often mention the detective, speaking warmly of her new friend. They asked when they were going to meet him. This evening was their first occasion. Everything had to be perfect. She had to harness her thoughts and the feeling that meeting Jack Bradley was no coincidence. It was distracting her. She worried Jack Bradley might be a threat to Danika. A threat no one would expect. She then laughed out loud at that thought. *'Oh, good god, woman. Get a grip! This is not a James Bond movie with covert villains popping up out of the blue. Your imagination is running wild!'*

A knock on the front door brought her back to reality. She took a deep breath, patted her hair in place and checked her appearance in the hall mirror, then opened the door to the detective. His face lit up at the sight of her. In his arms was an enormous bouquet of native flora. Emotion overwhelmed Eva when he handed her the flowers. She threw her arms around him, wanting so much to trust him, to confide in him her concern about Jack Bradley being a potential threat to Danika. She also wanted to tell him about Marcus. Guilt gnarled her. She said nothing. Just hugged him tight. Hoping he was the man she wanted him to be because her feelings for him were growing. And she needed a confidant.

"Hey," he said in a singsong way while juggling the bouquet as she grabbed hold of him. "I've missed you too," making light of her unusual behaviour, sensing something was amiss. He held her until she was ready to release him. "Are you okay?"

"Yes. Fine now. I just needed a hug," she said. "How was your day?"

"My day just got better. I'm open for hugs anytime of the day or night for you." Slipping his arm around Eva's waist, he drew her closer to him as they moved toward the kitchen. "Mmm! Whatever that is, it smells wonderful."

"Harry and Montana should be here any minute," Eva said, moving away from him to check the oven temperature. Before Eva had finished the sentence, Harry and Montana entered the kitchen. "Hey, Mum," they said in unison.

After introductions, they all sat down to eat. Harry noticed his mother struggling to stay focussed on what she was doing. "Are you okay, Mum?"

Eva looked at him for a moment. She missed what he had said. "What, love?"

"I asked if you were okay."

"Yes, yes. I'm fine, darling." She smiled warmly at him. "Just a little tired. We had a busy day at the senior's expo. You know how much energy it takes with all of us women talking and trying to get a word in," she joked.

They all laughed.

The evening was a success. The detective sat back feeling at ease, listening while Harry and Montana shared amusing moments about Eva with him. Their affection for her was unmistakable. She glowed with pride. Conversation flowed easily all evening. He knew he had passed their scrutiny. Later, he noticed Montana whispering something to Eva, giving her a thumbs up with a smile and a wink. When Eva blushed, Montana wrapped her arms around her, telling Eva she deserved to be happy and to go for it. "Mum, nothing would please Harry and me more than to see you happy. If Sam can add to that happiness, all the better. We like him. The way you refer to him as detective is kind of sweet."

Waving Harry and Montana off at the end of the evening triggered an unfamiliar sensation in the detective. He took a moment to analyse it. Something was missing from his life. Family! He had not expected not having a family would bother him until now. Being included in Eva's felt good. He liked that feeling and wanted it to last.

After Harry's car lights faded into the night, Eva turned and looked at Sam about to say something. She stopped. He wore a pensive expression. When watching old movies, Eva was in the habit of reading the subtext of the story and of character's emotions. Did she imagine she saw sadness and joy with a touch of loneliness flash across the detective's features? Softening her voice, she asked if he enjoyed the evening?

"Very much so," he replied, looking at the ground.

"Are you okay?"

"Can a person be happy and sad at the same time?"

"They certainly can."

"That's how I'm feeling. And, a little envious."

"Oh, why?"

"I envy you, your family. I was too busy to want one until now, when it's too late."

"Oh, never mind," Eva said, leaning into him. "I'll share mine with you. They like you very much."

The detective looked into Eva's eyes. "You truly are an amazing woman!"

She took him by the hand. "C'mon," she said, grinning, leading him inside. "We're about to discover just how amazing we both are."

Curled up in the bedsheets, Eva rolled over closer to Samuel. "Well, who is the amazing one now?" she asked, grinning from ear to ear.

"Glad to be of service, madame," he teased. "Is this where we pull out fags and take long drags on the death stick, exulting great satisfaction? It's such a pity I don't smoke. The scene is perfect for that."

Eva laughed, visualising the image in her mind. She unravelled herself from the sheet, rolling in the opposite direction and rose from the bed, naked. "Ciggies are off the menu. Aha! Wine isn't though!" She giggled. "I'll be back," she said, disappearing through the doorway.

A few minutes later, the detective heard glass on glass announcing Eva's return. The wine had ignited courage in Eva. Courage she would need to ask some serious questions.

While she thought about what she wanted to ask, Samuel commented, with a straight face, "You'd never be a successful crook, my darling."

"Oh, why would that be?"

"You're too easy to read, sweetheart. Want to tell me about it?"

"About what?"

"I don't know. I'm waiting for you to tell me."

"Are you a corrupt cop?" she blurted out, succoured by wine.

He laughed. "We just spent the best hour of lovemaking. Would you have done that if you thought I was corrupt?"

"No, I guess not," she said, childlike. "I don't want you to be corrupt. You must be honest and good and wonderful, as I imagine you are."

"I'm doing my best to master those fine qualities."

"Now that's settled. Want to share your concerns with me?"

Eva did not respond. She had rested her head on his shoulder and fallen asleep.

Dappled sunlight danced across Eva's face. She stirred. Then sat up in bed. The space beside her was empty. Her mind was foggy. *'Was he here with me last night?'* She could hear Maggie. Her warbling sounded like chatter. Eva left the bed and half staggered to the kitchen. She stopped in the doorway. The table was set. "So, he *was* here last night. It wasn't the fringe of a dream?" Eva moved to the sink to get a glass of water. She heard someone talking and leaned forward to look out of the window, surprised to see the detective hand feeding Maggie. She smiled. *'He fits like a glove.'* Eva knocked the glass over. The detective turned toward the sound.

"G'morning!" he said. "Didn't have the heart to interrupt your concert. You were giving a glowing rendition of something unfamiliar," he teased.

"Oh, wine makes me snore like that. Lots of trumpets, I bet," she laughed unashamedly.

"How do you know that?"

"I recorded myself once. Had a good laugh about it too."

He left Maggie with a titbit and joined Eva in the kitchen. "No wine tonight, then. As a test case, of course. I'm all about facts." He grinned and decided not to broach the subject Eva was about to embark on last night. Whatever it was, she would confide in him when she was ready. Unbeknown to Eva, he had an inkling of what it was.

Later that morning, Eva and Danika were working in the studio. Danika noticed Eva was all over the place. Out of character for a perfectionist. She would start folding papers and then leave that to do something trivial, for example, wipe over clean benches.

"Eva, you are distracting me. I can't work with you flitting back and forth around the studio. Do you want to talk about it?"

"About what?" she asked.

"That's what I'm trying to find out."

Eva came and sat down beside her. "I'm worried. No, I'm not just worried. I'm out of my mind with anxiety."

"Are you and Sam having trouble?"

"No! No, we're fine. Couldn't be better. My snoring doesn't bother him."

Danika raised her brows, thinking, *too much information*. Then smiled at the thought.

Eva realised what she said. Flustered, she cried out. "Oh god no! It's not him. Nothing to do with him." Eva paused. "Well, indirectly it is. But it's about YOU!"

"Me?"

"Did you not think that a very attractive, fit and healthy man in his late fifties visiting a seniors expo as odd?"

Danika shook her head. "Never gave it a second thought."

"Well, it bothers me. I cannot concentrate on anything else. I want to tell Sam your story. He can help you and keep you safe. With all my heart, I believe we can trust him."

"Let me think about it?"

"Okay, you've got an hour. I cannot do another thing until I confide in him. The worry is driving me bonkers. Your ex could have sent someone to harm you or worse to … Oh, God, I cannot even say it. You may have to hide out for a while at the city apartment. No one knows I have it."

"No one?"

"No, I was too ashamed to mention it. The story attached to it is too awful. I've been there only a couple times in the past two years. I have a caretaker looking after it. He is aware there are security cameras installed, so it does not tempt him to rent it out or do whatever unsavoury people do. Not that I'm saying he's one of them. I trust no one." Eva paused. "Tell me you have told no one."

"Only Abbi. She's not interested in your business. I told her only to explain where I was that night. She was fraught and concerned that something had happened to me. And besides that, she's in America. I'm so glad about that. One less thing to worry about."

Danika stared at Eva for a moment.

"Okay, out with it."

"Mary told me some very interesting things the other day. After the senior's expo, we met up for coffee at Flowers on the Bay."

"Go on. I'm listening."

"As we both know, Mary is into conspiracy theories; she calls them truths in disguise."

"Okay." Eva nodded.

"After recalling what Martin said years ago, about knowing of a group planning to control the planet. I now believe he was telling the truth. Especially with the information Mary has backed up by international experts on the subject, for example David Icke and Alex Jones, Dr David Martin for starters. It fits in with what Martin said." She paused. "I think I now know why he killed those men. They were part of the organisation." Danika turned to face Eva; eyes large as saucers. "Holy crap! My testimony put him in prison! For twenty years! Martin might have been trying to stop the group from growing in numbers, at least here in Australia. I might have stuffed that up!"

"Dani, from what you've told me about him, Martin doesn't sound like any kind of hero. He would've had his own agenda. So, don't beat yourself up over that, kiddo."

Danika nodded in agreement. "But all the same, there's a ring of truth in what Martin said. I can feel it in my bones. I can't see why I would be his target, though. If I was Martin, I'd become the invisible man and fade into the gathering twilight; not risk my life settling an old score. That would be suicide! You know, I'm not sure I'd recognise him if he walked past me in the street. I cannot remember what he looks like. All I can recall of him is that he was good looking, oh and tall."

"Well, Jack isn't tall," Eva said. "He is, ah, I'd say, very handsome though?"

"That he is. Those eyes of his are mesmerising. They draw you to him. I see strength and kindness and warning in them. Jack is a mixed bag of contradiction. I'd wouldn't like to be his enemy. Regardless, I like him. There's something familiar about him." She paused. "Hmm, now you've got me curious why our paths have crossed?"

In his city apartment, just a twenty-minute drive away from Manly, Jack was listening to Eva's and Danika's conversation. "Well done, ladies! You didn't disappoint," he said, pleased with himself for being an excellent judge of character.

Unbeknown to them, a listening and tracking device was inserted in the business cards he gave them at the expo. "You've nothing to fear, my beauties. One threat will soon be disabled, with another loose end to attend to before this party is over for good."

Chapter 25

Martin Hopkins was still not used to the new identity. The decision to come to Queensland, he soon realised, was not a wise one. Especially travelling around unfamiliar districts; Sydney was his territory. He knew every inch of the city and unlike Brisbane, he felt safe there. The humidity and heat drained his energy, slowing him in his search for Jane, which was not as easy as he had hoped, even with the intelligence he paid for.

There was a knock on his door. Moving with caution, he looked through the viewfinder. *'What the hell does he want?'*

He sighed heavily and called out, "Who is it?"

"Jack Bradley. Your neighbour on the next floor."

"Okay, hang on," Hopkins replied, scanning the room for anything he needed to conceal. Seeing that it was all clear, he opened the door. Keeping his voice steady, he asked, "What can I do for you, mate?"

Jack slowly edged his way into the apartment, asking if he would answer a couple of questions. "Mind if I come in?"

"Looks like you already are." Hopkins said, walking away.

Jack closed the door and followed him into the kitchen. He stood facing Hopkins, separated by the kitchen bench.

"Okay, you're inside, so what's the question?"

"Are you enjoying your freedom, Martin?"

Hopkins froze and then relaxed. Looking down at Jack, he smirked. "Good enough. Why do you ask?"

"You're not curious about where I got my intel from?"

"Should I be? I've paid my dues. I'm a free man."

"Free? Hmm." Jack paused. "Having money to burn doesn't make you a free man, buddy."

"Who are you? What do you want?" Hopkins demanded, as his anger mounted.

Jack's eyes never left Hopkins; his every movement was calculated. Hopkins let his anger get the better of him and made the fatal mistake of snatching his Ruger from the kitchen drawer beside him. Jack leaned forward, grabbed his arm, flipped him over and then propelled himself over the countertop to flick the side of his head with his hand. It was over in a split second. Martin Hopkins, aka Rhys James Winton, lay dead on the floor. Jack studied the lifeless body. No sign of damage. Clearly an accident. He pocketed the Ruger and then left.

Back at his apartment, he rebooted the building's security cameras, checked out the Ruger SP101. New, never been fired. Guess Marty was expecting a close encounter. The revolver was only effective up to 91.44 metres. Jack smiled. *'Well, that's something he won't have to worry about anymore.'*

The following day, Jack picked up his mobile and punched in Roma Street Police station's number.

"Detective Senior Sergeant Ruben, please," asked the man with an authentic Australian accent.

On the third ring, Ruben answered.

"Got a tip for you."

"I'm listening."

"Word has it Hoppy, aka Marty Hopkins, has a new ID."

"Okay and?"

The caller said nothing.

"Are you going to give me the name?"

"Yeah."

"What is it?"

"Oh, yeah, yeah. It's ah, Winton. Rhys Winton. Got himself flash digs someplace in the city," the caller said and then hung up.

The detective turned to his computer and typed in the name the informant gave him. Nothing. Next step, licensing. Bingo! A recent photo of the ex-con, with hair and eye colour change, appeared on the screen, along with an address.

Ruben called his new partner, Buddy McIntyre. Buddy's real name was Bubba. When first introduced, the detective told him he would not call a grown man Bubba.

Especially one as large as he. They settled for Buddy. Bubba was fine with that. Nothing fazed the good-natured, sweet-faced indigenous.

"Any idea who the rat is?" Buddy asked Ruben as they drove through the city to Winton's address.

"Nah, didn't recognise the voice. A plant, maybe. Very convenient. Hopkins has been flying under the radar for too many months not to be. There's more to this. You can take that to the bank."

Buddy laughed. "Not these days, mate. Ya get nothin' for ya dollar anymore."

Ruben smiled. "Yeah, guess you're right."

The detectives were an odd duo. Buddy, large and muscular. Ruben, the same height, muscular and lean. They were a good team and worked well together. Neither noticed the stares they got wherever they went; solving assignments they managed was their only focus.

Ruben found a park in proximity to the building where Hopkins lived. Getting in and out of the vehicle was a tight squeeze for Buddy. "A task and a half," he would say, with a beaming grin.

"Yep, you made it again this time too, mate," replied Ruben, shaking his head. "I'll have to request a larger vehicle. One day you might not!" he kidded. "C'mon, let's see what this piece of crap has been up to. This way," said Ruben, glancing at the address.

They made their way up Adelaide Street, stopping outside the building noted in Ruben's diary where Hopkins lived.

"Bit flash for an ex-con, wouldn't you say?"

"You read my mind, Buddy."

A man, short and stout, dressed in a valet uniform, pulled the door open as Ruben placed his hand on the handle. Both men stopped and glanced at one another with raised brows. Ruben thanked him and then asked if he knew Rhys Winton.

"Sure do." The doorman said warmly. "A fine gentleman, he is, too." He frowned. "Come to think of it, I saw Mr Winton come in, but he hasn't been out for a day or two."

"He could have slipped out while you weren't here."

"No. He wouldn't do that. I arrange transport for him every time he goes out. He's a man of habit. You don't do what I do for as long as I have without learning about people or their way of doing things. If you get what I mean."

Both men nodded.

"So, you're saying Mr Winton's home?"

"That's what I'm saying, sir."

"Okay then, we'll go up and surprise him."

The man in the uniform said nothing. A smile crept across his features as he watched them head for the elevator.

Ruben knocked several times with no response. Then began pounding. A neighbour opened her door and stuck her head out to see who it was making the racket.

"Must you?" Asked the elderly lady with sad brown eyes.

"Yes madam, I must. It's important that we get in contact with Mr Winton."

"Oh, is it about his ex-wife?" Her voice reflected concern.

"Why do you ask?"

"Rhys told me he was looking for her to make amends. He seemed very sincere. Tears filled his eyes whenever he mentioned her. I think he said her name was Jane. They also have a daughter." She paused for thought. "I cannot remember her name, sorry."

"Privacy laws prevent me from discussing that with you. But it would be helpful if you have any information," Ruben said, showing her his ID.

Buddy leaned forward. "I'm Detective Bubba McIntyre."

She looked at him and said, "McIntyre?"

"That's correct. My daddy was a big Scotsman and my mother was indigenous," he said, smiling with pride.

"My husband was Scottish too. Blair Mackenzie. How's that for a good Scottish name? He passed away last year," she added with a note of sadness. "Rhys has been good company for me. I hope what you have to tell him isn't bad news," she said, stepping back into her apartment and closing the door.

The men turned back to Hopkins's apartment. "What do you think?" asked Buddy, holding his mobile in his hand. "Call the manager?"

"Yep."

They went back downstairs to wait for him. His secretary said he was in a meeting. She would notify her boss and then message them when she heard from him. Fifteen minutes passed before she let them know he was on his way.

A medium height, chubby, dark-haired man about mid-sixties waddled into the building perspiring profusely. A large handkerchief dangled from his hand. He mopped at his face and neck and then wiped his hands on it.

"My apologies gentlemen, for keeping you waiting." the man said, offering his hand.

After introductions, Kalil Badaw ushered them into a small side office.

"Now, gentleman, how can I be of service?"

"We would like you to check on a resident here. There's reason to believe he could be in serious trouble?"

"Do you have a search warrant?"

"No, Mr Badaw. I can get one should you refuse to cooperate."

The short man began nervously dabbing at his face and neck with the handkerchief he still held. "I have to think of our resident's privacy."

"The doorman assured us Mr Winton was home." Ruben said.

The manager looked puzzled. "What doorman? There's no doorman here."

The detectives did not respond. Both stared down at him. Mr Badaw coughed to clear this dry throat. "Okay. You take full responsibility?"

Both men nodded.

"Follow me gentlemen," he said, emphasising gentlemen.

Outside the apartment, after unlocking the door, the manager said, stepping away. "If you don't mind, I'll wait here."

Detective Ruben nodded and called out to Winton, pushing the door open with his foot. The room was well lit, giving a wide view of the city. Nothing looked out of place. Glancing at one another, both men felt an eery sensation. Buddy moved to the kitchen as Sam headed for other parts of the apartment.

"Sam."

"Found something?" Ruben called from the main bedroom.

"Yep. Sure have. Come see for yourself."

Buddy and Sam looked at the lifeless body of Martin Hopkins, aka Rhys James Winton, sprawled on the kitchen tiled-floor.

"How long do you reckon?" Buddy asked.

"At least twenty-four hours."

"Yeah. I'd say that too."

"Murder or accident?"

"Now that's difficult to tell. He could've slipped and fell. The coroner will have to determine that."

"You call him while I go through the files I found in the bedroom."

Fifteen minutes later, the apartment was swarming with officials. Ruben had gathered the files he found and took them to his car, telling no one. Buddy saw him, but said nothing. He knew Ruben well enough to know that he had good reason and he would explain later.

On the way back to the station, Ruben told Buddy he wanted to go through the files he squirreled away from the apartment before anyone else got their mitts on them. "At a glance, they look like intricate plans of a new organisation. I can't be sure what it's all about until I read through everything. There's a long list of names. Mostly high-profile names."

"How high profile?"

"Politicians and high court judges, bishops, Masonic Lodge members …"

Buddy's eyes widened as he whistled. "No shit?"

221

"No shit." Echoed Ruben. "A note was left on my desk a few days ago saying a call came from Hopkins's PO reporting he had not seen or heard from Hopkins since he'd been released. I pulled up Hopkins's case file and went over it with a fine, tooth comb. Murdered two associates of his. Never said why, just that he had done the world a favour. He also said he was safe as long as he had the files. No one knew what he was talking about. No one cared enough to investigate, either. But the odd thing is, he was given special privileges and protection while inside. Someone was looking after him."

"So, if he was murdered, why were the files left behind?"

"One of three angles. First: He was topped for another reason. Second: The killer did not know about the files. Third: Someone wanted the files to be found."

"Yeah, but it doesn't look like murder."

"True, it doesn't. It's not meant to be. My guts say, Hopkins was executed by a professional. I'm looking forward to the autopsy report."

"What about the doorman that never was?"

"He could be our killer," Ruben said.

"What a short, sixty something Italian." Buddy laughed.

Ruben did not crack a smile.

"Mate, you can't be serious? He's old, stooped and unfit. Hopkins towered over him."

"I'm not ruling out anything. We've got to remember things are not always what they seem."

By the time the detectives arrived back at the office to write their reports, Winton's death had made headlines across the country. *'Wealthy businessman, Mr Rhys James Winton, passed away alone in his luxury apartment. No suspicious circumstances.'*

Chapter 26

"Holy shit!" Danika yelled, startling Eva.

"What is it?"

"Can you recall when I said I thought I didn't remember what Martin looks like? Well, I do." Pointing to the computer screen, she said, "I clicked on to the news by mistake and came across this. That's him! That's Martin. He has changed his name, his hair colour and is wearing colour contact lenses. But that's him. He's dead. That's what it says in this article. Here, read it for yourself."

Eva dropped what she was doing and came and stood behind Danika. She leaned in to read the article over her shoulder. "Hmm, a bastard he is, but all the same, that bugger's a looker."

"He was also once a good guy until drugs and greed corrupted his heart and he became a stranger," Danika said with remorse. "We might have had a good life together." She paused. "I really loved that scumbag!" She slumped forward with a heavy heart. "The poor bastard died all alone in his fancy apartment. A lot of good his ill-gotten gains did him." She paused. "Damn him! No, fuck it! Serves him right! Karma's a bitch!"

Eva rubbed Danika's shoulders. "They steal our hearts and trample all over them and think nothing of it. And yet, we can still find compassion for them in their demise."

"That's because we're decent human beings, Eva. Let's celebrate that."

Later that evening, when the detective joined Eva for dinner. He told her he could only stay for a quick meal as he had work to do.

Eva asked if it had anything to do with Rhys Winton's death. "Dani and I read about it on the office computer this afternoon. She clicked on the news link by mistake."

"The news bulletin also said his death was not suspicious. So, why ask about that?"

"Yes, it did. But what you don't know. The dead man was Dani's partner. His name isn't Rhys Winton, it's Martin Hopkins. Dani was offered witness protection to testify against him at his trial. Her testimony closed the case and put him in prison for twenty years." Eva went silent. The detective was not reacting, which surprised her. "You already know this, don't you?"

"Can't say I knew for certain. But I guessed. You've just confirmed my suspicion. And before you say anything, I know you tried to tell me. You were struggling between your loyalty to Danika and to me."

"I'm sorry I didn't trust you sooner. Dani was in fear of her life and I promised to keep her secret confidential."

"Okay, now that's out of the way. Did she say why her life was in danger?"

"Martin vowed to get her for dobbing him in to the police." She paused. "Oh, and that *they* had long tentacles and also had police on the payroll."

"Who are 'they'?"

"Dani never found out who *they* are. But she is scared these *invisibles* think she knows their secrets. She knows nothing. Martin hid everything from her. The only thing she can remember is she recalls Martin saying something about files he had would keep him safe from the people who were planning global control." Eva noticed a reaction from the detective. "Ha, so there is some truth to that?"

"Not sure about anything yet. I have a lot to do before I know anything for certain."

"So, I take it that's what you'll be working on tonight?"

The detective looked at his watch. "Yes. I have to leave and get cracking on it right now. I might not get back tonight. But I'll be over in the morning with fresh croissants and coffee."

Eva smiled. "I guess croissants are a nice substitute. Are you going back to the office now?"

He shook his head. "No. I'll be working from my apartment. I'm keeping the information belonging to Winton under wraps until I go through it. You understand I can't discuss the case with you?"

Eva nodded.

"If there's anything you need to know, I'll tell you. In the meantime, be cautious when moving about. At least, until I know what it is I'm dealing with."

Danika was expecting Lucas to be back by now. He had been away for over a week. One call during that time was unusual. She had given much thought to his behaviour and concluded he was withdrawing from her. After Martin's and her relationship disintegrated, she vowed that no one would have the power to steal her peace ever again, so she detached herself emotionally from Lucas. Regardless of how she felt about him, her senses screamed something was wrong. She was not about to call and ask where he was. Had he wanted her to know, he would have told her. Lucas was a free man. The only one stipulation she asked of him; if he met someone new, he would end their relationship before he got involved with the new woman. She told him that humiliating and lying to your partner was the lowest thing anyone could do to another person; it was a deal breaker for her.

Soft music filtered through her small home as she prepared the evening meal; garlic prawn salad. After dinner, she cleared the dishes away and then poured a glass of red wine and stretched out on the couch, unaware her every move was being watched.

The eyes in the night studied her features and thought how lovely she was. He was not about to allow anyone to harm this precious jewel. The eyes followed her when she got up and danced her way into the kitchen. He listened with pleasure; her singing the last few lyrics of *My Way*. Several times before, he had heard that lovely voice and wished she would sing more. Only when alone did her melody start. The house was now in darkness. Minutes passed before steady breathing told him she was asleep. No sound was heard while moving into position. The trap was set. It was only a matter of time before the end game. Maybe tonight, or maybe next week. It did not matter. Time was his friend for a change. No schedule demanded he be elsewhere.

Chapter 27

Sunlight sliced through the darkness, spreading slivers of golden rays along the dark, cloudless horizon. The bay was still. Not a whisper of a breeze. Another hot day ahead. The hours had dissolved so quickly; night left and morning arrived without warning.

Pages from the files covered Ruben's large oak dining table. He threw the last one aside indiscriminately after reading it. Try as he might, he could not digest the words written on those pages; they were beyond comprehension; words of an insane mind. Ruben rubbed his eyes. He was mentally and physically exhausted. He wanted to lay his head down on the table and erase every syllable from his thoughts, wishing he had left the file case in the apartment. But he knew it was well past that. The baton was handed to him and he had to run with it to God knows where. Feeling despondent, he pushed his chair away from the table. He stood and stretched the stiffness out of his long, lean, muscular body.

He made coffee and headed out to the balcony to watch the sunrise. The brew was hot and strong, just what he needed to wake him up. He glanced at his watch. Four-forty-five. The town was coming alive. In the distance, he could see early morning walkers with their dogs. It would not be long before the foreshore overflowed with joggers of all ages and elders who still have a tight hold on what's left of their vitality. Young mums with their toddlers came later in the morning.

The unimaginable scenes he saw on the DVDs and the words on the pages lying on his table, reflected nothing of the harmonious unsuspecting community just metres from his apartment; inconceivable details threatening the fabric of societies worldwide. Ruben studied the activity in front of him with a heavy heart. *'You poor bastards are about to embark on the fight of your lives. How many will fight the tyranny and how many will ignore it?'* Most poignantly, he thought, *'Who will believe what the near future holds for everyone?'* Shrugging, Ruben went back to the table and gathered up the papers and DVDs and put them back into the files where they were initially housed, but not before he first made copies of everything. With all he now knew, the reaction of his superiors will confirm a few things for him, if they are involved in this deception.

Showered and dressed, Ruben picked up his briefcase and left. First stop was the bakery, keeping his promise to Eva of fresh croissants and coffee for breakfast. She, too, was up and ready for the day ahead by the time he arrived.

"Aww, you're tired, detective Ruben. Partying all night by the looks of it," she teased, wrapping her arms around his neck kissing him. "Did you have a good time?"

"I would've had a better time here with you last night than going through that material." He put the coffees and croissants on the table to return her hug.

Eva noted the concern in his voice. "You've found something awful, haven't you?"

He said nothing.

"Anything to do with Danika? Is she in harm's way?"

"We're all in harm's way."

"What?" Eva paused. "I know you can't discuss police business with me."

He nodded. "At least for now."

She gave him a puzzled look.

"I'll explain later. It's *wait and see*, for now. I promise I won't keep you dangling. As soon as I can, I'll explain everything. For now, will you keep this between us? No girl talk, okay?"

She nodded.

They ate in unified silence.

On the way into the city, Ruben called Buddy on the car phone. In the background, he could hear Buddy's children playing and their mother telling them to be quiet, hearing her say, "Daddy's on the phone."

Buddy moved to another room. "Okay, mate, we can talk now."

"Are you prepared to trust me on what I'm about to do?"

"Ah, what are you about to do?"

"Conceal evidence."

"Uh-huh. Want to tell me why?"

"I can't right now, but I can show you later. My report, with a few details omitted, will be on your desk by the time you arrive this morning."

Buddy glanced at the bedroom clock. "You're early. Looking for the gold star from the teacher?" He laughed.

"I wish it was as simple as that, Buddy. I'm setting a trap for vermin that might be in the house."

"Uh-huh, okay. This better be good. See you later."

The office was almost deserted when Ruben arrived. While he waited for Buddy, he researched two of the names he found on Winton's lists. The first, he discovered, was one of the most highly respected judges in Australia who had committed suicide in 1996; guilty of paedophilia. The second, a retired politician; another paedophile. Ruben sat back, stunned. How long he sat there, he did not know.

'Christ,' he thought, 'if this is just the start, I dread to think who else I'll find.'

Ruben reacted to the sound of footsteps and quickly closed the page. Within minutes, the office came alive. Glancing at his watch and then at the door, he was relieved to see Buddy entering the room. Ruben's eyes followed him to his desk.

"Mornin' Sam," Buddy said, picking up the report. After reading it, he nodded and placed it in his in-tray. "Looks fine to me," he said, moving things around on his desk, looking for his pen. "What's on the agenda for today?"

"First up, have a chat with the boss about the evidence found in Winton's apartment. Then we get out of here."

Ruben waited an hour before heading into the boss's office, giving him time to settle into his morning routine. As soon as his office was clear, Ruben strolled over and knocked on the door.

"Got a minute, chief?"

James Kelly put his pen down. "Yep. What's up?"

"Came across this at Winton's ah, Hopkins' apartment yesterday," Ruben said, dropping a stack of files on the desk. "Hopkins was using an alias."

Kelly reached out and dragged it in closer. "What's in it?"

"Looks like a heap of conspiracy crap. I thought you might want upstairs to look it over. It's not my bag, besides that Hopkins' death looks like an accident. I'm fairly sure the autopsy will confirm it."

"Okay, leave it with me," Kelly said. Ruben noticed he was attempting to keep his voice steady. He went back to his desk and shuffled papers around to look busy while intermittently glancing over at Kelly's office. Ruben could see the strain on his boss's face; the reaction he was expecting to confirm his suspicion that this went deeper than anyone knew. Buddy caught on to what Ruben was doing. He said nothing as he put his mobile in the back pocket of his pants, aware there was a purpose to everything his partner did. He waited for his cue to role play. It came when Ruben sat on the edge of his desk holding a file, eager to discuss what intel they already had gathered about the next case. The conversation was loud enough for those close by to hear. After a reasonable time passed, Ruben told Buddy to get his things. "Duty calls."

On the way out, they playfully bantered with each other until they were out of the line of the security cameras and at the vehicle. Before unlocking the doors, Ruben attracted Buddy's attention and mouthed, "keep playing." Buddy gave the thumbs up.

They travelled out of the city towards the suburbs to Carindale Shopping Centre, where they grabbed coffee and something to eat. They then sat in the ground floor open cafeteria.

"Want to tell me what this is about?"

"Before I do, I have to caution you, if you're privy to this, it could place you and your family in danger. Also, our vehicle might be hot to see if we are curious about the Winton files. So be careful from now on."

Buddy nodded and then smiled. "I wasn't aware this job was risk free. Spill it."

"Okay. This is nothing either of us has ever come across before. This is insane stuff."

"Right. You've got my attention."

Over the next hour, Buddy was glued to his seat as Ruben revealed what was in the papers and what was on the DVD's. "I saw the most evil and insane things beyond anyone's imagination." Ruben fought back tears.

"I can't get the carnage of what I saw out of my head. *Horrific* isn't a strong enough word to describe what's on those DVD's. The people performing those heinous acts can't be human." Ruben went silent and looked at Buddy staring back at him in disbelief; wide-eyed with gaping mouth. He was shocked into silence. He cleared his throat. "Babies and children?" he said and buried his head in his hands. "I feel sick."

Ruben took in a long breath and then let it go. "That's just the tip of the iceberg. They are adding dangerous chemicals and aborted baby cells to junk food and drinks and processed food. They're poisoning the food chain anyway they can. Unhealthy people need medicine," he said. "Big pharma has an endless supply of drugs. Large corporations are driving this." Ruben went on to tell Buddy about the human experiments: "Changing our kids' gender is another focus of theirs to create a non-gender race. To dissolve the family unit as we know it. Education isn't about the three r's anymore. It's about the indoctrination of children, coaching and convincing them to make choices without parental consent, for example, to change their gender. These crazies have plans in place to depopulate the planet, so they can create *One World Order* by setting in motion bogus series of events, terrorising the community into complying with whatever the government instructs them to do under the guise of protecting them. Fearful people are easily controlled. Climate change is a hoax, another fear tactic mode of control. A fake virus is coming, so is digital currency, to replace notes and coins. This currency will be the same as food stamps, allowing us to purchase only certain items. The digital card won't work if the government disagrees with your purchase."

"Hang on, hang on." Buddy recovered enough to interrupt Ruben. "You said this information was over twenty years old. Since nothing has happened, it could be outdated now?"

"Ah, but a lot *has* happened right under our noses. We were too busy living our lives to pay attention. I realised the plan was active after opening the files on Hopkins's computer last night."

Buddy's eyes widened as large as saucers. "The computer was unlocked?"

"Uh-huh, still on when I found it. The killer must have interrupted Hopkins while he was updating the information.

Buddy looked puzzled. "How do you know that?"

"The files are current and so are the names on the lists. New names have recently been added. I crossed referenced a couple of older members with the hard copies. The Cabal cult recruited new members by blackmail, infiltrating every organisation of power and authority. Hand-picking politicians and judiciary because of their known fetishes and weaknesses: paedophilia and money and then drugs."

Saving Buddy from asking how he knew, Ruben explained Hopkins had many grotesque videos of these members in his files. "The videos are now in a secure place."

"Let me get my head around this," Buddy paused and then blurted out without taking a breath. "you're saying they are implanting the gender dysphoria syndrome in our kid's minds to create a non-gender race? The Cabal mega rich groups want to control humans and they've already started doing this by making sperm out of stem cells to eliminate families as we know it today?"

"That's what I'm saying. Child trafficking, child sacrifice and cannibalism's all part of it. From what I've read so far, the Freemasons are one of the main players. If you look around, freemasonry is everywhere from American dollars, the White House to Australia's Parliament House, the House of Lords, Vatican City ..."

"That's fucking insane!"

"It is and that's why it's called a conspiracy theory, because it's too fucking insane for ordinary people to comprehend. These monsters will succeed if people don't wake up and see what's taking place around them. You saw who's on that list. Several former Australian Prime Ministers, a leading Australian child psychologist (deceased), radio jocks, a bigwig in advertising and racing, police commissioners, priests and charity CEO's and a happy-clapper church. The names are endless. These evil bastards have infiltrated every fucking establishment like a cancer! Note those who insisted this Australian Cardinal," Ruben pointed to a photograph, "was innocent of paedophile charges, are also on the list along with him. These bastards look after each other. They have to. One falls, they all fall like a house of cards. They're powerful people. This scum was either bribed, compromised or are willing participants. It isn't just here in Australia. It's global. They have a five-phase plan in place, from killing tens of thousands of the elderly to paralysing the country with a bogus virus and then with food shortages. Do you recall a movie called Contagion? Dustin Hoffman was in it."

Buddy thought about that for a moment. "Fucking hell! You think it'll be like that?"

"I'm not sure what to think. Possibly they will try to make it seem like that. But I'm fairly certain life as we know it is about to change, big time."

Leaning back in the seat, Buddy took a sip of his coffee and then looked down at the black liquid and smiled. "You know, mate, I'm getting used to drinking cold coffee."

Ruben smiled.

"What can we do to stop this from happening?" Buddy asked.

"Nothing! It's already in progress."

"What? Nothing?"

"There are two reasons we can't: no one would believe us and we wouldn't last a minute after going public and neither would our families. There's been too many accidents and suicides of whistleblowers who have spoken out against big pharma and paedophilia in America recently. We don't want to start a list here in Australia with us at the top. Hopkins implied in a note among his files, this information will come to light in the event of his untimely death. We'll wait and see what he has put in place."

"I'm thinking you could be right about Hopkins being bumped for another reason. His place wasn't touched. The killer or killers had plenty of time to rip the apartment apart for the blackmail material."

"I've been thinking about that too." Ruben said. "I'll bet a month's pay the old Italian 'doorman' is our killer."

Buddy nodded. "Yeah. On second thought, you could be right. But for what reason?"

"Still working on that one, mate." Ruben went quiet.

"I can hear your wheels turning," Buddy said, looking at his partner. "What's on your mind?"

"Hopkins threatened his ex with payback when he got out of prison. I think his murder is connected to that somehow."

"You think his ex ordered the killing? Is she in the system?"

"No. She's in witness protection. But I know where we can find her."

"You do? Man, you're full of surprises. Where?"

"Jane Hopkins is Danika Bryce. She is a close friend of Eva's."

Buddy shook his head in amazement. "I'm awake, aren't I?" he asked. "This isn't the twilight zone?"

"I'm hearing you, mate. Nothing makes sense! I didn't sleep a wink last night. I'm running on coffee overload."

"So, we sit back and say nothing? You know we can't unsee any of it. My life changed the moment you shared this with me, as did yours, when you read those files and viewed the videos." Buddy sighed. "You know, I used to grumble when Angie refused to let the kids have takeaway. She'd say it was rubbish and she refused to feed her babies garbage. God love her! Angie was right. She'd spend hours looking at the ingredients of everything she bought. If it wasn't Australian, she wouldn't buy it. God, I love that woman!" Buddy paused. "How do I protect my kids by keeping silent?"

"We do nothing for now," Ruben said. "You have a better chance of protecting your kids because you know the truth and won't be influenced or controlled by government propaganda. That's the advantage here. From here on, we pay attention to everything going on around us and in other countries."

"You know, I've always left the schooling of the kids up to Angie. That will change as of tonight. No one's getting their hands on my kids as long as I have breath in me."

"Mate, I agree, but you've got to be careful not to become paranoid. You'll frighten Angie and the kids and drive them away. Your every move must be subtle. What we are dealing with here is psychological warfare: a well thought out mind control plan to brainwash people's perception of reality."

Buddy nodded. "Yeah, I guess you're right."

Chapter 28

That evening, during dinner, Ruben told Eva that Martin Hopkins was the victim found in the city apartment. He drew back in surprise when she said, "I know. Dani recognised him. She said he looked different, but it was him for sure. I told you about that this morning."

"Oh Yeah, I forgot. There's so much going on in my head. Sorry about that. How did she react?"

"What do you mean, react? How should she react?"

"Sweetheart, it's just a question. I guess the detective is still on duty. This case bothers me. Hopkin's death makes little sense. There's no visible rationale behind it."

"What do you mean?"

Ruben was tracing the pattern on his placemat with the tip of his butter knife. "There doesn't seem to be an obvious motive here that I can see. It wasn't a robbery. The apartment was untouched. None of his belongings were taken."

"Ah, so you think the killing was personal?"

Ruben paused, realising he had spoken his thoughts aloud. "Yes."

"That's why you wanted to know Dani's reaction. You thought she might have had him killed."

"It was just a question. Covering all possibilities."

"Well, Dani had nothing to do with his death. It shocked her to the point of feeling sorry for him."

"I'll need to talk with her. Would you mind if Buddy and I come to the studio in the morning?"

"Can I object?"

"Not really. It's routine. Eliminating possible suspects, you could say." Ruben raised his hand in surrender when Eva's expression changed to defiance. "Now, don't go jumping to conclusions. I'm not accusing Danika of anything. It's routine, like I just said, that's all."

She relaxed and then picked up her coffee cup, taking a sip.

"Are we okay?"

Eva peered over her cup. "Hmm, I guess so."

"Good. Buddy and I'll come by eleven, sharp. Okay?"

Eva nodded.

"There's no need for Danika to worry about her identity being exposed. This visit is off the record."

The following morning, the detectives drove out of the city bearing east to Bayside. Twenty minutes later, both were walking along the pathway to Eva's studio. Buddy looked around, admiring the yard. "Wow, the garden's amazing! God help me if Angie ever sees this. She'd nag the life out of me to create her a beautiful backyard just like this one," he said. "God help me!" Buddy sighed.

Ruben smiled with pride. "Eva's a talented gal!"

Hearing voices, Eva looked out of the window. "They're here."

Danika and Eva greeted the men at the door. After introductions, Buddy looked around the room. "Wow"! he exclaimed, inspecting one of the completed boxes. "This is beautiful! Angie loves this kind of stuff."

The women glanced at each other and smiled. Danika pulled a face mouthing *stuff* and grinned.

"If you think your wife would like it, detective, then you must give it to her."

The octagonal origami box dwarfed in Buddy's large hand. "She would love it! How much is it?" Buddy asked, reaching for his wallet.

"No charge. It's a gift."

"Now this is awkward," Buddy said, holding the box as if it were about to crumble.

"Only if you make it so, detective. I very much value your capability to appreciate the beauty of my work. That's admirable, especially coming from a man. Whereby most men would see just a box."

Buddy held it up for a closer look. "This is not just a box, Eva. It's a piece of art. The structure; every section fits perfectly together. The composition of colours in the flowers and flecks of gold touches are delicate and unique.

The fragrance in the paper is sensual. Angie will love this for sure."

All three were silent as they stared at him.

Buddy smiled. "I'm not just a big Bubba. I wanted to be an artist," he confessed shyly. "Thank you, Eva."

Turning to Danika. "Now, it's your turn to be under the spotlight," he quipped.

The trio moved over to the cherry red leather lounge and sat down while Eva made coffee. Ruben and Buddy were satisfied Danika was not involved in Hopkins' death after questioning her. Over coffee, they engaged in conversation. Out of the blue, Danika said she was having lunch with one of her friends and something her friend said triggered a memory of Martin telling her, years ago, he would be protected from 'them' while he was in prison.

"Did he say who *they* were?"

"No. I didn't take any notice. I thought the drugs had screwed his brain."

Ruben asked Danika what was it about the conversation that made her remember Hopkin's comment after all those years.

Danika faced Ruben. "You'll think Mary and I are nutters. Conspiracy theorists, or as Mary calls it, conspiracy truth. She was telling me what David Icke and Alex Jones predicted about the Cabal planning to take control of the planet and create a one world order."

Ruben and Buddy glanced at each other.

"Yeah, just as I thought. I can see you think I'm crazy. You've got that look in your eyes."

"No, you're wrong. I've read one of David Icke's books. You mentioning his name reminded me of that."

"Oh, okay. Well, Mary said, if I wanted to see the future of humanity, all I needed to do was read David Icke's books. When I arrived home that afternoon, I clicked on to Icke's website and spent several hours watching his videos. Then I clicked onto Infowars.com to watch Alex Jones. While doing that, I came across Dr. David Martin. My head was spinning by late evening. I could erase none of what I saw and heard from my mind. The worst part is, our apathy has eroded the fabric of our society. But," Danika said, "there's hope as long as we remain united." All of them were unanimous about that. "To answer your question," she said. "When Mary mentioned global control, it clicked with me that Martin had not lost his mind, nor was he crazy. He was telling the truth. Huh, for a change."

An uneasy silence fell between them. Each immersed in their own thoughts, wondering what the future really held. What will become of their families if this conspiracy is true? Daring to acknowledge the unthinkable; the government of the day was the enemy of the people.

Danika broke the silence. "There's not a damn thing we can do about any of this without losing credibility. People make horrible comments about Mary behind her back. I admire her for her courage, to not give a hoot what people think of her. Even her daughter called her toxic and won't have anything to do with her."

"Oh, I did not know that," Eva said, raising her voice a few octaves in surprise. "They were so close. How is she coping with the rejection?"

"I asked her that same question. Mary admitted she was hurt and angry, but now, all of that has turned in to acceptance."

Both detectives said nothing, but listened to the conversation with interest and then excused themselves, saying they had work to do.

"Before you go Buddy. As you know, Christmas is four weeks away. If you have not already made plans, would you and your family like to celebrate with us and our friends?"

Buddy hesitated, thinking about the garden he just walked through and all the work ahead of him when Angie sets her eyes on it. Ruben smiled, reading his mind.

Eva glanced at Ruben. "Is there a problem?"

"Well, sort of," replied Ruben. "It's your garden. If ..."

"If Angie sets her sights on it," interrupted Buddy, "she will nag the hell out of me until I build her one just as pretty as yours."

They all laughed.

"A gal after my heart!" Eva quipped.

"But I'm not one who would refuse an invitation to a meal," Buddy said, patting his belly. "I graciously accept. Thank you!"

Later that afternoon, Eva called Chelsea. "Oh, I was just about to email you an invitation to our Christmas party," she said. "I'm feeling better and I want to celebrate this year."

Eva was surprised. "Well, I was calling you with that same idea in mind." Eva paused. "Okay, that's not a problem. We will just combine our guests."

"Perfect!" Chelsea said with the enthusiasm she used to have.

A smile creased Eva's features as she thought, *'I had better call Sam to tell him of the change of venue to put Buddy's mind at ease, at least for now'*. She could not get a hold of the detective, so she left a voice message. Ending that call, Eva pondered the idea of inviting Jack Bradley. She wanted to satisfy her curiosity about him.

He answered on the third ring. Jack welcomed Eva's call like an old friend. Enquiring after her friends and sharing recent discoveries of what he admires about Brisbane. By the end of the conversation, Eva had succumbed to his charm. She held the mobile in her hand, staring at it, shaking her head. *'He did it again!'* she thought. *'His charm is intoxicating. That man has magical powers. I'm convinced of it. But the fact remains, I don't know who he is or what he's about. Is he a friend or foe? That is the* question! And I am going to find out either way!' Her determination was without doubt. 'Had I not known Danika's dilemma, would I be so curious about Jack?' Eva pondered that thought for a moment, concluding she would not. The probable danger Danika faced turned her intuition beacon to high alert. 'If I'm so attuned to Danika's danger, why did I not see the threats to my marriage? Why are warning bells ringing loud and clear this time and not during my marriage? Or did I ignore them, too afraid to face the truth?' Eva sighed. 'I guess I'll never know for sure. I'll just have to live with it and appreciate what I have.'

Eva doubted she would have even met Jack, convinced he was a key player in this scenario. She wanted him to be a *good guy* because she liked him. Not with any romantic notion; just liked him without explanation. Although her instincts implied Jack posed no threat to Danika, she was not brave enough to trust them. "Oh, my goodness!" she cried. "I forgot to tell Sam about Marcus. I will, first thing tonight!" She declared to the empty room.

The sound of tapping on the window snapped Eva back to the moment. It was Maggie. She was asking for treats. "Okay, my lovely," Eva said, in sing-song. "I'll be but a moment."

Maggie could see Eva in the kitchenette from where she was. Warbling began the moment Maggie sighted the container that housed her treats. "You are such a joy, my lovely lady," Eva said, as Maggie took tiny pieces of beef from her hand and flew away to her squawking baby. Then silence. Maggie came back for more treats when the chick started up again. This went on for a few minutes until both birds flew away.

Chapter 29

Eva's mobile pinged. A message from the detective said, 'Dinner date tonight. Pick you up at six, sharp! Kisses. P.S. Buddy is breathing easier!'

Eva checked the time on the mobile. Four-thirty. She dropped everything and headed for the house. The walk through the garden, no matter what kind of day she had, would soothe her spirit. She reached out and gently ran her hand through the lavender, stirring the scent to rise around her. After picking a small bunch, she then moved to the rose bushes and cut off several rosebuds. Holding them up to her nose, she breathed in their perfume. "Hmm. Perfect for my bath!"

Inside the house, Eva switched on her cd player. Her favourite discs of Stjepan Hauser were still in there. She pressed play. The music filtered into every room. She went to the bedroom and undressed. In her nakedness, she felt free, floating with the melody, as water from the shower cascaded down her body. Cupping a small amount of shampoo in her hand and working it into a lather, she massaged her hair and then moved under the shower, tilting her head back for the suds to float away. With a flick of her hand on the tap, the water stream vanished. Stepping out of the shower, Eva took two thick, soft towels from the shelf. One to wrap around herself and the other around her head.

Leaning over the bathtub, she turned on the hot water full blast and let it run until half full, then tore the roses apart and dropped them into the bath. She did the same with the lavender. The scolding heat from the water released the perfume. Before adding two cups of powdered milk, she turned on the cold water. Once the temperature was right, in went the milk and the towel was abandoned. She climbed into the tub and sunk deep into the opaque, scented liquid. There she remained for twenty minutes, serenaded by Hauser and his cello and a full string orchestra.

The timer sounded. Eva opened her eyes and stood up slowly, covered in rose petals. She brushed them off and retrieved her towel from the floor and wrapped herself in it. Unwinding the towel from her head, she shook her shoulder-length, honey curls free, to dry naturally. Her choice of outfit was simple; a knee-length navy linen dress with spaghetti straps and matching sandals. Glancing at the clock, she smiled, thinking the detective would be here any minute.

As the music continued, she stood in the doorway listening to the cello sing with her eyes closed, embracing the emotion of every sweet, harmonious note of

Unchained Melody, unaware Sam had entered the house through the back door. Spellbound, he watched her provocatively sway with the tune. She was encapsulated in a halo of light from a table lamp behind her that made the tips of her hair sparkle. Eva turned and saw him. She hesitated for a moment and then smiled, offering him her hand, inviting him into her imagination. No word spoken. The song was their voice. The dance was slow and sensual. Their bodies melted into one.

Earlier, Sam had booked a restaurant in the city for their dinner date. A ferry ride along the Brisbane River was also part of his plan. That would not happen tonight. He made a phone call instead. Forty minutes later, there was a knock on the door. Sam opened it and let two men in, carrying containers. While Eva enjoyed her second soak in the bath, the table was being set for a three-course meal.

Dressed and ready to leave, Eva entered the dining room in time to be seated at her candle-lit table.

"Oh, how lovely! I was not expecting this!" she exclaimed.

"Since we were delightfully detained, I thought it best I bring the restaurant to you," he smiled, pulling out the chair for her. "Madam, if you please."

"Thank you, kind sir," she said, pecking him on the cheek.

The room was set for romance. Soft lighting, background music serenading lovers dining in contented silence. Then Eva remembered her promise to tell Sam about Marcus.

"All this is," she said, with a sweeping hand. "Is wonderful. I'm overwhelmed with pleasure."

Sam was about to take another bite of his meal when he sensed a 'but' coming. He laid his knife and fork on his plate and gave Eva his full attention.

"I have to tell you something." She began and then paused and took a sip of her wine. "Now, this happened before I met you."

"Go on, I'm listening."

"It was when Danika set up my social media page to promote my business. Marcus, the man I want to tell you about, sent me a friend request. He wasn't the only one. There were several others," she blurted out and then covered her mouth with her hand. "Oh, that sounds so wrong."

The detective said nothing. He was motionless.

"I deleted all of them except for Marcus, because he asked if he could be my friend. I needed a friend. I was sad and very lonely. And I enjoyed his company in the evenings. We chatted about music, the books I read and topics of the day." She paused. "It felt good knowing someone cared about me. During our conversation, I noticed several anomalies. I suspected he was not who he said he was."

"Yet, you still continued the contact."

"Yes, I did. I was curious about the man in the photo. Who was he? His image was being used to solicit relationships with lonely women. I felt it was my mission to find out who he was and then you came along and I lost interest in my cause. Messages from Marcus arrived daily, some added up to fifty at a time. I imagine he panicked when he knew I wasn't interested in him. After weeks of ignoring him, I answered what was to be the last call. He sobbed, begging me to stay in contact with him, telling me he needed my help. Explaining how he borrowed money from friends to start his construction business and now they want to be paid back in full. He said he could repay most of what he owed them, but needed thirty thousand to cover the full amount." Eva smiled, raising her brows.

"And?"

Eva shrugged. "And, I laughed. He was furious. They will kill me! He screamed at me. I told him I have no money. He said you own a house. Sell that and give me the money. You can save my life! He cried. I hung up and blocked him. I'm telling you this just so you know. That's all."

"Okay. You know you're one of the lucky ones."

Eva gave him a questioning look.

"So many women fall for these cons and hand over their life savings to these people."

Eva nodded. "I know. That's why I deleted and blocked this person." She sighed. "We agreed on no secrets. That's why I'm telling you this now."

"Okay. Anything else?"

Eva shrugged and said tongue in cheek. "Nothing else comes to mind."

"Good." Sam pushed his chair away from the table. Offering her his hand.

"This is our song. May I?"

Chapter 30

Two weeks into December, Chelsea, Eva and Danika got together to plan the Christmas party.

"Oh," Danika gasped. "We've been so focused on party preparations, I forgot to call in to Simply Beauty and buy a dress."

"Go now," Chelsea said.

"Oh, I love that shop. It's pretty and smells so nice; walking into a wonderland of colour and bling. I'll come with you," Eva said. "C'mon, Dani. I'll drive." Eva looked at Chelsea with a cheeky grin. "We won't be long."

"Uh-huh." Chelsea nodded. She knew not to expect them back so soon.

They grabbed their bags and hurried to the car. The shop was on Bay Terrace, a short distance from Chelsea's house. But much faster by car, which meant they could spend more time trying on as many garments as they liked. Parking was often a problem, but fortunately a space was available right outside the dress shop.

"Can we take that as a sign the universe opened this spot for us? Danika asked.

"Of course! And I'm sure we'll find something wonderful to wear for Christmas Eve."

Upon entering the store, Isabell, the owner, a softly spoken, petite woman with a warm smile and flamboyant style, greeted them. "You two must be psychic!" she said.

The women's eyes lit up as they looked at one another. "A new shipment has arrived, right?"

Gail nodded. "This morning. I'm about to put the clothes on the racks now. Help yourselves!"

After trying on several outfits, Eva checked the time and was shocked to see they had been there well past an hour. She asked Danika if she had found something she liked. Danika nodded.

"Good. Because we have to go now."

They left the shop in high spirits, happy with their purchases and looking forward to celebrating Christmas with family and friends. However, life as they knew it was about to change.

Sam and Buddy watched every news channel waiting to hear what was about to befall the planet. They knew a fake virus would play a major role in the plan to depopulate earth.

"Looks like *the big lie* is starting," Buddy said to Sam over the phone, the first time he heard the weekend morning *Breaking News* report. '*Hundreds dying in the street …*' said the prim, solemn-faced news reader, parroting a universal scripted commentary, as video footage showed Chinese citizens falling to the ground in full view of the camera.

"If we didn't know this was bullshit," quipped Buddy, "we'd be worried. Who drops dead like that? It's almost comical, like watching a B-grade movie."

Sam said nothing. He was thinking about something he read in the files.

"Hey, mate," Buddy said, "You still there?"

"Yeah, yes," Sam responded. "You know where I live, right?

"You mean your new shack?

"Yeah."

"Never been there, but I've got the address."

"Can you get away and come here asap? I think I might know why those people died, but I'll need your help to find the information to substantiate my theory. We need to go through the files. Thoroughly this time. My hunch is that the cause of those deaths is in there."

Twenty minutes later, Sam paused from typing, glancing up at Buddy as he entered the apartment. He smiled when Buddy whistled, perusing his surroundings. "Man, I should live this rough!"

Sam shrugged in response as his fingers busily tapped at the keyboard. "Spoils of years of wise investments." Before Buddy could reply, Sam said, "These so-called conspiracy truth tellers David Icke, Alex Jones, Mike Adams and a few others have been ringing alarm bells for decades. I'm guessing their followers will recognise fact from fiction and warn their families and their friends."

"I dunno," Buddy replied. "Humanity is in an induced coma with internet, television and reality shows, video games, computers, smart phones and devices, transgenderism and so on. There are so many distractions going on around us, who's going to believe our government's part of the 'One World Order' and global depopulation. They're too indoctrinated to accept any of it. The Boomers were raised on soft television indoctrination and generational political parties. *Mum and Dad voted for 'them' all their lives, so will I!* is what I often hear at election time. Sleepers were conditioned to follow from childhood."

"They'll change their thinking when they lose their freedom." Sam responded. "There're consequences for ignorance and for stupidity. Millions will die before this is over that I can guarantee you."

"This reminds me of the Fort Dix 1918 swine flu; a pig virus harmless to humans. Pharmaceutical companies, through media, caused global hysteria, forecasting that fifty million would die. An invented lie to coerce the community to have the vaccine. This was not about health. It was about money. I read an article that Dr. Anthony Fauci co-wrote in 2008 about the Spanish flu epidemic that rates as one of the most devastating modern pandemics. It swept the entire planet in the wake of WW1 and caused millions of deaths. In studying this pandemic, Fauci and his colleagues found that most of the victims did not die from the Spanish flu, but from wearing masks. They caused bacterial pneumonia and death."

"Ahh, you have been doing your research too?" said Sam. "I see what you're getting at. The foe here is most likely a vaccine that follows the outbreak as the magic cure for the virus?"

"Yep. My bet that's our killer. A repeat of history!" They both went silent for a moment. "If everyone dropped dead after the vaccine was administered, people would know something was wrong. Hmm? They'd have to be subtle and administer fake vaccines as well. One document said a targeted race was planned."

"Did the article say which race?"

Sam shook his head.

"Okay. So, what caused the death of all those Chinese citizens?"

"It's common knowledge the Chinese government controls its citizens with an iron fist and would not think twice of using them as guinea pigs. In one of those files, I recall a reference to a G5 microwave weapon. You were correct in thinking a vaccine will be the weapon to depopulate the planet. I'm almost certain the G5 and this vaccine are bioweapons; combine the two and pow! Instant death, like we saw in that footage. I know nothing about the science or technical jargon regarding either of these and we can't risk any reprisals inquiring about it."

As Buddy picked up a file, his mobile buzzed. He read the message. It was from his wife.

"What is it?"

Buddy shrugged, looking awkward. "It's from Angie. Sorry, mate. She needs me at home."

"Go ahead, I'll see you later."

On his way out, Buddy, looking over his shoulder, said, "Call me when you come across that article." Sam gave him the thumbs up as Buddy closed the door behind him.

After Buddy had left, Eva called, asking Sam if he would like to join her at the Manly Jetty. Not wanting to disappoint her, he gathered together the files and then secured them in his bedroom wall safe, muttering that he'll have to get back to them later.

Eva said she would see him in twenty minutes, so he walked to the jetty. His heart was heavy as he made his way along the esplanade, taking in the world around him. He tuned out the chatter of the passing parade, observing his surroundings in slow motion, as people went about their daily activities, unaware that a sinister plot to eradicate them or destroy their lives was being actioned at that moment and the clock was ticking. While struggling with the anguish that tried to claim his joy, he wondered how many will recognise the truth and how many will believe the lie? The lie that will destroy them if they comply. A lump formed in his chest. For the first time in decades, tears escaped and ran down his cheeks; with a flick of his hand, they vanished as quickly as they appeared.

Sam cleared his throat and stood tall and looked out at the bay; the sky was bright blue, dotted with cotton balls and white ribbons. The despair that was about to befall upon humanity mocked the serenity surrounding him. Nothing was as it seemed! Never had Sam doubted an outcome. For him, no matter the circumstances, a light at the end of the tunnel was there, even if it were as small as a pinhead. He feared that the light had failed to shine for him this time.

Nearing the jetty, he spotted Eva among the crowd, recognising her fluid movements; she glided like a dancer when she walked. He looked on as the wind tousled her hair and tugged at her floral, cotton dress. His heart beat faster, thinking no woman had looked at him the way she did. She made sense to his life. At that moment, he knew Eva was his light at the end of the tunnel; she eradicated his fear of the unknown. Waving to attract her attention, a smile lit up her face the moment she saw him. As he quickened his gait, the dozens of gulls congregating on the footpath scattered and took flight, squawking their displeasure at being disturbed.

"I missed you," he whispered in her ear, hugging her close to him. "I can face anything with you by my side."

He loosened his hold enough to enable Eva to look into his eyes. "I've missed you too," she replied with a note of concern and then studied him.

"This conspiracy thing is real, isn't it?"

Sam nodded.

"Does it need your immediate attention?"

He shook his head.

"Okay, well, today it's just us. I want your full attention for the rest of the day. Deal?"

"Deal!"

She took hold of his hand. "C'mon."

"Where're we going?"

"To buy fresh prawns. The trawler's just come in. You like prawns, don't you?"

"Love 'em!"

"Okay then, c'mon."

Squinting into the sun, Eva guided Sam to the spot a friend was holding for her while she went to find him. They weaved their way through the maze of customers waiting for a table inside the restaurant or outside on the jetty to have breakfast overlooking the marina. Farther ahead was the very long line of seafood fans with their cooler bags and their esky's-on-wheels chatting to one another as they edged slowly toward the trawler.

"After we get the seafood, we can store it in the camping fridge and then come back here for breakfast."

Sam's eyes lit up. "Did you say camping?"

"Oh, don't get too excited. I drove Josh's Range Rover here. He decked it out with all the bells and whistles for camping. It was his passion, not mine. The fridge comes in handy from time to time; to keep the seafood from spoiling."

"I enjoy camping!"

Eva said nothing. She turned her face away and smiled. *'Oh, gawd no!'*

Chapter 31

The media relentlessly bombarded the Australian population via television, radio and the internet, with doom and gloom as the global crisis worsened. For many, it was difficult to get away from it; addicted to keeping up-to-date with current affairs and local news, which only instilled rampant fear in the community!

Mary Castle knew from over two decades of research that the media was intentionally hiding the truth from the community; stirring up a frenzy of terror in people's minds. Fearful people don't resist. They comply. Both Mary and Danika shared the information they found from creditable overseas websites and from creditable sources only with friends who were interested in knowing the truth about the hoax virus coming to their shores.

Many family members and friends they knew were so afraid that they dismissed everything other than the narrative as conspiracy theories. They would listen to and accept only what the media reported. Mary was convinced television and mainstream media were the virus! Both women found it frustrating interacting with the brainwashed. And both were mind boggled that only a few were questioning media reports. The Christmas party was the reprieve from the maddening crowd they needed. They momentarily shelved life outside.

Christmas Eve was stifling and the heat of the day lingered well into the evening. The guests arrived at the Harrison's home full of festive spirit. They expressed great delight at the sight of miniature lights twinkling around the walls amid subtle lighting as Christmas carols filtered around the room. A huge pine tree decorated in tinsel, colourful balls, bows and antique Christmas ornaments took pride of place in a corner of the room, beside an artificial fireplace with a flickering flame. Underneath the tree were presents, guests had dropped off during the week. Delicious aromas floated out from the kitchen alcove.

The house was buzzing with excitement as friends hugged and greeted one another. Some met for the first time. Buddy's children, Rikki and Shona, gazed wide-eyed at the wonderland before them; they had seen nothing like this before. The sight, the sounds, the food, the joy and the laughter made it all seem like a magical Christmas, just like the ones in movies.

Jeffery did not recognise Jack. The chances he would were slim: Jack's hair was now longer and darker to match his olive skin and eye colour. He had also altered the shape of his oval features to appear squarer. As a natural chameleon, Jack could be whoever he needed to be for however length of time. He was careful to not lose himself in any of the identities he created. After every assignment, the man of many identities would travel back to the mountains of Montana, to meditate and fast and detox the personality he assumed for allotted assignments. That routine would be challenging next time, as he wanted to keep Danika's image imprinted in his mind for the rest of his life.

Jack was also aware Eva was curious about him, but she posed no threat. She liked him and he wanted to keep it that way. It was crucial for all concerned. His new *friends* were good people. Sam and Buddy lived up to their flawless credentials. Both men were old school and he trusted them with the files. Neither was aware Jack was keeping close tabs on both of them; more for safety than anything else. He also monitored Lucas Johnson's activities for the same reason and discovered Lucas was not the man Danika thought he was. Knowing this did not give him credence to expose him. Interfering could be disastrous. Jack knew Danika was aware something was amiss with Lucas and whatever they once had together had run its course.

Jack wandered around the room, interacting with everyone, even the children. He smiled when overhearing Jeffrey encouraging his mate to join OzFish. One of them asked how he got involved with the organisation.

"Now that's a good question," Jeffrey replied with a grin. "While standing in line at the supermarket, gazing around the place, without a care in the world because I could. Living and working to a timetable did not allow me such frivolous time, anyway. While daydreaming, I failed to hear the lady at the checkout, say next please. But I felt a tap on my shoulder from a rather large younger man, Johnny Oyster of course, telling me I was next. I turned around to apologise and noticed a logo on his tee-shirt. "What's that about?" I asked pointing to the logo.

"If you've got time for a coffee, I'll tell you."

The rest of the conversation faded as Jack headed outside to the pool where Danika stood staring into the water. She was miles away in her thoughts.

"Am I interrupting?"

Danika spun around and stared at Jack. Neither spoke for several beats. She smiled at him. "It's good to see you, Jack. I'm glad you could make it. I've noticed you're a natural communicator and so at ease with people who were complete strangers five minutes ago and end up being your besties. You amaze me."

"You were miles away just a moment ago. Are you okay?"

Danika hesitated before responding. "I'm fine, Jack. Thank you for asking."

"Something is troubling you. I can see it in your eyes."

The surprised expression on Danika's faced had Jack apologising. "Oh, forgive me for prying. It's none of my business. Forgive me, Danika, for being so familiar."

Danika stared at him. "See what I mean? We've just met, yet you can read me so well. Who are you, Jack? Why are you so familiar to me?"

He looked up at the evening sky. "It's a beautiful evening Danika, it should be enjoyed."

Without another word, Danika looked up at the clear night sky and smiled. Mesmerised by trillions of tiny diamonds sparkling overhead, the sounds of merriment inside faded to a distant hum.

Jack was thinking, *'I'm just a guy enjoying the company of a lovely woman with sad, beautiful eyes. I've travelled far and wide and have experienced much in life to recognise pain, loss, joy, happiness and sadness.'*

Danika did not know Jack was speaking to her telepathically and reading her thoughts. She was wondering if they had met somewhere in the past because she felt comfortable in his company, which was not normal for her; suspicion and mistrust was her companion among strangers.

When he asked her if she believed in reincarnation. She glanced sideways at him, puzzled. He was still looking up at the stars, pretending not to notice her studying him.

'Reincarnation? What made me think of that? Of course, I believe in reincarnation. Is that where Jack and I met? In a past life?'

His smile that escaped was too brief for her to notice. He replied, 'We've shared many past lives, my sweet lady. This time I'm here to keep you safe.'

'Safe? From what?'

'You know the answer to that question,' he said, gently touching her arm before heading inside to join the others after noticing Eva watching them through the kitchen window. Jack smiled at Eva as she passed him. "It's a beautiful evening!" he said. "I was just telling Danika we should enjoy it."

Eva stopped. She drew in a deep breath and then released it. "The Bay air is clear too! My favourite time of the year," she sighed with gratitude. "Desserts are being served, if you're interested?" She said, as he headed inside to join the others.

"Thank you!" came his reply.

"Did I hear you say desserts?" Danika called from the other side of the pool. "I guess I've admired the stars long enough," she said, coming around to link arms with Eva, attempting to drag her inside to the dessert table. The manner in which Danika took control caused Eva's thoughts to zip back in time to when she dragged her off to lunch at the Deck restaurant four years prior.

Danika glanced at her friend. "Something wrong?"

"No. Nothing's wrong. I was just thinking that we've come a long way since the day you dragged me off to lunch and out of my pity party and now there's another year about to arrive."

"You know how you always write your list of goals for the New Year."

Eva nodded.

"Well, I plan to do that this New Year's Eve. It works for you. It might work for me, too."

Eva studied her friend for a moment. "What's going on with you?"

"Nothing. Why?"

"You and Jack are getting chummy. Are you attracted to him? Not that it would be a problem. I like Jack. We all do. It's just that ..."

"It's just what?"

"No one knows anything about him."

"There's no reason to worry. Jack and I are friends. And, yes, I like him. He's different from any man I've met. I like him. But he's a loner, which makes us as different as day and night. I'd be wasting my time wishing and hoping for something that can never be," she said. "That's life, I'm afraid. Well, that's my life!"

"Where's Lucas? You've not mentioned him in weeks."

"That's because I haven't seen him in weeks."

"Are you not worried that he hasn't called?"

"I was at first, but then I remembered his ex telling me he used to disappear for weeks at a time and never explained where he had been when he returned. It's a deal breaker; he's disrespecting me!"

"Did she ever find out where he went and what he did?"

"Yes, she did. He had been gambling. She discovered that when she went to the supermarket. Her card had nil funds. Fortunately, she was in the habit of squirreling a few dollars away each week, just in case of an emergency."

"You know, hon, once a gambler, always a gambler. I'm surprised you took a chance on him."

"To be honest, Eva, I didn't believe her."

"Why not?"

"I've known them as a couple for ten years. She was a drama queen, always seeking attention. Never taking responsibility for anything. It was always someone else's fault. She blamed Lucas for everything wrong in their marriage. Lucas did not fit the profile. He catered to her every whim."

"You're having doubts about him now?"

"It's odd. The feelings I had for him have faded into indifference. Perhaps it was just something left over from the past; infatuation maybe? Certainly not love. It was comfortable while it lasted. But I'm not sad that whatever we had is over."

Danika glanced at the house; through the glass she could see everyone had gathered around the dessert table. "OMG!" she gasped and grabbed Eva by the arm. "I'm not missing out on dessert. Chelsea has made all of my, ah, our favourites. C'mon."

As they stepped inside, a vortex of laughter, chatter and Christmas carols greeted them. Jack handed Danika a plate with small portions of all the desserts on the table. Delightfully surprised, she smiled her thanks.

Following suit, the detective chimed as he handed Eva an identical plate of deserts. "I trust this will keep me in your good books for a few days?"

"Oh, you treasure. This will keep you in my good books for life!"

"If that's a proposal? I accept."

Eva was about to set her plate on the bench.

"Nah, nah, not before you finish your dessert. We'll talk about this later," he grinned.

"Well, at least you've got your priorities right," she laughed.

"You're not eating?" Danika asked Jack.

"Aah, no. I don't eat sweets."

"And you only drink water, I notice."

Jack nodded.

"A health nut?"

"I wouldn't say a health nut. More like, careful what I consume. The body is a temple."

"Uh-Huh!" *'We all have our quirks,'* she thought.

After dessert, everyone pitched in to clear the dishes away before presents were exchanged. Buddy had brought his guitar. He positioned himself by the fireplace, picking at the strings and then began humming *Silent Night.* Everyone stopped what they were doing and quickly gathered around, found a seat or a place on the floor and joined in. A peaceful ambiance shrouded the room. Jack looked over at Danika, waiting to hear her sing; he loved her rich alto voice. She closed her eyes for a moment and then she joined in too. She harmonised well with Buddy's voice. The others stopped singing to listen to them. Buddy carried on and sang, *Oh Holy Night.* Danika followed him with ease. The room erupted into applause on the last note.

"Okay, okay, yeah, yeah, thanks everyone," Buddy said, clapping, looking over at Danika. "And to you, like WOW!" In her shyness, she brushed off the compliment.

"Anyone for hot chocolate?" Chelsea said, moving to the centre of the room. "The children have been very patient. So why don't we open the presents now?" Everyone cheered. The children cheered the loudest.

At midnight, the guests gathered their belongings together, wished each other a Merry Christmas and headed home, weary but happy. Mary lowered her voice as she spoke to Eva and Danika while hugging them.

"Tonight, was the best Christmas ever. Perhaps our last for a very long time. Who knows what the future holds for us? Regardless, tonight was wonderful. A treasured memory to store away to recall when times are not so great," she smiled. "And," she whispered, "I hope to receive an invitation to Chelsea's next spring luncheon. Her cooking is divine!"

"After that wonderful commendation, how can I not include you?" Chelsea said, coming up from behind.

Mary spun around. Her eyes twinkled with delight. "Thank you, Chelsea. I accept!"

The hostess took hold of Mary's hand, saying it was a pleasure to have finally met her, since Dani and Eva spoke so highly of her.

After Mary said her goodbyes, Jack offered Danika a ride home before Eva and Sam did.

"Oh, okay," Eva said, hesitating, unsure of Jack's intentions, when Danika told her she had just accepted Jack's offer.

"Come along, dear heart," Sam said, in a low voice that only Eva could hear. "Dani's a big girl and old enough to pick her playmate," he grinned.

"It's not like that," Eva snapped and then apologised. Softening her voice, she said, "They're just friends!"

"Hmm. If you say so. But by the way they look at one another, I ..."

Eva cut Sam off mid-sentence. "Yes, yes, it's obvious they like each other. But Dani knows Jack is, well, different."

"Different? In what way? I know 'us' men are odd creatures at the best of times, but 'different' sounds ominous."

"He is different. Not in a bad way. In a mysterious way. A loner. A drifter."

"I'll check him out to put your mind at ease. Although, he seems okay to me. I like him."

Eva gave Sam's offer some thought as he opened the car door for her.

"You can't do that. Jack's a friend. We cannot invade his privacy. But thanks for the offer," she said, settling in her seat and laying her head on his shoulder.

"Anyway, we have an important matter to discuss." he said.

Eva smiled. "Yes. You mean the proposal over dessert?"

"Uh-huh! Well, what do you think?"

"I gave you my answer," she said. "it's yes!" She then fell asleep.

Chapter 32

"You should sing more, Danika. You have a lovely voice," Jack said.

"Singing was never an ambition. My love of music is personal; not to entertain."

"Well, you're wasting that talent."

She ignored his comment.

"It's a beautiful evening, or I should say, morning. The stars are still shining brightly." She sighed. "It's magical." She paused and then sighed again. "It's a shame Christmas and Christmas trees and trimming is just a fairy-tale, a commercial enterprise; even the birth of Christ is incorrect. Everything we've been told is a lie! Nothing is as it seems!"

"Unfortunately, Jane, you're right about the deception."

She jerked her head sideways and stared at him. "What did you just call me?!"

"Jane. I called you, Jane. That's your name, isn't it?"

"Yes, but how do you know that?"

"I'm not at liberty to say. But you can take comfort in knowing I'm here to keep you safe."

She shook her head, puzzled.

"Something wrong?"

Danika said nothing. She was thinking, why did that statement sound familiar to her, but she could not remember where she had heard that.

"Do you mean by keeping me safe from Marty's crooked friends who think I know what his business dealings were and want to stop me from talking?"

Jack nodded.

"He never told me anything. I knew absolutely nothing about what he did. I asked him once. He was so angry. I was too afraid to mention anything about his work again. Marty kept everything from me. I knew nothing. So why would I be a threat to 'them', whoever they are?"

"It wouldn't matter to those people, regardless of you knowing anything about Marty's dealings. They're *cleaning house*; a warning to others not to step out of line. The bounty is still on your head."

Danika froze in her seat, staring out of the windscreen.

"No one will kill you, Jane. You have my word on that. And when this is over, you won't recall a thing."

"Oh, so just like magic, you'll wipe the drama from my memory," she said with the wave of her hand.

Jack nodded. "Yes, just like magic. You won't remember a thing."

"Do you realise how insane that sounds?"

"To you perhaps. For me, it's perfectly logical and will

save you a lot of pain and recurring nightmares."

"Who the hell are you?" she asked in frustration.

He reached over and gently touched her arm and she calmed down.

"We have shared many lifetimes. Our bond is strong. It has never been broken. That's why you were attracted to me and comfortable in my company. Your spirit recognised me."

"So, the feelings and attraction I have for you are real and from a past-life?"

Jack nodded.

"Ahh, that explains why I felt I had to protect my heart regardless of my feelings for you."

"For the record, Jane, Danika, by which name should I call you?"

"Danika."

"Your affection is reciprocated tenfold, Danika." He paused. "I'll remain with you until the threat has passed and then I will leave. You'll only have a vague recollection of me. Your contract must be fulfilled before we can be together again. In the meantime, another who holds you dear to his heart will come forward."

"Contract?"

"We all make a contract before birth. We choose our paths and challenges; it's our choice regarding everything we do in this life. Only minimum intervention is allowed. Unfortunately, the contract is forgotten after birth and we plough through life, wondering why we were born when things go wrong."

Shaking her head, she mumbled under her breath, "This is mind-boggling."

Pondering everything he said, she concluded it resonated with her. As he pulled up outside her place, she asked, "And who's this mysterious person who holds me dear to his heart?"

"All will be revealed in due course," he replied, before getting out of the car and walking around to the passenger's side. He opened the door for her. They stood facing each other. He took hold of Danika's hand, cupping it in both of his, erasing the conversation they just had from her memory. "Thank you for a wonderful evening, Danika."

"Oh, you're so welcome, Jack. Now you can share your Australian Christmas experience with your friends in Canada. Mind you, not everyone does it our way." She smiled and hugged him briefly. "Good night, Jack," were her parting words.

Jack waited beside the car until Danika went inside and closed the door before he moved. He then got in his car and drove to the street behind Danika's. He parked and then walked back to her house and waited in the shadows. Before too long, Lucas arrived and entered Danika's home. Jack heard her shouting at him to get out of the house. Then gun fire. He entered the house seconds before

Danika fell to the floor. He caught her, checked her pulse before calling triple zero.

Lucas stood in the middle of the room dumbfounded and in shock, still gripping the revolver in his right hand. Jack stood up and faced him. Dead calm. He took two steps towards him. In a split second, Lucas was lying dead on the floor. He then turned his attention back to Danika. Blood poured out of the gaping hole in her side. He packed the wound with paper towels and secured them with plastic wrap. He departed just before the ambulance arrived, but not before applying healing pressure around the wound and across Danika's forehead. "You won't remember a thing," he whispered in her ear and then left.

The noise had woken Danika's neighbour, Beverly Parker. She grabbed her mobile and ran from her house to the front garden. Scanning the area, she could not fathom where the sound of the gunshot came from. The only house in the street with lights on, other than hers, was Danika's. While heading over there, she called the police. During the conversation, she told the police someone must have called the ambos. "Because I can hear a siren. It's getting closer," she said, wondering who had done that, since there was no sign of activity elsewhere. The paramedics arrived as Beverley reached the house.

Bradley Wilson, an acquaintance of Danika's, greeted Beverley.

"Did you call triple zero?" Wilson asked as he and his

partner unloaded their gear.

"No. I called the police. I thought I heard shouting and then I definitely heard a gunshot. I don't know who called triple zero."

"Is this your place, ma'am?" Wilson asked, pointing to Danika's home.

"No. But please hurry and go inside and see if Dani is okay."

Wilson was shocked at the sight of Danika lying on the floor in a pool of blood. He knelt down beside her and then glanced over at his partner, puzzled.

"Looks like someone just saved Dani's life." Neither stopped to question it.

"C'mon, c'mon. On three. Let's go! Let's go!"

Before leaving, Wilson's partner, Bobby Johns, checked Lucas for a pulse. There was none. The police arrived as they were leaving. Bobby Johns leaned out of the driver's side window and told them there was a body inside.

Beverley made another call as she watched the ambulance drive away.

Danika was in surgery by the time Eva and the detective arrived at the hospital. Jack was not long behind them.

"Oh Jack, you're here."

"Thanks for calling me, Eva," he said, taking her hand. "As you know, I'm very fond of Danika. How is she?"

"She's in surgery. We're waiting to hear." Eva's voice quivered. "Danika's neighbour rose the alarm. After …

after she heard gunfire." Eva stopped talking.

The detective wrapped his arm around Eva to comfort her as he told Jack Lucas had shot Dani. "Did she give you any sign she felt threatened by Lucas when you two were together at the party?"

"No. Danika didn't mention her relationship or Lucas, or gave any hint she was in fear of anyone. I'm sorry I can't tell you anything more than that." He paused. "She was happy."

"Buddy and I will investigate this," Ruben said, handing Jack his card. "If you remember seeing anything unusual when you drove Dani home, please call me."

Jack looked puzzled.

"You were the last person to speak to Dani before Lucas shot her. You might have seen the person who killed Lucas without realising it."

"Danika's boyfriend shot her? And now he's dead?"

The detective nodded, mumbling. "Strange though. There's not a mark on him."

"How serious is Danika's injury?" Jack asked Ruben.

"She is very lucky. If it wasn't for an unknown person or persons, stopping the bleeding, we'd be making funeral arrangements."

Jack said nothing and Eva burst into tears.

Waiting for news of Danika was excruciating for all of them; each tuned into their own thoughts, looking up with expectation at every sound, only to watch a cleaner pushing a trolley down the deserted hallway; a nurse doing her rounds, the elevator door opening and closing. As the hours laboriously ticked away, the hospital slowly came back to life and people filled the hallways.

Morning had arrived by the time the surgeon came to the lounge area. The moment the trio saw him, they scrambled to their feet and rushed towards him. They said nothing. The expression on their faces spoke volumes. They sighed with relief when the surgeon smiled.

"Good morning, I'm Dr Ralf. Everything went well," he said. "It was the initial attention your friend received that saved her life. The bullet hit the spleen. I had to remove it. She would have bled to death if not for that person. Ms Bryce is fit and healthy and will be fine, physically."

"Fine physically?"

"Yes. After a life-threatening trauma, in most cases, emotional issues appear later on."

Eva nodded. "When can we see her?"

He smiled. "Now, if you like, but only for a few minutes."

Overwhelmed with emotion, Eva lunged for the surgeon and hugged him. The detective and Jack shook his hand.

"It's a good day!" he said, removing his surgical cap as he walked away.

Jack knew Danika's prognosis was good, but had to remain in character and play his part according to plan. He also knew the good detective and his partner would never solve Lucas Johnson's mysterious demise, nor would they solve Martin Hopkins' death either. Both cases would become the bane of their careers, which bothered Jack since both men were exceptional investigators.

The trio gathered around Danika's bed. She slept peacefully, attached to a machine monitoring her heartbeat. Eva pointed to the pattern on the monitor's screen. "She's strong," she said with confidence. "Dani will be okay."

"Of course, she will," replied Ruben.

All of them turned when Bradley Wilson opened the door. "Oh, sorry!" he said. "I didn't know anyone was here." He looked awkwardly at the flowers he held. "Ah, these are for Dani. We're mates, well, sort of. We met at a first-aid course a few years ago."

"Yes, yes. Come in. I remember Dani telling me how much she enjoyed that course and liking the instructor."

"Yeah, well, since then we've crossed paths around the town." He looked at each one of them, then continued. "I got a shock when we found her lying there on the floor, I ..." His voice broke and he cleared his throat. "For a minute there, I thought, well ..."

Eva's eyes widened. "You found Dani?"

Bradley Wilson nodded. "My heart sank. I thought ... she was ..."

"What you did for Dani saved her life."

"Nah, it wasn't us. I wish I could say we were the heroes of the hour. But that honour belongs to someone else. I'd like to shake his hand and thank him personally. Whatever took place in her home last night, Dani surely didn't deserve this. She's kind and always thoughtful and considerate to everyone she meets."

Eva glanced up at Ruben and smiled. She liked Bradley Wilson and his strong square jaw and dark brown eyes and broad shoulders.

Detective Ruben introduced himself and asked if he had a minute to answer a few questions before he left.

Eva stood up and took the flowers from Wilson. "How about I find a vase for these, while you two have your chat outside?"

"If you don't mind, I'll go?"

"Oh, Jack, no, not at all! You must be exhausted, too. I'll let Dani know you were here."

"Ok thanks, Eva."

Wilson studied Jack, wondering if he and Danika were a couple. To put his mind at ease. Jack introduced himself and offered his hand and thanked him for looking after Danika last night. "She's dear to all of us. It's good to know she has you looking out for her as well."

Bradley stood taller and said, "You can count on it, mate!"

When Eva came back to the room with the flowers in a vase, she lowered her voice and said, "Merry Christmas, everyone!"

Jack did not head for the city to his apartment, instead

he made a detour to Wynnum Creek and parked his car on the Esplanade, got out and looked toward Detective Ruben's apartment.

It was still early and little activity in his street, given it was Christmas morning; inside homes nearby, people were probably sitting around the Christmas tree exchanging presents or enjoying a special breakfast with loved ones. While others experienced domestic dysfunctional pain and suffering, wanting no part of Christmas, oblivious to the contract they chose before their birth.

While Ruben investigated Lucas Johnson's murder, Jack strolled over to Ruben's apartment complex with a centre courtyard pool. Before entering the grounds, he removed a small device from his pocket and aimed it at the building, disarming the security system. He then climbed the stairs two at a time to the first floor, turned right and strolled to the end of the building and entered the detective's home.

Jack went to the main bedroom, opened the safe and removed all the files and DVD's Ruben found in Martin Hopkins' city apartment. He replaced them with an envelope, closed the safe and left the premises.

Chapter 33

Several days had passed before Ruben could spend more than an hour in his apartment showering and changing into fresh clothes. The frustration of no clue or evidence of who killed Lucas Johnson gnarled him. Keeping busy delayed the disappointment of facing that failure. Nothing of significance came out of the coroner's report. It was identical to Martin Hopkins; *No clear evidence of foul play.* The outstanding detail in Lucas Johnson's report was a high amount of alcohol and cocaine in his system, leading Ruben to believe he may have been leading a double life and wondered if Danika knew anything. He made a note in his work diary to contact her after she had fully recuperated.

Although Danika's speedy recovery was remarkable, Dr Ralf scheduled her for counselling with the hospital's psychologist. "You're not showing signs of depression or ill effects from the shooting, which is rare. I still want you to have a few sessions with David White as a precaution," he told her and she agreed only to appease him. She really wanted to go home.

Three hours later, Danika was sitting opposite David

White in his small, neutral-coloured room. A silky oak coffee table with a box of tissues, a water jug and two glasses on a tray, in the centre of an oblong natural weave rug, separated them. In the corner, next to the large window flooding the room with natural light, was a bookshelf full of various academic authors and two tan leather chairs identical to the one Danika and the therapist occupied.

He resembled an outdoors man more than a psychologist; tall, tanned face, broad shoulders, thick biceps and thighs and huge hands. She smiled when she first saw him.

"Ah, you also find me amusing. I get it all the time. I'm often told I look more like Grizzly Adams than a pale-faced head shrinker."

"No, no," she giggled. "I wasn't thinking anything like that. But that is a better description, though. Honestly," she laughed. "I thought you didn't fit the profile of a psychologist."

"Uh-huh and what would that be?"

"Bearded, overweight and balding, or anaemic, pencil thin with glasses and very sensitive."

He grinned. "Grizzly Adams is more fitting with all the bushwalking and rock climbing I do in my spare time. Getting close to nature is my antidote for everything. But we're not here to discuss my hobbies."

"Well, your hobbies sound more interesting as opposed

to what you want me to talk about."

"And what is it specifically, Danika, you think I want you to talk about?"

"The shooting."

His bushy brows rose and fell. "Really?"

She nodded.

"It may surprise you to know, if you'd rather not talk about that, then that's okay with me. You may talk about anything you like."

She said nothing.

"Okay, how are you feeling? Ready to go home?"

"I am."

"Your file says you have a daughter."

"Yes. That's correct. Abbi is currently working in Florida. Initially, she was based in New York and then an opportunity and better incentives to move to another office was offered to her. She grabbed it with both hands."

"You must miss her a lot."

"Yes, I do. But Abbi has her life path to follow. That may mean I'm not a part of that chapter of her life."

"And you're fine with that?"

"Yes, I am. Being the main lead in your child's life has a use-by date. One has to step back and become only an extra, similar to that in a play. Just be there when she needs me. My daughter is her own person and has to be free to accomplish all she wants to do. It's impossible for her to achieve that if she's standing still."

David White said nothing as he scribbled in his notebook. Danika leaned forward and filled both glasses with water from the jug on the tray. She pushed one toward him and then picked up the other. Leaning back in her chair, she took a sip from her glass and waited for him to finish writing.

"Well," he said, breaking the silence. "Same time next week suit you? Oh, and thank you for thinking of me," he smiled.

She looked confused. "In what way?"

"The water."

"Really?"

"One day, I will explain. So, same time next week?"

"Okay," she shrugged and walked gingerly back to her room and found Chelsea and Eva waiting for her.

"Dani, you're a fraud," Chelsea exclaimed, hugging her. "You look wonderful! There's no need to ask how you are. I can see that for myself."

Eva looked on, smiling. "She's a cat, with eight lives now, after this near miss."

"A nice red would go down well right now."

"A nice red like this one?" Eva replied, pulling out a bottle and three plastic wine cups from her bag. Chelsea offered her French cheese, champagne ham, and mini sourdough rolls, along with a few other delectables.

Danika's eyes lit up like headlights and hobbled as fast as she could to her bed, scrambling across it as would a child eager to be fed, moaning from the discomfort of the wound, while laughing at the same time.

"Oh, shit!" She exclaimed, holding her side. "I forgot I'm a walking wounded." Danika paused and gave Eva a suspicious look. "Huh," she grinned, "Is this payback for getting you sloshed that day I forgot you were on medication?"

"You'd deserve that if it was," replied Eva.

The trio chatted and laughed while enjoying their bedroom picnic, avoiding the elephant in the room. A nurse, passing by, stuck her head in to say hello to Danika, spied the wine, spun around saying, "I was not here!" and promptly walked away. The ladies chuckled.

"So, when do you get the all clear to go home?" Asked Eva. "I have to say, I'm surprised you've recovered so quickly?"

"I'm not sure when I can leave. Dr Ralf signed me up for counselling. I was having a session with the therapist while you were waiting for me."

"How did that go?"

Danika looked over at Chelsea. "Yeah, fine. That's just it. I'm fine. I wish people would believe me. The wound is a little tender but healing well."

Eva and Chelsea glanced at each other.

"So, man or woman?"

Danika looked puzzled.

Eva sighed. "Is your therapist a man or a woman?"

Danika giggled. "Man. And he's a mountain of a man. He actually looks like Grizzly Adams. Remember that TV series in the '70's, where this big guy lived in the mountains and fought bears and bad guys?"

They laughed. "He sounds scary," added Eva.

"No, not at all. He actually has kind eyes. I like him even though I can't see his face. Pity he has that beard. I loathe beards. Germ carriers. Yuk!" she shuddered.

"Married?"

"Didn't notice a wedding ring. Oh, anyway, he's not my type. I can just imagine him ruffing it in the wild and stripping off to his birthday suit to bathe in a freezing raging river in the middle of winter. My idea of camping would be a hot tub and private loo and fine dining. Chelsea's lifestyle has rubbed off on me," she grinned. "Beside all of that, David White is my therapist; a no-go zone!"

Chewing on a sourdough roll, Danika glance out of her room. She had a clear view of the nurse's station. Mouth full, she lowered her voice, holding a hand over her mouth. "Look, look," she said. "There he is, David White, my therapist."

Eva and Chelsea craned their necks. "Hmm, he's a bit of alright," Eva said.

"Hmmm, I'd go camping with him."

Danika and Chelsea looked over at Eva.

"I mean, if I wasn't, wasn't with the detective," she

stammered, embarrassed and her friends laughed.

When they turned their attention back to the nurse's station, Mary was standing in the doorway, blocking the view.

"Thanks very much for letting me know what happened to Dani," she huffed.

"Oh, Mary." Eva said. "You can blame me for that. I didn't know where to find you. Dani is the only one who has your contact numbers."

"Well, okay. Luckily, Brad Wilson saw me in the street. He gave me the gruesome details this morning. I almost keeled over with shock," she said.

No one spoke.

Mary continued. "It's difficult to believe you were knocking on death's door a few days ago. Now look at you, sitting cross-legged on the bed, drinking wine and eating something delicious by the look of it." She leaned forward. "Mmm, what is that? It looks and smells yummy."

Chelsea invited Mary to help herself, while Eva poured her a wine.

"Anyway, how ya doin' kiddo?" Mary asked, sipping her wine.

"I'm doin' just fine."

"Dani, I'm not sure if you know this, but Brad really cares a lot about you. We went to school together, so I know him well. He's a matter-of-fact kind of fella. I have to tell you he was all teary while telling me what had happened to you."

"Have I met him?" Chelsea chipped in.

"No," Mary smiled. "Brad's a beer and barbeque fella. Not the little soiree kind. But," she glanced over at Danika, adding, "I'm sure he'd adapt."

Heads turned towards the door at the sound of light tapping. "Am I interrupting?"

The women glanced at one another and raised their brows.

"Not at all, Brad, Come in. If you recall, we met a few days ago. That day, I'd rather forget.

"Yes, Eva, I recall."

"Anyway, how are you?"

"I'm fine, Eva. Thanks for asking."

"This lovely lady is our other friend, Chelsea," Eva said, pointing to her. "And of course, you know Mary."

Chelsea gave a little wave and smiled at him. Brad nodded in return.

"You must feel overwhelmed being surrounded by so many females," quipped Eva. "We should give you and Dani privacy."

"Thanks. I can't stay. I'm AWOL and have to get back." He turned to Danika. "I took a minute to drop by to see you. If you don't mind, I'll come back after my shift."

"I'll look forward to seeing you then, Brad. Have a great day, mate."

He winked at her and then left.

"I like Brad," Chelsea said.

"So, you all approve?"

"We do!" They cried in unison, laughing.

"Oh," Mary said, checking her watch. "I'd better go. I'm meeting a friend for coffee."

After Mary left, Danika turned to Chelsea. "And how are you progressing with your treatment?"

"I'm fine and feeling so much better now that I'm managing the medication myself."

Eva's eyes widened. "What do you mean, you're managing your medication?"

"Just that. If you remember, Dani, I told you the dosage the first oncologist prescribed for me was too high and how it made me feel awful and horribly nauseous all the time.

Danika nodded.

"Well, that was the start of my research in to Polycythaemia Vera and sacking three oncologists since this illness surfaced. The oncologist I see now is working with me. I take the medication every second day instead of every day. This oncologist also prescribed a phlebotomy which means a certain amount of blood is taken out, (a transfusion in reverse) every few months because my blood has thickened. This method prevents clotting," she added, "So far so, good! I rest when I'm tired and don't push myself the way I did in the past."

"It's wonderful there's no telltale signs of a serious illness." Eva said. "You look marvellous and never have a hair out of place."

Chelsea smiled and thanked Eva, thinking, *'if you only knew how hard I'm fighting this disease.'* "I must go. Jeffery will be home soon. He might even be there now, waiting for me."

"Is he still volunteering at OzFish?" inquired Danika.

Chelsea nodded. "Yes. That's all he talks about these days. Did you not hear him chewing everybody's ear about getting involved and protecting the bay at the Christmas party? Before Danika could respond, Chelsea continued, "Jeffery enjoys being out in the open air and sunshine and being productive. It's wonderful to see him so happy. I'm not ready to get involved just yet. I will one day. Okay, I'll see you both later," she said, waving as she left the room. A few minutes later, she appeared in the doorway. Danika and Eva jumped when she spoke.

"Oh, sorry." Chelsea laughed. "I wish you two could have seen the look on your faces just now."

They said nothing.

"I forgot to ask how Abbi is. Your news would have been a tremendous shock for her."

"It was, but she's fine now that she knows I'm safe and on the mend."

"Is she planning to come home to see you?"

"Abbi tried booking a flight back home. But, with all this BS going on with this virus, she faces too many restrictions. So, the answer to that question is no, unfortunately."

"How do you feel about that?"

"It's out of my control, so I have to be okay with it. Besides everything else, Abbi has her own path to follow. America could be her destiny." Danika shrugged. "Who knows anything for certain?"

Chelsea nodded and waved and then left, thinking, 'Dani's doing just fine!'

Eva leaned back in the chair beside the bed, studying Danika.

"What?" Danika asked, when she noticed.

"I was thinking you are different. Softer. The *edge* you had is gone. The *alert* in your demeanour isn't present either. I've never seen you more relaxed. Mind if I ask a personal question? Don't answer if it upsets you."

"Go ahead, ask away."

"Why did Lucas try to kill you?"

Danika shook her head. "I can't answer that because I don't know. All I remember is saying good night to Jack, walking inside and waking up in hospital."

"I've been giving this some serious thought." Eva paused. "Stop me if my probing disturbs or upsets you. Okay?"

Danika nodded.

"Lucas knew you were in witness protection, didn't he?"

Danika nodded and looked towards the door. The detective and Buddy stood there listening.

"Mind if we come in? We'd like to hear what you have to say."

Danika waved them in. "Yes, he knew I was in witness protection. We had a twenty-year friendship. I trusted him."

"Were you aware he had a gambling addiction?"

Danika hung her head. "Well, sort of."

The detective waited for her to explain what 'sort of' means.

"His ex-wife mentioned it to me years ago. I didn't believe her because she was often loose with the truth and was no Mary Poppins. She blamed Lucas for the marriage breakdown when she slept with any man who smiled at her."

"Our investigation uncovered Lucas was in debt for one hundred and seventy-five thousand dollars. He had an offer to wipe it." The detective could not finish the sentence.

"To kill me?"

He nodded.

Danika said nothing.

Eva clutched her friend's hand. "Are you alright?"

"It's over now, isn't it?"

The detective nodded. "Yes Dani. It is over now."

Danika turned to Eva. "I'm fine, hon. Really," she said, wondering when she should remove the wig and contact lenses.

Chapter 34

"I want to take another look at those files before we head back to the office." Ruben told Buddy as they left the hospital.

"Okay. What do you hope to find?"

"Not sure yet."

Twenty minutes later, on their way up to his apartment, Ruben waved to a neighbour, passing by.

"How ya doin' captain, keeping the wolves from our doors?"

"Doing all we can, Max. How are you?" Before Max had time to respond, Ruben pointed to Buddy. "Detective McIntyre."

"Right," Max said, nodding. He gave the *thumbs up* and was about to move on. Then he stopped. "By the way, you had a visitor Christmas morning. I was too far away to see who it was. I thought about calling out to let the person know you weren't home, but decided against it in case I woke the neighbours. I'm not popular Pete around here, as you know. You must be the only one who hasn't complained about my Harley being too noisy."

Buddy and Ruben glanced at one another.

"Thanks for the heads up, Max. You'll never hear me complain about your Harley. Had one myself a few years back. They sing like a bird. Catch you later!"

"Too bloody right they do! Yeah, yeah, see ya!"

Inside the apartment, Ruben checked the security camera, rewinding it back to Christmas morning. Ruben noticed the tape jumped from four-fifty-five am to five am. He then went to his bedroom and opened the safe. All the files were gone; an envelope sat on top of his private papers where the missing evidence had been.

"I got a nasty feeling when Max mentioned the visitor. I knew then the files were the target. My hunch was right." Ruben said, holding up the envelope as he came out of the bedroom. "Look what my visitor left in their place." Ruben slid the typed letter out of the envelope and began reading it.

"Hey, how about sharing the news, or is it private?"

"It's not private. It's to the both of us." Ruben paused and looked at Buddy. "It's from our friend."

"Does *our friend* have a name?"

"No."

"Okay, I'll read it. Here goes."

My apologies for invading your home, Detective Ruben, and removing the evidence from your safe. I did this to protect you and Detective McIntyre and your families from dangerous, vile people, who would eliminate you all in the blink of an eye and celebrate your demise, if it were ever discovered either of you had any knowledge of their existence.

I left the files in the apartment for you both to read and to be informed of what is soon to take place, to show you who the enemies are and what you're dealing with.

Horrific events must take place and run their course for sleepers to wake up.

Ignore mainstream media. Don't get distracted by the lies they spread.

Good will overcome evil, but not without a fight, emotionally and physically. The next few years will be difficult. Never lose heart or faith. The evil ones will be destroyed. Every one of them. Remain calm when dealing with the enemy. Take care not to give them your power by embracing fear and complying to their demands. Death and misery await those who do. Remain joyful and loving, but firm in your beliefs. Keep company with like-minded people.

Both of you will face many challenges before this battle ends. Accept every challenge with gratitude. Each one you overcome will rise you to a higher consciousness. Nothing will harm either of you, unless it's part of your soul contract; the one you made before birth.

Many will simply drop dead on the world stage for the truth to be known. Soon, all the lies and deceit will be revealed.

Find your tribe. Unity is your strength. When in doubt,

seek guidance through meditation. The creator is in control!

Destroy this letter!

"Better memorise this before I burn it," Ruben said, handing the letter to Buddy. He took a few minutes to read it, looking for a clue as to whom the author might be. Handing it back to Ruben, Buddy asked if he had any idea who the *friend* might be?

"Nope. Not one!"

Ruben struck a match and held the flame under the letter over the kitchen sink. Both watched the paper shrivel and curl in the heat, turning to ashes in seconds and float downwards into the sink. Ruben turned on the tap and watched the last fragment swirl down the drain.

"Okay, that's done." Ruben said, wiping his hands on a paper towel. "We'd better get back to the office."

They moved toward the front door, then Ruben stopped and turned to Buddy. "Do you remember the day I took the files into the boss's office?"

"I sure do. I've got a video of it," he said, patting his hip pocket where his mobile was.

"You have?"

Buddy nodded with pride. "Yep! Just a feeling I had. I decided we can't trust anyone. Good thing I did, because we now know who the enemies are," he winked.

"I could kiss you, bro!" said Ruben.

"Ahh, nah, I wouldn't do that if I were you."

Ruben laughed. "Just a figure of speech, my friend. You're a champion! I've got a feeling I'm going to need that video as proof I handed in the files."

"Where did that come from?"

"Our friend's warning about remaining calm when evil comes to our door and having to destroy the letter. I'll bet my apartment will be searched. I could be wrong or just have an overactive imagination." He shrugged. "There's no harm in being prepared for battle."

Back at the office, Ruben took his time writing the report, while Buddy looked over the file of another case. From his office, James Kelly sporadically glanced over at Ruben, assuring Ruben that something was about to happen. The chief was now standing and looking directly at him. Ruben glanced up and saw him tap on his window, summoning him to his office.

"You rang?" Ruben joked.

"Always the smartarse. What's happening with the Winton case?"

"Here," Ruben said, handing Kelly the report. He remained silent until his boss had finished reading it.

"Is that it? He was using an alias?"

Ruben nodded. "Real name was Martin Hopkins. An ex-con and model prisoner. Served twenty years for killing his business partners, Rod Raymond and Thomas Barker. The coroner ruled Hopkin's death as accidental. All that was found in the apartment were those files full of conspiracy theories."

"Hmm, why the alias?"

"At a guess, I'd say to find his ex. It's the only explanation."

"Hmm. Did you go through the files?

"No. It's not my thing. It's bullshit! It does my head in. That's why I passed that stuff on to you to figure out. Did they get anything from that pile of crap?"

The chief shook his head and shrugged. "Nothing."

Ruben studied his boss and thought he looked uncomfortable.

"Ok, well, that's a closed case, then?" Ruben said, turning to leave.

"What's the go with the Lucas Johnson case?" Kelly asked.

"I'm working on the report now, chief," he said, as he stood in the doorway. "Johnson shot his ex-girlfriend, Danika Bryce, who was in witness protection for testifying against her former partner, Martin Hopkins. After he was released, Hopkins went looking for her under the alias. Couldn't find her, so he put a two hundred thou bounty on her head; a revenge killing. In the meantime, Hopkins slips over in his kitchen and dies. Johnson, who was in debt to the sum of one hundred and seventy-five thousand and his creditors were breathing down his neck, took up the contract to clear his debt, because the relationship between him and Bryce had crashed and burned. He botches the kill, wounding her, instead. Bryce survives with no memory of the shooting or her past."

James Kelly let out a few profanities, shaking his head. "And I thought my life was shit!"

Ruben laughed. "Karma's a bitch!"

Kelly glared at Rubens' back as he walked out of his office.

Buddy was discreetly watching Ruben and the chief from his desk. He thought things between the pair looked tense and then sighed with relief to see his partner grinning as he came towards him. When Ruben reached his desk, he picked up a current case file and nodded to Buddy, signalling things were back on track. "We can get cracking on this one today."

"I've made it clear to the chief the case is closed. Implying there was no point in pursuing Danika Bryce since she has no memory of her past. I've given him a few things to think about before he talks to his puppet masters; closing the case is best for all concerned."

Ruben's mobile pinged. A message and photo from his neighbour.

"Hey Captain! A couple of suits were knocking on your door. Know them? I suggested they try you at Roma Street. Got nothing from them and they left."

"Thanks, mate. Good work." replied Ruben.

"What's up?" Buddy asked.

"Wolves at my door."

Ruben looked over at James Kelly in his office and felt

contempt rise within him. He shook his head in disgust. Buddy asked Ruben if he was okay.

"Nah, mate, I'm not. It turns my stomach knowing the powers that be are so corrupt. I'll be tendering my resignation soon. Staying here and following orders, knowing what I know, is only condoning their depraved insanity."

Buddy grabbed his jacket from the back of his chair. "C'mon, Sam, let's get some air."

Outside, the detectives stood in silence, leaning up against the building, watching heavy traffic snail along the street as the lunchtime crowd rushed to get a bite to eat. Everything seemed normal; traffic lights pulsed in readiness to change from green to yellow to red in the melting heat of midday. On the surface, everything appeared *normal* when it was not. A dark cloud was about to descend upon the country at the fault of the Gate Keepers. It bothered Ruben that he could do nothing other than to wait and see.

"Sam, neither of us can save the world. As our friend said, people have to learn the hard way."

Ruben scratched his head. "Yeah, I know you're right, mate. I've never in my life thought violence was the way to solve anything. But I have to be honest, Buddy, when I know who the enemy is, makes me want to pick up my pistol and wipe the lot of them from the face of the earth."

"My sentiments exactly." Buddy, said. "But that's what

they want us to do. They get off on people's pain and suffering. Our strength's not to react to the bullshit and lies. We'll win this war. It won't be easy. But we'll win in the end. Good versus evil." Buddy paused and then laughed. "Mate, the baddies have never won in the movies! We're living in a 'B' grade movie at the moment. Well, at least it feels like it."

Ruben laughed out loud, releasing the tension he felt. "You're right, c'mon, let's get a bite to eat before I hand in my resignation."

"That's what I want to talk to you about."

"You too?"

"Yeah. Angie and I were talking about my leaving the force last night."

Ruben's brows shot upwards. "You told her?"

"Nah. Just that I was thinking about changing careers. Over the years, we've made good investments and can afford to move in another direction now. Angie was thrilled. It means more family time together."

"We're on the same page then. Now is a good time for me too. So, I guess, there's no better time than today." Ruben paused and then said, "You know, mate. We have a nice little group of like-minded friends. As long as we look after each other, we'll be fine."

Buddy nodded in agreement, chuckling. "Let's go eat! All that thinking has given me an appetite."

Chapter 35

David White was at the reception desk finishing a report when a paramedic hurried past him and turned into Danika's room.

'Hmm, that was my next stop. I guess it won't be today,' he shrugged.

Danika saw David at the desk and hoped he would come in, but Brad blocked her view from attracting his attention. She wanted to know if David was ready to give her doctor the *okay* to discharge her.

"Hi Dani!" Brad chirped. "You are looking better by the minute."

She smiled. "Two bunches of flowers? You're spoiling me!" She teased.

He looked embarrassed. "Ahh, just one bunch for you."

"Oh?" she grinned mischievously.

"The other flowers are for Patty, my partner. She broke her leg this morning. She's kinda special. We've been a team for over five years. I took it for granted she'd always be there until today. I realise that only a fool takes things for granted." His tone was serious.

Danika smiled. "You're no fool, Brad. You're everybody's hero; always thinking of others. Patty will appreciate your thoughtful gesture, as do I."

"I hope so Dani. I hope she knows what she means to me."

"Just be clear about your feelings, mate, so there's no miscommunication."

"Right." Brad thought about Danika's comment. "Right! Yeah. Okay. I'll do that. See you later, Dani."

"Good luck!" Danika shouted, just before he vanished from sight.

David White and the nurse at the desk looked up as Brad dashed out of Danika's room and rushed down the corridor. David White stopped writing and walked over to her room and stood in the doorway. "Is everything okay?" he asked.

"It sure is," Danika replied, grinning.

He nodded.

"While you're here, David. I want you to know I'd like to go home today. You can make that happen if you clear me with my doctor."

"I could, but I don't think you're ready to be discharged just yet."

Danika looked puzzled. "Its New Year's Eve," she said, as if that would be the deciding factor.

"So, you have a shindig to attend tonight?"

311

She shook her head. "I just want to go home, that's all." There was a sense of urgency in her voice.

"Danika, give yourself time to heal, physically and mentally. A few days ago, you were clinging to life by a thread."

"But ..."

"I know what you're going to say; you've made a full recovery. Physically, yes. Which is astounding. But there may be some deep-rooted trauma that could surface. I have to be sure that doesn't happen. Be patient. Give me a few more days."

She hung her head.

"Are your friends visiting tonight?"

She shook her head. "I told them not to come in. I thought I'd be home enjoying a quiet evening watching a movie."

"What did you have in mind?"

She looked puzzled.

"The movie. What movie were you planning to watch?"

"Oh."

She said nothing for a moment. "A random choice."

"Okay. I've got work to catch up on. So, I'll come by and wish you a Happy New Year, before I leave for home. Since you loathe beards, it will be handshakes only."

Danika turned bright crimson. "You heard us talking?"

"Every word," he said. "See you later!" He waved as he left and smiled at the sound of Danika's laughter.

She sat cross-legged on the bed, wondering if she should resume her real identity now that the danger is no longer imminent. *'Maybe keep the name, though. I like this name, just lose the wig and contact lenses. Everyone's entitled to a makeover at least a few times in their life.'*

With a sense of excitement, Danika scrambled off the bed and headed for the bathroom. She had to tug at the raven wig to remove it. She tossed it aside and shook her platinum blond locks free and then stepped into the shower.

Just as Danika wandered out of the bathroom dressed in a bathrobe and towel around her head, Eva came in, carrying a bag.

"Going somewhere?" Danika asked when she saw the bag.

"No. This is for you."

"Me?"

"Yes. I was having breakfast when suddenly, I had this feeling you needed clothes. Since I didn't have the keys to your place, I gathered a few of my things together for you I know you like," she said. "You've always admired this dimity print."

"You must be psychic, Eva!" Danika said. "Oh, yes, I love that dress, but on you. Those tiny blue flowers are so sweet," she quipped, holding the dress up against her towelled frame, with one hand while removing the towel from her head with the other, shaking her hair loose.

"The dress is perfect for you, too!" Eva's eyes widened. "WOW!!!" she repeated several times. "You look amazing! Your hair's beautiful!"

"I'm reclaiming my identity," Danika smiled, still holding the dress up against her. "I will remain Danika Bryce since everyone knows me by that name. Oh, it feels good to be free and to be myself again!"

"No more hiding behind a disguise?"

Danika did not respond right away. She was gazing out of the window.

"No more hiding. No more disguise," she said and then turned around. "Do you have a notepad and pen?"

Fossicking in her bag, Eva pulled out a notebook with a pen attached. "Like this one?"

"Yes!"

"To list your goals for the New Year?"

"Yes!"

"Well then, you had better have one of my special hexagonal boxes to keep those precious goals in until next year."

Danika's eyes filled with gratified tears. "How can I ever thank you, Eva?"

"You have, many times, over."

Eva glanced at her watch. "I have to go," she said. Before hurrying away, she hugged Danika. "Happy New Year, sweetie!"

After slipping the dress on and brushing her hair, Danika sat in the chair by the window. Jack's image popped into her thoughts. She smiled. *'I've not forgotten you, my dear heart,'* she whispered, aware he could hear her. She picked up the pen and began writing. When finished, she tore the sheet from the notebook and rolled it up and put it inside the box Eva had given her and then laid on the bed and closed her eyes.

"Are you sure, Dani?" Jack whispered.

"Yes. I want to go home. I want to be with you."

Jack took her by the hand and her spirit rose from her body. She turned and looked down at the figure lying there on the bed.

"That's just a vehicle you chose for the journey," he said.

She turned back to him and rested her head on his shoulder. "Yes. I remember."

They walked hand in hand toward the light.

"Dani." Jack stopped walking. "You have a choice. You can turn around and look back at the universe or you can continue on towards the light."

She turned around. The life she had lived ran like a movie among the stars. She saw herself as a child, the day she fell from the swing. Jack was there in the park that day. He picked her up and comforted her. He was there the day she was lost in the supermarket. He took her by the hand and led her back to her fraught mother, so angry she was about to slap her child. Jack touched her mother's arm, calming her. Jack's spirit had been with her every step of the way, protecting her from Martin's violent outbursts. She had felt a presence, but thought it was her imagination. The love encompassing her while watching her life flash before her eyes was not her imagination; it was real and comforting.

Jack released her hand. "You must now choose. Would you like to reincarnate and go back to live another life or stay here?"

"With you?"

"Yes, stay here with me."

She reached for his hand. "I want to stay with you. I recognised who you were Christmas Eve. I felt your love. A love I've never known; pure and spiritual. Why would I trade that for an uncharted life when I'm already where I want to be?" She moved closer to him and they continued their journey together.

Chapter 36

Eva was home getting ready for her evening with Ruben. They planned to have a quiet night at home, celebrating New Year's together. An overwhelming feeling to go back to the hospital niggled at her. She called the detective and asked him the meet her there after sending a message to Chelsea and Mary.

David White was in his office; he too, had that same feeling to see Danika, but continued working since he planned to see her shortly. The feeling persisted and disturbed his concentration. He dropped his pen and hurried to the hospital. The others arrived at the same time as he. They looked at one another. No one spoke. They then rushed to Danika's room.

Chelsea let out a huge sigh. "It's okay. Dani's sleeping,' she said, lowering her voice. "She looks so angelic."

When Danika did not move, David went to the side of her bed. He touched her face with the back of his hand. He then wrapped his hand around her wrist, feeling for a pulse. He looked over at her friends and shook his head.

"No, no, Dani's just sleeping." Eva said. "She looks so peaceful. So beautiful. She can't be ..."

The detective pulled Eva closer to him and held her tight and let her tears flow.

"She was ready to be discharged. I was planning to surprise her tonight, telling her she could leave in the morning." David White spoke so low the others just heard him. "I don't understand," he said, "All she wanted to do was to go home."

Mary moved about the room looking for something that would explain what had happened. She saw the hexagonal box on the cabinet beside the bed and opened it. Inside was a tiny, rolled up scroll. Mary unravelled it. "This should explain things," she said. "It's Dani's wish list. In large letters, she wrote she wants to go home to be with Jack." Mary paused to look directly at each of her friends. "Dani transitioned."

All of them looked back at Mary, puzzled.

It was Eva who asked, "What does *transitioned* mean?"

"It means Dani's spirit left her body."

"What, she just laid on the bed, closed her eyes and died?" David asked, sarcastically.

"Not die, exactly. Not in the way you mean." Mary paused to take a breath. "This will probably be difficult for you all to grasp. But we are spirits. Only the body dies, not our spirit." Mary stopped talking. She could see the confusion in her friends' eyes.

"Go on." David urged.

"Are you sure?" Mary asked. "You're all eyeing me like I'm some kind of nutter."

David nodded.

"Okay, Dani and I talked about this at length. She was curious why her life went in the direction that it had. We did heaps of research and came across information that satisfied our curiosity; explaining that before we were born, we made a contract and chose the life and challenges we would need to learn certain lessons. But most of us forgot why we chose our life."

"So, what's Jack's involvement in this?" Chelsea politely asked, grappling with Mary's mumbo-jumbo nonsense.

"I'm not sure if any of you noticed the connection between Dani and Jack," Mary said.

Eva looked at the others and nodded. "I did. It was difficult to describe what they shared because I knew they were strangers." Eva dabbed at her eyes. "Whatever it was, they both seemed to glow in one another's company."

"Yes, I remember they connected from their first meeting." Mary said. "I noticed it too. I think Jack and Dani shared many lifetimes together. I would say he came to take her home." Mary turned toward the bed. "Look at her. Look how peaceful she appears. Wherever Dani is, she is happy."

David shook his head, trying to make sense of what Mary was telling them. "Are you saying this Jack person who took Danika *home* was an angel, a spirit, or an alien?"

Mary shrugged. "I can't say that for sure. All I know is they connected in a way that's difficult to explain." Mary sighed. "Have you ever met someone you felt you've known them all your life, that you've instantaneously connected with?"

Eva and the detective looked at one another and nodded. Chelsea wrapped her arm around Jeffery as they too nodded. Mary looked into David White's eyes and smiled warmly. He returned her smile as if seeing the pretty, petite redhead for the first time. "Yes, I do understand what you mean."

On January 30th 2020, The World Health Organisation declared the outbreak of the mysterious Covid-19 was a Public Health Emergency of International Concern and further declared a pandemic on March 11, 2020. By April, half of the world's population was under some form of lockdown.

www.ingramcontent.com/pod-product-compliance
Lightning Source LLC
Chambersburg PA
CBHW030525120726
47904CB00005B/1634